The Reluctant

Doppelgänger

by

Nick Hilliard

Visit:

NickHilliard.com

The Library of Congress Control Number:
2018909224

Dedication

To Janet and Rob: Amazing friends and work partners for nearly two decades now. Rob without your evil editor's pen, editing marks (I had to learn to understand), your seemingly endless supply of yellow highlighters and infinite patience I would have never finished this project. I owe you so much and freely offer-up a lifetime of gratitude.

To Sharon and Myra: Thank you both so much for being beta readers. Your positive and affirmative comments along with your constructive criticism was greatly appreciated. It seems I've known you both forever and I wouldn't have it any other way. How blessed I am to have wonderful friends!

To Diana: There aren't words to express what you've meant to me in my life. I would do it all over again if given the opportunity. Life together hasn't always been the easiest of journeys but God couldn't have given me a better companion for the trip.

1

Mrs. Haskins, my landlady, called to me from the parlor when I came through the front door of the boarding house. I peeked around the doorway to see she was holding a small yellow sheet of paper that I immediately recognized as a telegram. I'm not sure why my sense of recognition came so readily - it wasn't like I had ever received a telegram before. Along with that recognition came a certain sense of foreboding, not because of any knowledge of what the message might contain, but for the sheer fact that it was indeed a telegram. It could only be from one person: my father. A very thrifty man, my father would only send a telegram for one of three reasons: if someone was seriously ill, if there had been a death or if it was urgent business. It had to be the latter because, if it had been the serious illness of a family member, he would have telephoned. And if someone had died, he would have made the eleven-mile forty-five-minute automobile trip to deliver his message to me personally. Therefore, even before I was handed the telegram that Mrs. Haskins was currently waiving in the air, I had come to the conclusion that it would certainly contain some kind of urgent business.

"We don't get many a telegram around this house," she said in her lilting Irish brogue as she handed the message to me.

"To be quite honest with you Mrs. Haskins, this is the first one I have ever received," I said, absently staring down at the message.

The pale-yellow paper was emblazoned boldly with the Western Union Telegram letterhead. Under that was the date and time: "Oct. 10 1927=1005A." It read: "Mr. Edward M Standish=1433 Bernice St=Westwood Village Calf. Be in my office no later than 3:00P this Friday STOP. B. Standish. 12:13P"

"Have ya done something to make your pa out of sorts with ya?"

I looked up at her. It was obvious from the question that she had read my telegram. But giving the devil his due, being that the telegram was a single sheet of paper, most everyone would have been hard pressed not to read it. It wasn't until later that I would learn that telegrams were delivered in envelopes, which, for this particular missive, had gone conveniently missing.

"I don't think so Ma'am. My father is nothing if not thrifty and Western Union charges by the word. I am certain that explains his curtness." *However, it appears that he does command my presence.* This last bit I kept to myself.

Perhaps I should take a moment to introduce myself. I am Edward M. Standish. The M stands for McPherson. It was my mother's maiden name. And it was given to me by my father, Bertram Standish. No middle initial. I, too, might have escaped the fate of having a middle name if it hadn't been for the fact that my mother died in childbirth, my childbirth lest you think I might have younger siblings. And I am an only child lest you might wonder that I have older ones as well.

The Reluctant Doppelganger

My middle name was given to me in hopes that it would show a sign of respect for my mother's family, therefore, forging a strong bond with said family.

My mother was the fifth of five daughters of a wealthy apothecary owner. My grandfather, Elias Patrick McPherson, was very much the patriarch and ruled not only his businesses with a firm hand but his family as well, the latter being no small feat in a household comprised solely of women. My grandfather had a string of what we today call drug stores across Orange County. He was of the old school of thought and found the use of the word "drug" in place of "apothecary" to be vulgar and offensive — until one evening when my grandfather happened across a window-cleaner plying his trade on the front windows of one of his shops. He greeted the man, whom he had known for many years. Owl Drugs, my grandfather's largest competitor, had just opened a new store a short distance down the street from his shop. As he spoke to the window-cleaner, he looked over the man's shoulder and noticed the lighted sign. The word "DRUG" ran down the marquee vertically in huge block letters.

My grandfather let out a disgusted, "Harumf! Drug indeed. What a vulgar term."

He was still grumbling when the other man turned to see what had drawn my grandfather's attention away from their conversation.

"I have to agree with you, Mr. McPherson, that "apothecary" is much classier, but ya gotta admit that sign can be read easy from where we are standing, right here, nearly two blocks away."

A month later every one of my grandfather's stores had a marquee-style sign with the word "DRUG" constructed of mammoth channeled letters painted pink with hundreds of clear electric lights filling each letter's channel. Evening sales rose over ten percent in less than ninety days. Suddenly the word "drug" didn't seem quite so vulgar after all.

My father, Bertram Standish, is a motion picture agent. And a very successful Hollywood motion picture agent, too. With the invention and almost overnight success of the moving pictures, associated industries came suddenly into being and the Hollywood agent was one of them. My father saw an opportunity and created his niche. He assures that actors and actresses are being well represented in the terms of their contracts with the motion picture studios. Plus, he promotes as well as protects their public image. It is an enormous and constant task for which he is highly paid.

My father and mother met at an event to raise money for a new hospital wing. The wing was to bear my grandfather's name due in no small part to his very sizable contribution, but perhaps more because it had been stipulated as a condition for said sizable donation. My grandfather had required every member of his family to be in attendance that evening.

My father had arranged for several of his clients, the new Hollywood dynasty, to be present at that same event. Their job was to sign autographs and pose for photographs with attendees of the event. Those attendees posing for photographs were substantial donors to the hospital fund. They had to be generous donors in order to secure what turned out to be a sought-after photo with a moving picture star.

It was there, while she was posing for a photograph with Gilbert Anderson, the star of the Broncho Billy series, that my father caught sight of my then eighteen-year-old mother. He asked her to dance and lost his heart. They were quite the pair, my father standing six feet four inches tall and my mother barely five feet.

By the time my father met my mother, he had already become quite successful. But my grandfather had not seen it that way. Because my father was pioneering an industry, my grandfather perceived him as a ne'er-do-well because he wasn't part of an established profession that had had long term successes. Combine this with the fact that my father was fifteen years my mother's senior and was known around Hollywood as quite the lady's man, one can see why my staunch grandfather would not be accepting of the match to his youngest daughter.

But it seems that my mother was every bit as stubborn as her father. She, along with my grandmother and her sisters, had literally worn the poor man down. Like I said before, a man living in a household of six women was outnumbered no matter how stern his constitution. In the end, my grandfather acquiesced and agreed to the marriage. Two years later, I was born, and she was gone. That very act of God placed my life at a crossroads. It would take one of two extreme paths. Either my father would love me with all his heart because he loved my mother so much or because he loved my mother, he would blame me for her death and would forever despise me. Thank goodness for my sake it was the former.

In fact, I was greatly loved. I had an almost idyllic childhood. There was a strong bond with my grandparents and four aunts. I doubt honestly, however, that it was because my middle name was McPherson.

My father taught me to hunt, shoot, ride horses and deep-sea fish. He and I also took up two new sports that had just come to the coast of California around the time I was born, surfing and judo. My father is a strapping man. Like I mentioned earlier, he is tall, has broad shoulders and a narrow waist. He could easily pass for one of the more mature Norse Gods. I take after my father in many ways. I share his reddish-blonde full head of hair, pale skin, searing blue eyes, sharp features and his quick wit. But alas, I shared my mother's diminutive stature standing a towering five foot three inches tall. When puberty struck, while all the other boys were gaining facial and body hair, I did not. My father attributed this to our Scandinavian heritage. Whatever the reason, I never developed facial hair, therefore I could not grow the long sideburns that were so popular at the time. And at twenty-two years of age, I still cannot grow sideburns. Thank God, they are no longer the rage. So today, I'm classified as a pretty boy. I still have no facial hair or body hair to speak of and my voice never lowered much either. When I was younger, this lack of manliness caused me to feel very insecure. I can still hear my grandmother saying, "The good Lord made each and every one of us different, yet we are all beautiful in His sight." She said it to me over and over and over again. I am pretty sure she was trying to instill a sense of courage and perseverance. And I think it worked.

My father started grooming me to become a Hollywood agent very early in life. His plan was to incorporate me into his business and for me to take over that business when the time came. He always insisted on me being well educated. I had private tutors for all of my primary education. My father had opted for a private education over the more common boarding school for young men from wealthy families because he had wanted me close. He, himself, taught me how to work with people. And more importantly, how to understand what people are really saying even when they are not saying it. His philosophy is that every business owner needs to understand the fundamental process of business itself and its operation. In this belief, he and my grandfather are in total agreement.

So, that brings me to where I am today, enrolled in The Bentley School of Business in Westwood Village California. I have completed nearly two and a half years of the three years it requires to earn a degree. I had finished my classes for the day and was returning to my lodgings at the Haskins' Boarding House for Young Men when Mrs. Haskins stopped me to deliver the telegram.

"Thank you, Mrs. Haskins, for signing for the delivery." I said this cheerfully and in no way acknowledging her nosiness.

I took my telegram and headed up the stairs to my room, where I would spend the next four days fretting and pondering about what in the world my father could possibly want.

2

On Friday, I boarded the Red Car Trolley at 1:30 PM for the thirty-minute ride to Hollywood. I wanted to be early. For my father, on time was the same as late. At 2:45 PM precisely, I stepped through the door of my father's office. The reception area was small. There was no need for a large waiting room. My father never saw more than one client at a time, and they were never scheduled to meet in passing unless it was my father's intention. He is a master tactician. The secretary's desk was off to one side of the reception area leaving my father's office door front and center. My father's secretary, Gertrude Myers, was seated behind her desk typing when I appeared in front of her.

I walked around the desk and gave her a hug and peck on the cheek.

"Hello my sweet, Gertie! How is the most beautiful woman in all of Hollywood doing today?"

"You've got some nerve, young man."

Her voice was stern, but her mouth broke into a wide grin even as she spoke.

"Yes Ma'am, I surely do at that."

The Reluctant Doppelganger

Gertie had been my father's secretary ever since he started his business and I had known her all my life. She was a bit older than my father and had played mother to me many a night when my father had to be out on business. Her hair was all gray now and she still wore it up in a bun on top of her head in the old-fashioned style. She was dressed in a smart navy wool suit with a white silk blouse. Her face bore fine lines around her eyes. To me, fine lines around the eyes signified that either one had bad eye sight or spent a great deal of time laughing and smiling. For Gertie, it was laughter and smiles.

"I'll let your father know you are here."

She reached over and lifted the earpiece on my father's newly installed inter-office communication system. She fastened the single earpiece over her right ear and held a horn in front of her mouth with one hand, as she pressed a button on a large wooden box with the other. The box sported three lights – one green, one yellow and one red along with two large toggle switches. She waited a moment. I could hear a tone sound inside my father's office. Then she spoke into the horn.

"Eddie is here, sir."

There was no voice reply but the green light flashed on the large box. She removed the earpiece and stood wordlessly. We moved together back around her desk. She ushered me to my father's office door.

"You know I could see myself in, don't you?" I asked with a wink.

"Old habits die hard." She sighed. "It's show time!" she said it in an excited conspiratorial whisper. "Get that smile in place." She looked at me with an exaggerated grin.

She was imitating my father. Those were the lines he used on his clients just before they greeted the public or headed into an important meeting.

Nick Hilliard

The door to father's private office was large and imposing, made of solid mahogany. It had gleaming brass hardware. It was designed to make an unforgettable opulent first impression and it did its job well. Gertie turned the ornate knob and stepped back. The door swung open on well-oiled hinges. The room was cavernous. It was paneled in the same rich mahogany as the door. A mammoth mahogany desk with ornate carvings sat in front of a bank of floor-to-ceiling windows. A huge dark green leather chair sat behind the desk, and there were two oversized wing-backed chairs that were not nearly as imposing sitting across the desk facing the windows. One of those chairs was draped with what appeared to be a full-length mink coat. My father's visitor's chairs were always placed facing the windows. He wanted the light to be in his visitor's eyes. He said that squinting into the light made it harder for them to lie.

On the opposite side of the room, two long burgundy tufted leather sofas faced each other across a long hand-carved wooden table. Sitting side by side on one sofa were my father and, nearer to me, a woman I instantly recognized from the cinema. It was none other than Theodora Desmond.

My father stood and gestured in my direction with an extended arm.

"I would like to introduce my son, Edward." He was smiling. "Edward, this is..."

I cut him off. A slight look of annoyance crossed his face. He never liked being interrupted or moreover upstaged. But I continued.

"This beautiful lady needs no introduction. How are you Miss Desmond? I am a huge fan," I said, closing the distance and holding out my hand to shake hers. As our palms slid one into the other, mine bare and hers gloved, in one fluid movement, she turned the back of her hand skyward forcing mine to turn down. My father has always maintained that this was a woman's way of letting you know she is in charge. Right at this moment, I had to agree with him. This woman radiated power.

"You must call me Eddie."

"Then you must call me Theo." She gave me that stunning smile for which she was so noted.

I noticed that her smile went all the way to her eyes. In this city, there is a great deal of smiling but rarely is it the sincere kind that goes all the way to one's eyes. Her smile was open and sincere. That, or she was a great actress.

Oh, my God! What am I thinking? She is a great actress!

My defenses immediately went up.

Why have I been called here and what am I in for? I wondered, praying that my thoughts were not being displayed openly on my face.

"Please join us." My father motioned for me to have a seat on the sofa across from them.

If my guard wasn't already up, it was now. As I've said, my father is a magician when it comes to tactics. This particular move of two people on one side of a table and one person on the other was what he had dubbed, using a pugilist term, "the old one-two punch." It was especially useful during an actor's contract negotiation with a studio's attorney. Or when a public spat erupted between two of the temperamental and highly-strung artistic types that we here in Hollywood have begun to call "movie stars." It's a rather catchy *nom de guerre* and I'm betting it will stick.

Warily, I sat. My father started in immediately after I was seated.

"I am going to lay everyone's cards on the table right up front." He said.

Good God I am in trouble! First the one-two punch and now the cards on the table ploy.

Suddenly there was a sinking feeling in the pit of my

stomach. I wasn't sure what was about to transpire, but I now knew the situation was one of dire straits. My father was pulling out all the stops, using every tactic in his arsenal. His "cards on the table up front" analogy meant there was about to be an ultimatum delivered. It might be candy coated but none the less it would be an ultimatum.

I wanted to close my eyes tight, clench my fists and scream *Just spit it out! Get it over with!*

But of course, I didn't. Young well-bred, well-educated men did not behave in such a manner.

So, calmly and with great composure I said, "Please do. I am sure Theo and I would appreciate your open direct candor."

I was sure that Theo already knew what was about to be discussed but I, myself, am no slouch when it comes to strategic maneuvers. After all, I learned from a true master of the craft. By including Miss Desmond in my response, I had openly aligned her with me, therefore, pulling the two to one approach into more of a triangle. It wasn't the ideal situation, but it was far better than being ganged up on.

My father cocked an eyebrow. I smirked and Theo leaned back a bit as if she was getting ready to watch two well matched chess players ply their talents.

"Well then," I said, "the game's afoot." And at that moment, I came to a startling awareness that I had just used my Sherlock Holmes voice out loud. I am a huge follower of the British sleuth and had the delightful opportunity of meeting the author during his speaking tour when he visited Los Angeles several years prior. I oft times use the phrase when embarking on a new challenge, but I had never intended to say it aloud. Any advantage I may have gained, I feared I just lost. Oh well, I am merely the student tactician after all.

Theo looked a bit puzzled, but my father only smiled. And

with that, the game was truly afoot.

"Son." Father said in a very serious tone followed by a long pause. "We have several very delicate matters to discuss. So, I'm asking you to give me your word that what is said in this room today will go no further than this room, no matter what the outcome."

Then he looked at me with that look. He was serious.

What in the world could be of such portents? I wondered to myself, as I nodded my consent.

He started, then hesitated and rubbed his forehead, then started again. That was very unlike my father. He always planned out what he was going to say before any meeting. I could not imagine this meeting being any different.

"I'm not sure where to begin. Eddie, as you know, this is Theodora Desmond."

Again, I nodded, wondering why he was re-stating the obvious.

"Theodora is just her stage name."

Although I did not know this, it was certainly not unusual in Hollywood. Studios required their stars to change their names all the time. It was to make them more marketable to the public. At least that has always been the studio's position. Even Greta Garbo changed her last name from Gustafsson to Garbo.

"Her given name is Molly."

He took a deep breath and paused. The next sentence rushed out of him as if it were on fire.

"She is your sister."

For a moment, I sat there, nonplussed.

"She's my what?"

I drew the words out, sounding somewhat contradictory. But most definitely puzzled and stunned.

"Truthfully, she is your half-sister." He stated calmly but emphatically now.

All the standard questions bubbled instantly to mind. Where? When? How? But what came out was something altogether different.

"And you didn't think to tell me until I was twenty-two years old?"

I guess my mind had simply skipped over the part about how and when. It had accepted the declaration as truth, probably because it was my father raining this down upon my head. I am certain I looked incredulous because I most assuredly felt that way.

"Perhaps I should start from the beginning."

"Perhaps? Perhaps?" I drew out the second for effect. "I dare say Father, it is the only place you can start."

He pursed his lips then licked them—thought for a moment and began.

"A few years before I met your mother, I met Molly's mother. She was a seamstress for one of the studios."

He began to fumble for words.

"We had—well a—a dalliance." He finally said sheepishly.

Again, he stopped to put his thoughts in order. I filled the silence.

"Yes, yes, everyone in Hollywood knows of your libertine nature," I spewed very confrontationally.

"Well, be that as it may." He bit out.

My father's face moved through a range of emotions in rapid succession: surprise, hurt and finally anger. His words came sharp and curt now. And the register of his voice dropped dramatically, which always signifies he is past angry, but I was not backing down. I was shocked, hurt and angry myself.

"Gentlemen!" Theo shouted.

We both looked up in surprise.

"I know you both consider this a matter between the two of you, but it's not. It is a matter that concerns all three of us."

She looked directly at me.

"Dear Eddie," she began again in what I considered to be a very patronizing tone.

I was not sure I liked the sound of her calling me *dear* either. I really did not know this woman at all. She must have sensed this and started again.

"Edward, my mother and our father…," She was saying.

I was only half listening now. I had not approved of the term *dear* used in the current situation. And I most definitely did not like her saying *our* father. I realized that I had drifted from the conversation and had to excuse myself. Once again, she started over, this time with a bit of an annoyance in her voice.

"My mother and *our* father," she pointed the word, "had a rather torrid dalliance before he met your mother."

My father was nodding now.

"Torrid?" he questioned, placing his thumb under his chin as he stroked his upper lip with a crooked index finger, looking at Theo quizzically.

"Those were her words."

She answered his question almost as an aside while never taking her eyes off mine.

The man actually smiled behind his stroking finger. He was shameless. He was taking pleasure in knowing that Theo's mother had called their tryst "torrid."

"My mother did not want to be married to our father. She had just been looking for a little fun. However, our father convinced her to marry him, thereby, doing the honorable thing. And shortly afterwards, they promptly divorced per their prearranged agreement. She left California and headed home to Oklahoma. Pops had been very wise indeed. My mother found it much easier to gain acceptance as a pregnant divorcee whose no-account husband back in California had left upon finding she was in the family way."

Her face reddened a bit. I was not sure if it was because of emotion or embarrassment.

"Her family would have never taken her in if she had been a shamed woman. Mama's recent past had all been manufactured by Pops, before she left California for that very reason. Mama would have never thought of it on her own," She said with some finality.

It seemed her story had been told. Pops? Now that was a new term of endearment. I looked at my father. He only looked like a *Father* to me. He watched me, gauging my reactions before he spoke.

"I always made sure that Margaret, or Molly, as everyone calls her at home, and her mother were financially secure. Her mother remarried when she was two, so I'm Pops and he's Daddy," He said reading my mind.

He had always been very good at anticipating my questions.

"You will excuse me if I move things right along," I was trying to maintain my composure. "But why now? You've had twenty-two years to get to it. So, again, why now?"

"I did not tell you because I saw nothing good that could come of it. If your grandfather had known, he never would have consented to your mother's and my marriage. I could not run the risk of you telling anyone in your mother's family when you were younger because I knew it would cause a rift in their relations with me. And I certainly did not want you to incur any wrath because of my short comings." He was speaking like a college professor now.

"Pops even offered to send me to college. But Mama got it into her head that I should be an actress. You see, she had always wanted to be an actress herself. She thought that Pops could make it happen for me because of his connections. So, five years ago, when I was twenty, I came to Hollywood.

The Reluctant Doppelganger

Pops really did make it happen for me. He had wanted to introduce us then, but I asked him not to. I was new here and scared to death. I was on my own for the first time ever, and I was half a world away from my home. I sure didn't want to meet a brother I had never known. And especially one that didn't even know I existed."

I hated myself for it but I was beginning to like her. And I had already forgiven Father. I just wasn't going to let him know it quite yet.

"Once again, it begs the question, why now?"

They looked at one another. There was a very long pause. My father was the first to speak.

"Recently Molly went back home between motion picture shoots. She was there for about four months. She became reacquainted with a young man she has known most of her life."

"I've known Will since we were just kids. His name is really William—William Morgan. He used to be called Billy, but when we got older, he made everyone start calling him Will, after Will Rogers. Because Will Rogers is from Oklahoma, too."

"And?" I asked, trying to get this woman to share something of relevance to the topic at hand.

My lord, she was my father's child, alright. Not only does she favor him greatly as I was just now noticing but she shares his propensity to prattle on. Tag! Now it was time for my father to speak once again.

Damn! I lost all my advantage when I used my Sherlock Holmes voice. I thought sulkily.

"Upon being reunited, Molly and Will consummated their love for each other." Father spoke once again, still using his teacher voice.

Then comprehension charged into my mind like Pershing leading his troops.

"You're pregnant," I gasped in horror.

"Thank you for your delicacy, son," My father said reprovingly.

Even I knew that it was in every actresses' contract that she would not become pregnant during the life of said contract without the studio's permission. And the studio never gave their permission.

"I'm afraid it gets even worse. Upon learning of her pregnancy, it seems that Will wanted to do the "right thing" so he and Molly were secretly married."

And there it was, Cardinal Rule Number One in every actor or actresses' contract alike. No one is allowed to marry without first obtaining studio permission.

"My God girl! What were you thinking?" I barked out in amazement.

Theo's or Molly's, or whatever the damn girl's name was, eyes began to fill with tears. *She picks now to cry?* Since she was already crying, I didn't feel it would be putting her out any to add to the tears.

"Well, sister. It would appear that you have made a royal mess of things."

I had been right about the increase in tears. I knew I was being a cad, but dang it all, why was she bringing her troubles to my door step?

My father had reached over and put his arm around her, trying to calm her down. It seemed to be working. She was now sobbing softly into his shoulder.

"Theo," I said calmly, looking first at her. "Father," I said, tilting my head up to look at him and then returning my gaze to Theo. "Although I can certainly appreciate the pickle you are in, I am not sure anything short of a miracle can help you at this point."

"I agree with you, son. You might just be that miracle. Remember last Halloween when you attended the Film

The Reluctant Doppelganger

Guild's masked ball? "

"Oh my God!" I exclaimed, as unbelievable horror jolted through me.

And the shoe dropped. In that moment, everything became as clear as crystal. Last Halloween, on a dare from my best friend, Cecilia Schofield, Seedy to everyone who knows her, I attended the Film Guild's masked ball as Theodora Desmond. I had been so convincing that my photo had run in one of the local tabloids the next morning.

The reporter said that it was his wife who assured him that the girl was not the real Theodora Desmond, because she was wearing a ready-made Woolworth's frock. She knew that, because she had purchased one just like it two weeks past, and she was sure a rich movie star wouldn't be caught dead in a ready-made.

The next day Seedy and I had had a great laugh. Not because the reporter thought I might have been Theodora Desmond, but the fact that he was sure I was a girl. That same morning, I had received a telephone call from my father. He had been apoplectic with rage. He couldn't believe that I would go out in public dressed as a woman. I had tried to explain to him that it was just a dare, and nothing would come of it. I had always wondered how he knew it was me. I had never been identified in the article. Now I knew. Miss Theodora Desmond and I share an uncanny family resemblance.

"Have you lost your mind?" I sputtered in my father's direction.

When no reply was forthcoming, I began to look back and forth at each of them with a look of ardent terror on my face.

"Hear me out, son."

Out of respect for my father, which was quickly evaporating, I sat fuming with my eyes narrowed and arms crossed over my chest.

"This could turn into a very volatile state of affairs."

We were back to the teacher's voice.

"A state of affairs not of my causing nor my concern," I snapped back.

"You are absolutely correct about this situation not being of your causing; however, you are not correct about it not being your concern."

I started to protest, but he silenced me by putting his index finger to his lips.

Damn! He used that index finger a lot.

"This is a matter of family honor and that same family's monetary wellbeing."

He paused to let those words sink in. The family thing was simply subterfuge as far as I was concerned. His true reason lay in the latter half of his pronouncement. This was all about money. Living a student's life funded solely from an allowance given to me by my father, I fully understood the meaning in his words "monetary wellbeing." I relaxed just a bit and uncrossed my arms. With that move he knew he was winning. I hated the fact that he could play this game so well.

"Your sister, Theo, is one of the studio's top paid starlets. I receive a commission on that salary, and you receive an allowance from me."

Ah, the trickle-down effect. I was familiar with the concept. I was just now studying it in my business marketing class. And that was that. He had me. I directly profited from my newly discovered sister's career. However, I wasn't quite ready to give up and become a girl.

"So, exactly how much money is at stake here?"

"A small fortune. Theo is one of the highest paid actresses at her studio. That is due in no small part to me."

I wanted to cut in and say, "Don't break your arm patting yourself on the back," but I thought better of it.

The Reluctant Doppelganger

"She earns twelve times the average educated man's monthly salary—per week. And I receive twenty percent of that."

I would never have used the word "small" to describe it. If Theodora Desmond earns over twelve times the monthly salary of the average well educated man, per week, then my father was talking about a very substantial fortune. Dear God, was he talking about a lot of money!

It was time. I slumped slightly forward releasing all the tension, and allowed my body posture to show that I acquiesced.

The moment comprehension dawned, he started in. "Good! Here's what we are going to do."

"Wait." I held up the palm of my hand in a stop gesture. "What about me? I do have my own life. And I do have school."

"It's for less than a year. Your education can easily be put on hold. What about your social life? Do you have a large quantity of friends and acquaintances who will miss you?"

He already knew the answer.

"Well, no I don't," I said grudgingly.

And with that, he launched into his plan. I always marveled at the way my father's mind worked. He was always thinking at least three moves ahead.

"Theo has purchased a large cattle ranch in Texas. Will is already there running the ranch as its new lord and master. We could not have her going home to Oklahoma where she is celebrated. The whole world would know she is pregnant in a matter of weeks."

He was getting excited. Maybe my father should start using the phrase *The game is afoot*, too.

"With Pop's help, I found an eleven-hundred-twenty-acre cattle ranch. Will thinks he has died and gone to heaven. It's only a two-day car trip to get to my mama and daddy's house."

"After Theo has the baby, she will need a month or so to get back on her feet. She can be back in Hollywood by next June in time for her scheduled summer motion picture filming."

I thought about it for a minute.

"So, I can lay low and make a few public appearances impersonating Theodora Desmond. This truly might be easier than I had thought. After all, Theo is noted for being Hollywood's Little Goody Two-Shoes." I was getting caught up in the plan too.

Theo looked peeved.

"I'm Little Goody Two-Shoes, as you say, because I am in love with Will. I've never wanted another man. I have been in love with Will for … well, forever, I think." She went wistful at the thought.

"You cannot lay low, son. The reason I insisted on meeting today is that matters are urgent. Theo is nearly three months pregnant. She is beginning to show slightly. Her six films have been such a success that the studio is wanting to move her from the ingénue to more powerful and thought-provoking roles. She is about to play Delilah in Rodrick Crawford's production of Samson and Delilah."

Everyone in Hollywood knew the name Rodrick Crawford. If you were cast in a Rodrick Crawford production, you were the crème de la crème. You had arrived at the top.

"Congratulations! That is an amazing accomplishment. I'm sure you will be marvelous," I gushed as an unabashed fan.

She smiled brightly at first and then the sparkle faded out of her smile.

"She cannot shoot the picture," My father said almost sadly, placing one of his big hands on top of both of her gloved ones, that were clasped demurely in her lap. The costumes for Delilah are … dare I say, scant. Not to mention the filming could take the better part of three months."

Horror now had me in its grips.

"You expect me to impersonate Theodora Desmond the actress as an actress? An actress in a Rodrick Crawford film wearing scanty costumes?"

My hands were gesticulating wildly now as my voice rose in both volume and pitch.

"Are you insane? Have you thought about the equipment I don't have and more over the equipment I do?"

I pointed first to my chest and then downward towards my…. well you know.

"Yes, I have. The first is not much of an issue." He gestured to Theodora's chest. "Thank God, no bosom is the height of fashion right now."

Theo blushed.

"And as for the second part, I have a few ideas. You will just need to trust me for the moment." He tried to sound reassuring.

This time his cheeks reddened.

"Here is how I think we should carry out the switch. First, everything must happen in the light of day. Any time Theo goes out she is mobbed by photographers, but it is especially so in the evening. When we leave here, I will accompany Theo to her home in Beverly Hills. She already has her essentials packed. She has placed her valise in a packing crate and addressed it to her mother. While she has been here, I arranged for the crate to be picked up by the postal service. The few things she is taking with her should already be on their way. Now we have only to get her on a train to Texas and you in her place."

I shook my head as this sank in.

"Her things are headed to Oklahoma, but she is going to Texas?" Suddenly I grasped the fact that this entire plan had been in place long before I had been included.

"They are and she is. We cannot risk anyone who might be interested in paying someone to find out where the parcel is going, getting the real story. Reporters will do damn near anything short of murder to get a scoop on a movie star."

"Don't you think you are being a little paranoid?"

"This is Hollywood, son. Everyone is paranoid and with good reason. Wealthy and famous people are always watched. And Theodora Desmond is both. Do you still have that dress that you wore on Halloween?"

I nodded my head yes.

"Sitting in the corner next to my desk is a case that contains a blonde wig. I want you dressed as a girl wearing that wig and the dress you wore last year."

"Oh my, I normally would not be caught dead in last year's fashions," I drawled dryly.

Theo giggled.

"I totally understand, "daaahling," she said, tilting her head and looking down her nose.

She had taken the R out and add a series of H sounds like so many of the society girls did these days. I really was liking Theo more and more. My father just shook his head. He was very focused now and I could tell he wanted us to stay on target.

"It is absolutely crucial that you do not look like Theodora. I want you to arrive at her home fully dressed at 8:00 am tomorrow morning. With tomorrow being Saturday, the early hour should find a great many of the reporters and photographers still in their beds. And if she is not seen out and about tonight, perhaps she will be out-of-sight-out-of-mind. You will find the address written on a note inside in the case with the wig. Do you think you can do that?"

I nodded my affirmation.

"Good!" He stood, encouraging both Theo and me to do

the same. "As you so aptly put it, the game is afoot."

With that he took Theo by the elbow and led her into the center of the office. I followed. Now my father was on a mission and the time for pleasantries had passed. He had already gathered Theo's fur from the chair across from his desk and was helping her into it. Theo was trying unsuccessfully to tell me that it had been a pleasure meeting me, and to thank me for my help, but my father's bustling about was making that pretty much impossible. In moments, he had her by the elbow, once again ushering her towards the office door. He stopped to collect his coat and hat from the hall tree at the door. Once he had them on, he crossed back to me and gave me a monstrous hug. He smelled of cigar smoke and of a spiced cologne that he had custom made. Just when I expected him to let me go, he did something very out of character. He clasped my cheeks in both hands, looked me in the eyes and bent his head forward and kissed me on my forehead.

"Thank you, son." He whispered in my ear as he released me.

He turned, offered his arm to Theodora Desmond, the actress, and escorted her out of his office, tipping his hat to Gertie. He closed the door behind them, and they were gone.

3

I stood there for a minute, stunned at what had just transpired. I walked over to the bank of windows behind my father's desk, looked down towards the street, and watched as Theodora's chauffeur opened the door of a shiny sleek black Daimler Royal limousine. He helped her into the soft dove gray leather interior and my father climbed in behind her, sitting in one of the two swiveling jump seats so that he could face her. The chauffeur closed the door, walked to the front of the automobile and slipped into the driver's seat. It was an English drive with the driver on the right-hand side. As the big auto drove out of sight, I wondered if it was hard to maneuver here in America where our drivers sit on the left. I watched the big black automobile until it disappeared around a corner.

I was lost in thought when I sensed someone looking at me.

"What are your thoughts?" I asked, without looking back.

"My thoughts on what?" Gertie replied.

Again, without looking back, I pointed to the large box on my father's desk where a light still glowed bright yellow.

The Reluctant Doppelganger

"I assume you were listening." I made it more of a statement of fact than a question.

She did not respond; therefore, I had my answer.

"Do you think he knows she's not coming back?"

"I think he is all too aware of it." Her tone was matter of fact.

"*Patrem eum, et cibavit leonis et lupi*?" I queried to the universe with a heavy sigh.

"I don't think your father has any intention of feeding his lion to the wolves." Her voice was solemn.

I looked over my shoulder at her, somewhat surprised.

"Don't forget, pup, who first introduced you to Latin."

The corners of her mouth quirked up in something just shy of a smirk. Gertie was the closest thing to a mother I had ever had. I loved her because she never added sugar to make taking your medicine easier to swallow. She was always logical, but most of all I loved her because she loved me. I turned around.

"So, my dear Gertie, am I to assume he has a grand plan?" I asked in my brightest timbre wearing an exuberant smile I didn't feel.

"Honestly?" She paused. "I think he moved heaven and earth to get her where she is today. He did it because he felt guilty about not being there for her as a father. It's not because he didn't want to be a part of her life, but after her mother left and remarried, he didn't feel it would be good for any of those involved. He sent her mother money every month until Molly came to Hollywood. The sad thing about our Molly is she never wanted to come to Hollywood at all. And she most certainly never wanted to be Theodora Desmond. That was her mother's dream. A dream she foisted off on Molly. Dora really isn't a bad sort. Dora is Molly's mother. It just seems she has never been able to make a good decision.

"Your father created the name Theodora Desmond. He wanted to use her mother's name, but he thought the name Dora was too common for a starlet, so he made it more exotic. He knew it would make Dora happy and perhaps she'd quit pestering Molly. It worked too. So, you see Eddie, Theodora Desmond isn't anyone. It has been a façade for Molly to hide behind. Now she has finally grown up. She knows where she wants to be and who she wants to be with. You surely cannot fault her for that."

"I don't fault her for anything, I don't think. But I just keep asking, why me?"

"The answer to that, dear boy, should be obvious to you as well."

I cocked an eyebrow. That is another thing I inherited from my father. The ability to raise one eyebrow. And it's been a damned useful tool to have in one's arsenal.

"You just stated it a moment ago. You are a lion. Molly is a lamb. She has survived the wolves. You can too. Perhaps, you will even conquer them."

I knew Gertie and there was still something she wasn't saying.

"And?"

"And I think you know that too."

Suddenly my face felt flush. I could feel the heat rising off it.

"I – I – I'm sure I don't know what you mean." I stammered.

"Oh, I'm sure you do. This day has been rough sailing for you already, no doubt. But I think between you and me it is high time we get this out in the open. I know your secret. And it's safe with me."

And with that pronouncement, my life had changed yet again today. She was right about the rough sailing.

"How long have you known?" I asked sheepishly.

The Reluctant Doppelganger

I never allowed my eyes to leave hers. I would be damned if I was going to be ashamed.

"Since you were around twelve. Remember that Saturday when you were staying with me because your father was away on business and we went to the beach?"

I nodded yes.

"You only had eyes for the boys. It was hard to miss. It's a common problem with the male sex in general. They find it very "hard" not to show their interest, if you take my meaning."

Her eyes were soft and glowed with compassion.

"Oh my, have I been that obvious? You know, I've never acted on it." I assured her hurriedly.

"You may not have acted on it yet. But you are a young man, and if you are anything like your father you will, and my guess is sooner rather than later."

"Do you think Father knows?"

"He has never confided his thoughts on that subject to me. But once again guessing, I would say yes. Why in the world do you think he had you involved in every manly sport in the state of California? Thank God, the caber toss wasn't an American sport or the two of you would been out in some field tossing trees around."

We both chuckled at the thought of that.

"I can't see Father in a kilt. And not because it is a skirt either." I grinned.

The bountifulness of my father's manhood is as well publicized as any Hollywood moving picture star. I did say he was touted around Hollywood as a lady's man. That could be a "big" reason why.

"You have become a damn good shot, an accomplished horseman; you are a great surfer and I would not want to meet up with you in a dark alley."

She was referring to my training in Judo. I started my

training at seven years of age and I now hold a tenth-degree black belt.

"There was a bonus to the two of you becoming sportsmen. You and your father grew close. And since it has always just been the two of you, that was a wonderful bonus, indeed. Now, I think, you can ease your mind about that as well. We both know your secret, we love you, and we don't care." She said it in a tone that brooked no argument.

"I don't care?" I blew up. "He's about to make me pretend to be a girl. Have I ever expressed any desire to either of you about wishing to be a woman?"

"No Edward, you have not. You did, however, become a woman, a very famous woman, for the whole world to see. And you did it well. It's my guess he thought you did desire it. And like with your sister, he simply wanted to make you happy. And in this case, he was killing two birds with one stone."

"You are certainly doing a great deal of guessing today, my dear Gertie."

"Perhaps. However, I have always been a good guesser." She smiled.

"I don't want to be a woman and it's not going to make me happy!"

It was an answer that came out as more of a whine than a declaration.

Gertie looked me straight in the eyes.

"*Leonis et Lupi Occiderent!*" The lion shall slay the wolves.

With that, Gertie turned and headed out of my father's office and back towards her desk. As she exited, she pointed back over her shoulder without turning or missing a step.

"Don't forget your hair, dear."

I snatched up the case in the corner, passed out of the office, then through the main door and was gone in a huff.

4

Once I was down on the street, I found a coin operated telephone and dropped a penny in the slot.

"Operator give me Clearbrook 6-8-5," I barked into the mouth piece.

My best friend, Seedy Schofield, lived in a lady's boarding house with four other women along with the lady of the house, Mrs. Winters, as frosty an old bird as her name implied. She had been known to shred the composure of many a young man calling on her boarders. I had been very fortunate. She liked me for some unknown reason. I knew she would be the one answering the telephone. She always did.

"Winters' boarding house. Mrs. Viola Winters speaking," she said, her voice tinged with ice.

"Hello and good day to you, Mrs. Winters. This is Edward Standish. Could I please speak with Cecilia?"

Her voice softened instantly as I knew it would.

"Hello Edward. I will call Cecilia for you," was her warm reply.

It was only a moment before Seedy was on the line.

"Heidi Ho, Eddie."

Seedy's voice was rich and surprisingly deep for a girl. She always sounded happy and bubbly. And to tell the truth, she was.

"Heidi Ho, Seedy! Listen, I must be brief. Do you have plans for this evening?"

"I was hoping you would call and suggest something wonderfully scrumptious and oh so exciting to do. If not, I'm going to read through the latest issue of *The Ladies Home Journal*. It will be a frightfully dull Friday evening, if that turns out to be the case."

"Would you like to meet me at the soda fountain at my grandfather's drug store at 6:30? I need to talk with you."

Going to my grandfather's store always made dinner and a milkshake easy. I got the grandchild's discount — free for me and my guests.

"That sounds keen. I will see you there at 6:30."

The operator came back on the line. "Please deposit another penny if you wish to continue the call."

"See you there," I said hurriedly and hung up.

I hopped on the next Red Car trolley headed towards the school. I had made the decision to tell Seedy everything. I would need at least one confidante besides Gertie and my father in this folly. There was no way I thought this could work. No one would ever think I was Theodora Desmond. I sat lost in thought staring through the window of the trolley oblivious to everything, as it wound its way back to the place that, for a short time longer, I called home.

When I arrived back at my rooms it was fast approaching six o'clock. I freshened up, slicked my hair back and changed into a more festive bow tie. I took a taxi to my grandfather's drug store in Westwood Village. When I arrived in front of the store, Seedy was already waiting outside on the sidewalk.

Cecilia Schofield and I had met nearly three years ago on

the first day of our freshman year at school. We instantly struck up a friendship. She was one of a small minority of women in the three-year degree program at the Bentley School of Business. She had inherited a modest sum from her grandfather on her mother's side of the family. When she announced to her family, she was going to use the money to go to college, at first, they were elated thinking she was going there to find and secure an educated husband. But as the years went by and she excelled in her business studies and showed no signs of finding a husband, their exultation began to wane.

Seedy's intent is to get her degree in business and hopefully secure a position as a personal secretary to an accomplished woman. And if that fails, to work as an executive secretary to a large company executive. She has a great work ethic combined with a commanding presence that is sure to help her with managing other people.

We share so many things in common. We both are five foot three inches tall. So, we look eye to eye. We both have blue eyes and we each have reddish blonde hair—hers is curly and mine straight. We share a head for figures, and we are each working towards a degree in business. Seedy is the only person to whom I've ever confided my dark secret. I'm not sure why I told her. But to my surprise, she wasn't offended at all. I had asked her to please keep it to herself because I could go to jail if anyone ever found out.

But Seedy always maintained, "One cannot go to jail for what is only in one's mind and heart."

Today, she was wearing a blue rayon dress that shimmered in the setting sun. It had a pink lace collar that set off her sparkling eyes. She was wearing silk stockings and low-heeled shoes. She was always so thoughtful for thinking of me when she dressed. She tried never to appear taller than me. I waved as I approached.

"You're looking swell tonight." I gave her a quick hug as I walked up.

"You're looking awfully dapper yourself. You're the bee's knees."

When she spoke, it always made me think of the sultry and seductive song of a bassoon. Seedy is contradiction incarnate. She has the face of an angel, the body of a tiny porcelain china doll and the voice of a siren. Or at least she sounds like how I think a siren would sound.

"Do you think that, after we get a bite to eat, you might be interested in going to the movie theater tonight? There is an eight o'clock showing of *The Flesh and the Devil*."

"I've seen that movie with you three times. How many times have you seen *The Flesh and the Devil*?" I asked, laughing.

"Does it really matter? It is a great movie. Garbo and Gilbert are so romantic." She swooned, clasping her hands to her face and swaying from side to side. She giggled girlishly before she instantly regained her composure.

I'm pretty sure she had a crush on John Gilbert. But that was okay because secretly, I did too.

"I would love to, but there is something very serious I need to talk with you about. And we need to go somewhere private to have this discussion." I gave her a grave look.

Her smiled dimmed. We hardly ever had need of serious conversations. And those few we had, all seemed to center around difficult classes or professors. We both loved school and were easy going, so we rarely had issues with those either.

"Sure. Would you like to do that first and come back for supper?"

"I think that would be the best idea."

There was a small park about two blocks down. She put her hand in mine and we walked, chatting about things that had happened since we last saw each other, which was this morning in class. We arrived and settled on an isolated bench.

She turned to me.

"So, spill the beans, what's going on?"

"I told you that my father wanted to see me today."

"I knew that was what this was all about. I hope he's not having money problems. I would hate for you to have to drop out of school in your senior year." Her voice filled with concern.

This was a very real issue for her. She was supporting herself. She had worked three jobs during the summer so that she could have enough money to pay room and board as well as her tuition for her senior year. It seemed that her grandfather's bequest had run shy.

"No, that's not it at all. My father had…." I paused, not sure how to tell this story. "My father had news for me, today." I elongated the word "news".

"What kind of news?" She asked, parroting back my tone.

"I'm going to ask you to contain your gasps and comments until I'm finished."

She nodded, but even as she did, I knew full well that this would not be occurring. So, I wasn't even sure why I was bothering to ask.

"My father called me into his office to meet my sister." I said calmly.

"Your sister? I thought you were an only child."

I knew she couldn't wait.

"Yes, I am an only child. But it seems that my father had an assignation with a studio seamstress a few years before he met my mother."

"And they had a love child?" She gasped.

"Yes. My father married her, but she didn't really want to be married, so they divorced. She went back to her family home in Oklahoma. That's where she had the baby, a girl, my sister." I stumbled over my words as I tried to relay my story in a calm even timbre. "Her mother remarried, but my father stayed in touch and sent her money over the years. When the girl was grown, he offered to send her to college, but her mother wanted her to move to Hollywood and wanted my father to make her a star."

"Was her mother insane? Does she know how many people come out here thinking they will be discovered?"

"Her mother had been one of those people. So yes, she knew. But she thought my father—because of his position, could make the introductions to all the right people for her. My sister, that sounds odd to say. My sister, Molly, that's her name, didn't want to be in motion pictures. She wanted the college education, but her mother would hear nothing of it. So, she came to Hollywood."

"That poor girl. I bet she was scared to death. I know I was when I came to Los Angeles. I had never been more than twenty miles from home. I came here by train, by myself. I enrolled in school, found a place to live and found a job all on my own. I must have considered tucking my tail and heading back home a hundred times. It was hard, and I wanted to be here. That poor girl." She sighed heavily.

"Molly really did prove to be tough. My father did use all his connections to get her in the door. But it was her own talent that helped her succeed."

Seedy looked confused for a moment, then, in an instant, her expression change. Seedy had grasped the gravitas of my last statement.

"She succeeded? Just who is your sister?"

Before the words could leave my mouth, I could tell she had put two and two together.

"Oh, good Lord! Your sister is Theodora Desmond?"

A smile crossed my face.

The Reluctant Doppelganger

"Theodora Desmond is your sister," she said again in amazement, just a bit too loudly.

"Sssh. Don't say it so loudly. It has to be a secret. I wasn't supposed to tell anyone."

"Why didn't he tell you long before now?" She whispered.

"That's a long story for another time. But there is more to this story that I need to tell you now and then I'm going to ask for your help."

She nodded with what I thought was an affirming nod, but I was not one hundred percent sure.

"Theodora went back to Oklahoma to visit between motion picture shoots this last summer. She rekindled the flame of a long-lost love. Now she is with child."

"She's pregnant?" she shouted in a whisper.

I proceeded to finish giving her all the details. When I got to the part about my father's solution to the situation, her mouth dropped open.

"Does he understand how dangerous that is for you? What if someone found out? You could go to jail!" She looked horrified.

"Actually," I said trying to sound like I believed it myself, "no I can't. I cannot go to jail for impersonating a woman. I could go to jail for being involved in sodomy and – or other lewd and lascivious behaviors. But I could go to jail if I did that now." I said more matter-of-factly than I felt.

"So where do I come in?"

"You are not in my father's plan, but you are in mine. I need someone to stay with me. Someone to make sure I don't lose my mind before June of next year."

"You want me to just drop everything in my senior year? Just quit in the middle of a semester that I worked like a plow horse to be able to afford? I can't do that."

"If we pull it off, there will be plenty of money to reimburse you for your tuition. And the added bonus is that

Theodora Desmond would write you a glowing letter of recommendation. After all, you would have been her personal secretary for almost nine months. And that letter by a famous movie star—I'm liking that term more and more every time I use it—would carry more weight than a college business degree. Who knows? Maybe Molly will keep you on once she returns and you may never need your senior year at all."

I felt guilty telling her that last part. I was pretty sure that Molly would never be coming back. And I wasn't sure, at all, how we were going to get ourselves out of the mess we were about to create. But I'd cross that bridge when I got there.

I could tell she was pondering the idea. She was silent for a long while. I was going to let her think it through for as long as she needed.

Finally, she spoke. "I'll do it! You're right about that letter of recommendation. And with as many public appearances as she makes, I am bound to be seen in the background. Maybe some rich and famous woman will hire me away."

"That would be great, but you cannot allow yourself to be hired away until next June."

She turned to me and stuck out her hand. I clasped hers and we shook.

"Deal!" we each said at the same time.

5

At eight o'clock the next morning, our taxi arrived at the front gate of the Beverly Hills address that had been scrawled on the note inside the case that held the wig. The house sat well off the road, but even from this vantage point it looked mammoth.

Seedy had flat refused to let me dress as the woman, when we had the "Real McCoy" as she put it. It did make perfect sense to me, so I had agreed. Seedy had donned the now infamous off-the-rack dress and fastened the blonde bob-cut wig over her own reddish-gold curly locks.

The driver wound his window down to speak to the guard at the gate.

"Who's calling?" the old guard asked the taxi driver.

The driver looked over his shoulder at me, causing the stooping guard to do so as well.

"I am Edward Standish, and this is Miss Cecilia Schofield. Miss Desmond is expecting us." I said, leaning forward.

The guard went back to the gate house and leafed through what I assumed was an appointment book. He returned to the car.

"Neither of you appear to be on the list. I would telephone the house to ask but this is not considered to be a reasonable hour. If you'd like to come back around ten o'clock, I will be more than happy to telephone up to the house."

I was at a total loss. My father had never given me a name to use at the gate. And he had no idea Seedy was with me. At that very moment, the telephone rang in the guard house. The guard went to answer it. In just a few moments, he returned to the car. When he reached the window again, he bent low and looked in, smiling.

"That was Miss Desmond herself." He sounded impressed. "She said to go on up to the house, and that she would meet you at the front door."

He looked at the taxi driver. "Just give me a minute to get the gates open."

Then he stood up and turned around, moving spryly towards the huge wrought iron gates. It was only as I watched him go that I noticed the gates themselves. The left gate had a massive letter "T" in script at its center and the right gate had a matching letter "D." A guarded front gate was impressive, but a monogrammed guarded front gate was a bit on the grandiose side. The guard pulled a large key from his pocket and unlocked first one side then the other. He pushed each gate open in turn and motioned for us to go through. With a bump, we rolled over the metal threshold as we motored up the long driveway, finally pulling up to a set of marble steps that led up to the front door.

Theodora and a gentleman dressed very formally in a black suit and white gloves were standing on the front landing, at the top of the stairs. I guess you'd call it a front porch, but it didn't look like any front porch I had ever seen before. The gentleman hurried down the front steps, opened the door for Seedy and helped her out of the taxi. By the time, he got to my side of the automobile I was already out, as was the taxi driver. I started to pull out my wallet to pay the driver, but the gentlemen in the black suit handed him a five-dollar bill and told him to keep the change. The fare had only been a dollar and seventy cents. I'm not sure whose jaw dropped first — mine or the driver's. He thanked the gentleman profusely, then got back in his taxi and motored back down the long driveway. The gentleman and I made our way up the stairs. Cecilia was standing next to Molly. Her mouth seemed to be gaping open.

As we reached the top of the stairs, Molly said, "That will be all, Wallace. Thank you."

Wallace gave a slight bow and went back into the house, leaving the door open.

Molly was smiling, "Eddie, would you like to introduce me to your friend?"

"Oh, pardon my manners Theo; this is Cecilia Schofield. Cecilia, this is my sister, Theodora Desmond."

"Nice to meet you Cecilia."

"And it's a pleasure meeting you too, Miss Desmond. I'm a huge fan. I loved your last picture, *Passions of the Night*."

"Thank you so much. I'm glad you enjoyed it. You must call me Theo." Molly held out her hand.

"Then please call me Seedy. Everybody does." And she shook the proffered hand.

"Let's go on in. Pops is waiting for us upstairs in the long gallery."

Theo was already moving, ushering us through the open front door. She flowed in behind us, leaving the door wide open. I felt an urge to go back and close the door, but by the time we had reached the bottom of the enormous mahogany and gilded staircase, Wallace had appeared, seemingly out of nowhere, and was closing, with ease, the massive wooden door that stood nearly two stories tall.

All I could think was, "WOW!" as it clicked shut.

Nick Hilliard

Upstairs in the long gallery my father was pacing the floor and, as expected, he was fuming.

Once Molly had closed the door, he looked up and bellowed at me, "What in the devil is Seedy doing here? I gave you one simple instruction, and you couldn't seem to carry it out."

"First, the instruction was far from simple; and second, if my life is going to change forever, then I need to have some say in the matter," I bellowed right back.

"Boys!" Theo hissed. "There are servants in the house. Could you please keep your voices down?"

Both Father and I immediately fell silent.

I started this time, in a much softer and more civil tone of voice, "I would go crazy trying to pull this caper off alone."

I held up my hand as my father started to interrupt.

"I know I have you, Father. But you cannot be with me twenty-four hours a day and Seedy can. She has agreed to work as my personal secretary and to live here in the house. She is my best friend and she will give me someone I can confide in. In return, I have promised to give her a glowing letter of recommendation as Theodora Desmond's personal secretary when it's all said and done."

I could tell my father was mulling it over. I looked over at Seedy and she had gone white as a sheet.

"You know Son, that's a great idea. Just goes to show, you really are a chip off the old block." He grinned.

The mood in the room relaxed almost instantly.

"It was Seedy's idea for her to come dressed as you had instructed. And I thought it was a smashing idea. You can see all three of us are about the same height and build. Well, except Seedy had to bind her breasts in order to appear flat chested."

"And that is something I'm willing to remedy as soon as possible, if you take my meaning," said Seedy, shifting her bindings uncomfortably.

We all chuckled.

"Now that I think about it, this might work out even better. Seedy, are you courageous enough to stay here at the house in Theo's room, dressed as Theo while Eddie, Theo and I get her on the train? Then Eddie and I have an errand to run. The whole thing should take about three hours."

"As long as I don't have to talk to any of the servants, I guess I can do that." Her face was alight with a mixture of both fear and excitement.

"You will have to interact with one servant." Theo told her. "But she's in on everything. Her name is Claudette and she is my personal lady's maid."

With that, Theo walked over to a bell cord that hung on the wall. She gave it three tugs.

"Always remember, three pulls of the cord rings for Claudette."

Just then the door opened quietly and a beautiful petite woman wearing a black uniform with a white apron glided into the room. She had dark bobbed hair. Her skin was olive and her eyes were as green and sparkling as faceted emeralds.

"Yes, mademoiselle?" she purred in a lush sultry French accent.

"Claudette, this young man is my half-brother, Mr. Standish. He will be taking my place. This is his friend and personal secretary, Miss Schofield," Theo introduced.

"How do you do, Monsieur and Mademoiselle?"

We both gave her a slight nod as my father started spouting out orders.

"Theo, you have a train to catch, so we had better get to it. You and Seedy should go trade places and I'm sure Claudette will be needed to help. Eddie and I'll stay here."

And with that the ladies left the room.

About twenty minutes later, Theo and Seedy came back into the room. The switch had been made, and at a considerable distance and if the viewer was very near-sighted, Seedy could pass for Theo. The biggest transformation was with Molly. Theo was gone. Before us stood a natural blonde beauty. She wore very little make-up and the ready-made dress was well suited for the new person she had become.

"Molly," Father embraced her, "you look stunning."

"You don't look like Theodora at all. You look like a completely different person," I said smiling.

"This is what I really look like. When I'm at home in Oklahoma, this is how I dress."

"That Will is one lucky man," Father said. "It's time for us to get going. I had Wallace call us a taxi. Seedy, you get back to Theo's room and stay there. If you need anything at all, just ask Claudette."

A horn honked.

"Wallace will shoot that taxi driver for honking if we don't get down there quickly. It's not like the cabbie is pulling up at an address where he's not sure that anyone will know he's there. Honestly, it's as if he didn't think the gatehouse would telephone up and announce his arrival. I guess it's just my nerves today, but it always annoys me when people don't think things through before they act.

Now, there was the pot calling the kettle black, if I had ever heard it.

6

Five minutes later, all three of us were piling into the taxi. I sat up front with the driver. It just happened to be the same driver that had brought us to the house.

"Did you have a good visit?" the driver asked politely.

"We had a splendid visit," I said, making light conversation.

"That's got to be one of Beverly Hills' biggest mansions."

Until he said it, I had not thought of that mammoth house with its multi-acre estate as a mansion, but it sure as the devil was.

And I was about to take up residence there. Wow!

In the back, I could make out Father going over a list of instructions with Molly. And knowing Father, it was for the hundredth time, too. To keep the cabbie's thoughts off the backseat and possibly overhearing something he shouldn't, I kept up a running conversation with him. I found out about his wife, their four children, and their dog they called Mutt. He told me all about how his brother-in-law helped build and then helped demolish the Beverly Hills Speedway. And how his eldest son was one of the construction crew that had already started to work on a new hotel on the old speedway site. He told me the new hotel was to be called the Beverly Wilshire Hotel. It sounded as if it was going to be like all things Beverly Hills, lavish to the extreme. I was glad when we pulled up in front of the train station. If the trip had been much longer, I was afraid of what else I might have learned about the man.

We all got out. My father palmed me a ten-dollar bill and then put his arm around Molly and started walking her towards the main gate and platforms.

"How much do I owe you?"

"It'll be two dollars and fifty cents."

I handed him the ten-dollar bill and told him to give me five back, and he could keep the rest. He smiled and was happy to do it. I was betting that the fiver I got back was the same one Wallace had given him this morning.

The taxi drove off and I walked through the gates. I spotted Father and Molly near the far end of one of the platforms. They were staying well out of the main crush of people, which was comprised of both travelers and their loved ones seeing them off. I'm sure it was because they wanted to minimize the chance of anyone recognizing Molly.

The conversation was light and casual as we waited for the train to start boarding.

"All aboard!" we heard the conductor yell down the platform.

We began to move back towards the front of the train and the first-class compartments. Molly had no luggage, but if the porter in first-class thought it was strange, he said nothing. Then it was time to say good-bye. Father gave Molly a hug and kissed her on both cheeks, holding her tight. He knew she wasn't coming back.

"I'll see you after the baby gets here. I'll miss you, honey. I've gotten used to having you around." He hugged her one last time.

Now it was my turn. As my father and I jockeyed for position, Molly reached into her handbag and produced a very large diamond ring. She slipped it on her ring finger.

"Presto Change-O, I'm Mrs. William Morgan," She beamed at me.

She leaned in to kiss me on the cheek, then placed both hands on my shoulders and looked me in the eyes.

"You'll never know how grateful I am. I so appreciate you for doing this." Her eyes puddled with tears. "Daaahling, I think you are going to be so good at this." She kissed me again. "Be good, little brother. Now the two of you get out of here before you cause me to actually cry and ruin what little make-up I have on."

With that, she shooed us off the train. Once we were back on the platform, she blew us a kiss and disappeared back inside the train, only to reappear at the window, waving. The train began to hiss its way into motion. Then chugging, it picked up speed and soon it was gone from the station. We waved until we couldn't see Molly anymore.

When the train was almost out of sight, my dad slapped me across the chest.

"Let's go Eddie, we have places to go and people to see. We need to make sure we get a different taxi driver this time. Where we're going, I don't want anyone to recognize us."

Now if that wasn't an ominous statement, I'd never heard one before.

We walked all the way to the other side of the station to secure our taxi. Father selected a cab after passing several by and we got in.

"Where to?" asked the driver in a deep gravelly voice.

"Take us to the Drakestone Hotel in East Hollywood," Father said.

"The Drakestone? Are you sure, Mac?"

"Yes sir, the Drakestone."

The driver looked hard at the both of us in his rear-view mirror as he pulled away from the curb. Even I had heard of the Drakestone. It was a notorious hotel and speakeasy that catered to homosexuals.

I didn't say a word, but I was surely wondering, *Why on earth are we going there?*

Nearly forty-five minutes later we arrived in front of a shabby three-story building. The sign painted on its façade proclaimed in peeling pastel letters that we were now indeed, in front of the Drakestone Hotel. There was a very mean looking, very muscular man sprawled in a white wooden slatted lawn chair in front of the entrance. He looked like a strong man from a circus. I mean that literally, too. He appeared to be in a swimming costume, and he was bare chested. He was wearing dark glasses, as if he was sitting on the beach or by a swimming pool.

We got out of the cab. The driver didn't. My father leaned into his window and asked him how much. He paid the man but didn't tip him. The taxi drove away quickly.

After the taxi had passed, my father walked over to the curb and stepped up onto the sidewalk.

"Did I have any change from the last taxi ride?"

I put my hand in my pocket and pulled out the fiver and made to hand it to him. He kept walking towards the door.

"Keep it." He looked back to see how much I still had. "I just wanted to see if you had given the driver a really good tip or if you had tipped him like your last name was Rockefeller."

I laughed.

"With you as my father, I'm all too aware my last name is NOT Rockefeller."

With Father in the lead we reached the huge, half naked man, silent behind his dark glasses.

The Reluctant Doppelganger

"Hello, Tiny. Is she in?"

Tiny?

"Good afternoon, Bertie."

Here was a case where the voice didn't fit with the body. It was unusually high and squeaky. "She is," he squeaked.

We walked right past him and headed to the front door. He never moved a muscle. The door was a revolving one. Father set it spinning first and I hopped in the compartment right behind him. When it spat us out into the lobby, I saw that the interior of the hotel was right in line with its exterior. The entire lobby seemed to have been caught in time. Everything looked to be at least fifty years out-of-date and heavily worn. But it was clean. Behind a large registration desk that once might have held several clerks, now sat a heavy-set woman wearing flapper evening wear and loads of make-up. As we drew closer, I realized that it wasn't a woman at all. There was beard stubble sticking through an overly made up face and a cigarette dangled from the corner of his mouth. It had a long ash that somehow hung precariously   balanced   off   its   glowing   tip.

"Well, well, well, if it isn't Bertie Standish in the flesh. I don't recall you representing any of my girls," said the more than obvious man dressed like a woman. His voice was all scratchy like someone who has smoked for most of his life.

With every word, the cigarette bobbed up and down. I found myself mesmerized with morbid curiosity. I kept waiting for the ash to fall, but it never did.

"Good day, Madame Rochelle, did you get my message to Georgie?" Father spoke in a pleasant easy fashion and wore a polite smile.

I waited for my father to introduce us, but no introduction was forthcoming. I could only assume that Madame Rochelle was the proprietress of this establishment.

Nick Hilliard

"He's waiting for you in the sewing room." Madame Rochelle nodded her head in the direction of a hallway that led somewhere into the dark depths of the building.

Even while nodding her head, the cigarette still didn't drop its ash. It just grew longer and longer.

"Can we go on back?"

"Well, the sewing room ain't gonna come up here to you, honey."

My father bobbed his head in a thank you and we headed down a tattered carpeted hallway. We passed the public areas and pushed through a door that took us, as I feared, into the bowels of the building. My father made a right turn and moved into a different hallway. These floors were covered in old worn but highly polished tiles. We turned at least two more times. By now I was thoroughly lost. He pushed through two swinging doors and we were in a large open ballroom or at least what use to be a ballroom. Suffused sunlight poured through a wall of windows that were covered on the outside with a thick viscous grime. It bathed the room in a dingy grayness. The room was filled with rows and rows of racks overflowing with clothes—lady's clothes. There seemed to be frocks in every size and color of the rainbow with a definite preponderance of extra hefty sizes.

At the far end of the enormous room stood a woman in a sparkling beaded very fashionable evening gown. She was pinning fabric onto a dress maker's form. Her hair was straight, nearly black, and cut in a bob. She had her back to us. As she worked, I first thought I heard her growling, but I then recognized the tune. She was humming.

"Georgie," my father called out.

The woman gave a slight jump letting me know we had startled her. She turned and once again she wasn't a she at all, but a he. He had the deep olive skin of the Italians with strong Romanesque features, including a large hooked nose.

The Reluctant Doppelganger

Hooked nose notwithstanding, his face was that of a cherub —albeit a cherub with dark thick beard stubble.

What is with this place? Is it a house-of-horrors?

"Oh Bertie, you scared me half to death," she said.

She might have looked Italian, but her slow drawl most certainly pegged her as coming from the deep south. Her voice was almost lilting. The voice was definitely that of a young man, but it seemed as if he was trying hard to make it feminine. He—She? I was getting so confused.

"I'm so sorry Georgie," Father said. And he sounded sincere. "This is Edward, the young man I was telling you about. He's the one who is going to impersonate Theodora while she is on her private sabbatical."

Suddenly for some reason I felt betrayed.

"I thought you said we were to tell no one about this. To my reckoning there are currently six people who seem to know all about your little deception. And I'm pretty damn good at reckoning."

I rarely cursed in front of my father out of respect, but this had gone as far as it could go. I quickly learned, however, that this situation was nowhere near as far as it was going to go. Before my father could reply, Georgie had moved to stand directly in front of me. He stood looking down at me with a calculating appraising stare. He drew uncomfortably close to me. He was a good deal taller than me but nowhere nearly as tall as my father. This man, in a dress, was looming over me. He placed a crooked finger under my chin and lifted my face up to his. Normally, I would have considered this a very intimate gesture, but in this case, he was simply appraising my face. He turned my head from side to side. I tried not to meet his eyes for some reason, but they were hard to miss with the intensity of his gaze. They were a deep watery blue, blue as the Pacific Ocean on a bright and sunny California day, and currently they were fixed hard on me.

"He's got really pretty skin," he drawled. "And he sure does have that boyish body that all the women in this town long to have."

With that, he dropped to his knees and grabbed the waistband of my pants.

"Let's see what we have to hide."

And with that he gave an almighty tug on both my pants and drawers and I was suddenly naked from the waist down with my trousers and drawers bunched at my ankles.

"Great God Almighty!" Georgie exclaimed. "Who would have ever thought that something this big could be attached to such a little guy." He was staring straight at my...well, you know.

I looked up in horror at my father, who was looking down and smiling with a great deal of pride. I may have forgotten to mention that this was yet another attribute I had inherited from him. The truth of the matter is the man could shame a stallion. And now, as it was oh so obvious to all of us in the room, I could as well.

"The only way to hide this big old thing is with a Prince Albert," Georgie stated with the same detachment a parent would use when talking about hiding Christmas presents from their children.

Now my father was staring down at me, stroking his chin with his brow furrowed. He looked like a mathematician pondering a very interesting equation. And before I could ask the most obvious question myself, he was posing the query in a very analytical manner to Georgie.

"What is a Prince Albert?" he asked, still stroking his chin and peering down at me.

"It is a piercing. There are many rumors as to how it got its name, but as for its use, it would be perfect for this." Georgie was looking up at my father now.

"Explain," my father said.

The Reluctant Doppelganger

I was beginning to come unnerved. There were two men staring at my exposed body, discussing it candidly and casually and one of them was my father.

"It goes through here and out here." Georgie began to explain.

He was actually holding my—my, well, credentials in his hand. Pointing out to my father where it should be pierced.

"Then we place a ring through here and we have a counter ring on the back of the garment that we fasten it to. We push these up inside." And with that he pushed my rather sizable huevos up inside me.

"We pull him back like so," he said, pulling my manhood backwards between my legs. "And lastly we fasten it to the back of the garment and voila, he disappears."

"I've had enough!" I shouted, pushing Georgie's hands off me, while grabbing at my trousers and my underpants and hauling them back in place. "There will be NO piercing!"

"I tend to agree with the boy," my father said. "We'll need to come up with another idea."

"That is an awful lot to hide. I'm not sure how effective anything else might be, but I'll see what I can do." Georgie shrugged.

"Is this why we came here?" I asked, rather disgusted. Currently, I was feeling more than a tad bit violated.

"No, we came here so Georgie could get a feel for a style that might work for you. He can create any look. He also works at the studio in the costume department. He will be helping us keep our secret by making sure your costumes don't put your very sizable…." He trailed off for a moment embarrassed, then gestured downward. "Your sizable manhood on display," he finally finished. He still had that look of pride on his face.

"And that won't be easy," interjected Georgie. "Trying to alter a costume designed by Ethel Welch will be next to impossible. She is always on the movie set just in case a costume doesn't photograph well or if a particular line of a garment does not flow correctly on a particular actor or actress. She has an eagle eye for detail. And that big ole thang of yours won't require an eagle eye. I just don't think it can be done without the Prince Albert," he said emphatically. "As for a style that will work for you, that one is easy. Coco Chanel will be your Paris designer of choice. Her designs were meant for a body like yours."

"That's great, but where am I to find French designs from Paris in Hollywood?"

"That's easy too - Beverly Hills. But the question you should be asking is, where can I find Coco Chanel inspired designs — designed as originals just for me and a seamstress that can keep my *not-so-little-secret*— a secret."

He folded his arms across his chest, stuck out his right hip and smirked. "That is why you and so many others come to Georgie."

We dispensed with any further talk, and Georgie measured every square inch of my body. Twenty minutes later, my father and I were in yet another taxi headed back to Theodora's mansion. I mentally made a correction in that thought. We were headed back to MY mansion.

7

When we arrived back at the house, the guard opened the gate the minute he recognized my father. I learned that his name was Truman, although Molly had always called him Mr. Truman out of respect. She often gave him small gifts of homemade baked goods. Seems Molly enjoyed cooking, which is why both Wallace and the housekeeper and cook, Mrs. Reid, were off on Sunday, something that was unheard of and had raised many an eyebrow at first. Molly enjoyed having the house to herself, and she usually baked on the weekends. I was afraid that Mr. Truman might be doing without his treats if he would be relying on me to cook them.

The cab pulled up to the house, but this time, Wallace was not waiting on the front landing. Father paid the taxi driver and we climbed the steps together. I rang the doorbell. I was sure Wallace had been alerted by Mr. Truman because the moment the bell rang, he opened the door. My father stepped right in without being acknowledged. I followed in his wake.

"Is Miss Desmond upstairs in the long gallery?"

He had expected Wallace to say no, that she was in her room. But to his surprise, Wallace confirmed that she was indeed in the long gallery and had been all afternoon. A flash of annoyance crossed my father's face, but only briefly. He didn't like it when his stars did not do as they were told. And Theodora Desmond was one of his stars, no matter who was playing the part.

"I'll show you up to the gallery, sir." Wallace moved towards the staircase.

"Never mind Wallace. I know the way."

My father started taking the stairs two at a time. I hated it when he did that. With his long legs and robust frame, he bounded up the stairs with grace. I took the steps one at a time, but I moved quickly. I didn't want him to tear into Seedy before I could get there. As we neared the door, I could hear Marion Harris' voice on the Victrola, singing *There'll Be Some Changes Made.*

How appropriate, I thought, and snickered to myself.

Father opened the door. When we stepped into the room, we could see Seedy dressed as Theodora and Claudette seated at the card table playing gin rummy.

"Why didn't you stay in Theodora's room like I asked you to?" Father barked.

It was Claudette who answered.

"This was Mrs. Reid's day to change the bed linens. I thought it best that we not interrupt her regular schedule. I told her that Miss Desmond had a slight case of melancholia and that we would retire to the long gallery because she did not wish to be disturbed. We have been here ever since, Monsieur Bertie."

"Quick thinking Claudette." He turned to me. "It's time to get you ready.

"Claudette, would you take Eddie to his new bedroom and help him change? Seedy, I guess you need to change too. How did you explain your presence to the staff?"

"Claudette told Wallace and Mrs. Reid, when she went

The Reluctant Doppelganger

down for coffee, that I was being interviewed for the position of personal secretary," answered Seedy.

"And they were none too happy about it either. Mrs. Reid told me that the studio was supposed to hire any additional staff other than her personal maid. They have never been happy about me being here, but we get along fairly well. I told them perhaps because the position had the word 'personal' in its title, that Miss Desmond felt she needed to pay the wage and therefore she had the choice of whom to hire." Claudette gave a haughty little smile and turned up her nose.

"Well then, Miss Personal Secretary, once we get you changed, I'll take you down to the house manager's office and let you get a bit familiar. That will also keep the staff's minds off their Mistress, giving Claudette ample time to work her magic." Father winked and smiled conspiratorially at both Seedy and Claudette.

"There's just one little hitch. I didn't know you were going to send Molly off in the dress I was wearing this morning and I have nothing to change into," Seedy frowned.

"You come with me as well then," Claudette beckoned as she headed out of the room. "There is a blue business suit in Miss Desmond's closet. She calls it her going-to-the-lawyer suit. It will be perfect for you. It will make you look very professional."

It seemed her French accent got thicker when she got excited. Seedy and I followed Claudette out, leaving Father standing there alone as the door closed. We turned left, went down a long hallway, where it appeared to turn right again on to yet another corridor. But when we arrived at the bend, what we found instead, was a deeply set alcove that sequestered a pair of ornately carved and gilded doors. Claudette stepped in front of us, gave both knobs a twist, and threw open both doors at once. What I saw took my breath away. The massive bedroom was opulently decorated in shades of blue with gold-leaf accents. There was a sky filled with fluffy white clouds that floated across the entire ceiling.

"When mademoiselle first moved in, this room was decorated for a man. Everything was too dark and too heavy. Mademoiselle loves blue. Every shade of blue as you can see. I was the one who suggested the gold-leaf touches and the clouds. It is very popular in English manor houses. And I had hoped it might soften the blue. Blue can be so harsh, don't you think?" She didn't wait for us to reply before continuing on. "I think it worked well. And the artwork helped too."

"That bed is enormous. I've never seen a bed that big." I said, amazed.

Centered on one wall directly across from where we stood at the entrance was the gigantic bed.

"It is called a king-size bed. It must have custom linens because it is so large. Mademoiselle saw one like it at an exhibit; she had to have one. She said her Will was a tall man and that he always complained that his feet hung off the bed." Claudette laughed softly as she remembered their long-ago conversation.

Across from the bed on one wall sat a huge dressing table with three mirrors running half way up the wall and set so the viewer could see herself from almost any angle. There was an open door on either side of the dressing table. I could tell one was a bathroom that seemed to be sculpted from white marble. The other opened into a closet where a raised fitting platform was surrounded by still more mirrors that went all the way to the ceiling. From the reflection in those mirrors, I could see a cavernous space filled with clothes, hats and shoes. As I continued to look around the room, I saw that beautiful artwork adorned every wall. I was drawn to a portrait of a naked woman. She was seated in a green striped chair and had her arms raised over her head. The picture had an unusual perspective and was rich in bright fluid colors. It was awe-inspiring in its provocative boldness.

"That painting is by an artist who is very popular in France right now. Mademoiselle purchased it when she was in Paris just this last summer. Several members of the party she was traveling with said she had been robbed by the artist and that she was insane to pay the price she did. But Mademoiselle is gifted with an eye for these things. She thinks it will be very valuable someday. The artist is a man by the name of Henri Matisse."

There was a full-length, life-size portrait of Theodora Desmond on the wall across from the bed. The artist had captured her arresting beauty with incredible accuracy. The portrait was so detailed and to such perfect scale it appeared that Theodora might walk right out of the canvas and into the room. The absolute beauty of the painting was marred by its garish frame. The massive frame was covered in gold-leaf and was set with what appeared to be a cornucopia of jewels. There was what looked like a huge dull red stone at the very top center of the frame. Diamonds, sapphires, emeralds and pearls of all cuts and sizes spewed forth encrusting the entire perimeter with no rhyme or reason. I grimaced.

Claudette chuckled as she took in my reaction. "The frame was a gift. Mademoiselle's contract with the studio promised her this house. At the time, however, it was the home of Reginald Montgrieve, the movie actor. Mr. Crawford had acquired a larger Spanish style property for the studio, and he offered it to Mr. Montgrieve. Mr. Crawford brought Mademoiselle to this house so that she could see it before Mr. Montgrieve had moved to his new home. He had a painting of himself done by the same artist. It had an identical frame. Mademoiselle was being polite and complimented the painting. Mr. Montgrieve then insisted that she should have her portrait painted so she too could have one to hang above the fireplace in the long gallery. Mademoiselle agreed to sit for the portrait. When the portrait was complete, Mr. Montgrieve delivered it himself. It had been placed in this hideous monstrosity of a frame.

"It seems that Mr. Montgrieve's father had been a jewel cutter and he and his brother had been trained as cutters and designers as well in England. When they joined their father's business, they each specialized in a particular facet of the business. His brother was trained as a master craftsman at creating paste replicas. He was employed by many wealthy families to create paste copies of their jewels so that the gentry could keep the real jewels locked safely away. When their father died, the brothers split up. Mr. Montgrieve's brother began to create paste jewels for exclusive fashion designers. According to Mr. Montgrieve, it is a very lucrative career without any of the risk of shattering precious gem stones while attempting to cleave them. Mr. Montgrieve came to America to make his fortune as an actor. The gems in the frame were created by Mr. Montgrieve's brother. He told Mademoiselle every motion picture star should have something that reflects their stardom and their youth."

"So why is it in her bedroom and not the long gallery?" Seedy asked.

"Mademoiselle thought the frame was too ugly. But she has a kind heart and would not change the frame because it had been a gift. So, she hung it here and told Mr. Montgrieve that she hung it in her boudoir because she loved it so much, she wanted to look upon it always. Enough about the decorations," she declared, changing her mood instantly. "You will have plenty of time to study them if you like."

Then she was suddenly all business. "Take off the wig and give it to me, Seedy." Seedy's name sounded sensual with Claudette's sexy French cadence.

The Reluctant Doppelganger

She walked into the closet and returned with a navy blue worsted wool suit. Molly was right on target when she called it her lawyer dress. Claudette paired it with a white silk blouse and handed them to Seedy. She went back into the closet and came out with a black garter belt and a new pair of silk stockings which she gave to Seedy as well.

"Go in there and change." She pointed to the open closet door. "There is a chaise lounge in the sitting area towards the back."

"There's a sitting area in the closet?" Seedy sounded amazed, echoing my own thoughts.

Seedy did as she was told and closed the door when she entered. In just a few minutes she had returned.

"Dang, Seedy! You really do look like a very successful personal secretary."

"You really think so?"

She twirled in place showing off and beaming. She pressed the jacket flaps down with the palms of her hands and stood up straight. "This really is a beautiful suit. And it does make me feel like a professional business woman."

"Run along now," Claudette said, giving Seedy a shooing motion. "I must help Mademoiselle Desmond dress."

Seedy shot to the door and was gone. The time had finally come. I had only pulled off looking like Theodora Desmond once. I was not sure I could do it again, not to mention sustain the illusion. Claudette moved quickly back into the closet and this time when she returned, she had in her hand a simple black dress.

"This is also from Paris. It will look stunning on you. It is an original by the French designer, Coco Chanel."

I laughed out loud.

"What is so amusing?"

"Nothing really. It's just the second time today that I've been told that Coco Chanel would be a good fit for me."

"Whoever told you the first time was right. Come over here and sit down at the dressing table and take off your shirt."

I did as I was told. Somehow, I felt a great deal more at ease taking my shirt off for Claudette than I did having my pants pulled down by Georgie. But I guess they each were working on different elements of my disguise.

As she worked, I asked her, "How in the world did a trained French lady's maid end up in Hollywood California? And moreover, how did you end up here?"

She chuckled. "I grew up in a small town just outside of Paris. When my sister and I were old enough, we were put into service and trained as lady's maids. One year, my sister and I went to Nice in December. It is where the wealthy English take their winters. We thought it would be easy to get work, and it was. We went to work for different families. When the season ended, both my sister and I were asked by our mistresses to accompany them back to England and stay on as their lady's maids. We both agreed. My sister ended up in a castle in Scotland and I in London in a house in Mayfair. After about a year, my mistress decided to go live in Spain. She was tired of the cold and damp. She desired a warmer climate. I did not want to move to Spain, so I resigned my position.

"My second mistress was an elderly dowager duchess. While I was in her service, an American motion picture actress came to England and the duchess invited her to stay in her home. She regaled Her Grace with stories of California and talked about how warm it always was. England is such a cold place no matter the time of year, always damp and foggy." She shivered. "You know, now that I think about it, I really should have gone to Spain."

"Anyway, the actress told Her Grace that film stars were America's Royalty. I took her meaning literally, so when Her

The Reluctant Doppelganger

Grace passed away, I came to the United States. I landed in New York City. I was there for almost a full year doing odd jobs before I finally earned enough to purchase a train ticket to California. When I got here, I found that the so-called Hollywood Royalty placed no value on a lady's maid unless they could steal her away from someone else. Then they expected her to do house work. I was unable to find work in the service for which I had been trained. So, I found a job as a cosmetics clerk for the Owl Drug Company."

"They are one of my grandfather's biggest competitors."

"The novelist and screen actress Elinor Glyn judges beauty contests for them — the winner of the contest gets a screen test. Clerks from the cosmetics department always help the contestants with their makeup while the public watches. Sales go up every time. Your father entered Molly, and I was the clerk who assisted her. While I was doing her makeup, we discovered we were living in the same apartment building, only two doors apart, and we became fast friends. She won the beauty contest and the screen test. Your father pulled many strings and made sure the screen test was noticed by all the right people. Rodrick Crawford saw the test film and Theodora Desmond was born. She is a good actress."

"I know. I've seen all six of her pictures."

"The studio put her under contract. Her first movie was an instant success. The studio gave her this house. On moving day, I went to say good-bye and congratulate her. Your father was there, helping or getting in the movers' way, I'm not sure which." She laughed. "Molly introduced us. She told him where we met and that I had been trained as a lady's maid. She also told him that I was born in Paris and worked in England. He questioned me. I'm sure of all people, you know how he is when he wants to gain information."

"I sure do."

"He must have been satisfied with my answers because he offered me this job right on the spot. He wanted someone who could watch out for Molly's interests as well as someone who could train her to dress and act like a lady. So, I was here the day we both walked into this house." She sounded almost sad now as comprehension set in and she knew her friend and mistress was really gone.

She dusted my face with powder using a large very soft brush. She reached over and picked up the blonde bobbed wig that Seedy had been wearing and pulled it onto my head. She made sure all my own reddish-blonde locks disappeared. She took the large brush once again and spun it around my hair line. Then she stood back.

"Mon Dieu! I would not have believed it possible."

I had been sitting with my back to the mirror. I turned, and staring back at me was Theodora Desmond. My transformation was complete. I took off my pants and Claudette helped me slide into the little black dress. She produced two unbelievably long strands of pearls from a jewel case in the closet. One set consisted of large perfectly shaped pearls, and the other set was made of pearls equal in quality only much smaller in size. Each strand must have made a three-foot loop. She draped them over my head several times, then pulled and tugged on them until they hung equally as low in the front as they did in the back. I slipped on a pair of black satin heels with large rhinestone buckles and stood up. I walked over to the full-length mirror in the closet, turned, and inspected every inch.

"We are going to have to hide that better." Claudette said with a mischievous grin, pointing at a prominent bulge in the front of the sleek black dress. "Give me a minute."

Back into the closet she went and returned in moments holding an undergarment. I wasn't sure what it was. It appeared to be a garter belt attached to something that looked very restrictive.

"It's called a girdle. It is a replacement for the corset. It won't work under most of today's modern fashions, they are too clingy; but I think it will work with this dress."

She helped take the dress off again, held out the girdle, and nodded towards the bathroom door. I took the device into the bathroom and closed the door. I removed my drawers and started working the girdle up my legs. It was unbelievably tight. I was constantly trying to keep my credentials out of the way. Then I remembered what Georgie had said to do. I pushed the huevos up and inside and then I pulled the rest of my manhood backwards between my legs, all the while tugging at the girdle. Once the task was complete, I was exhausted but there was no telltale bulge. It was damned uncomfortable to walk too, but I made my way back out to Claudette. This time she handed me a pair of silk stockings.

"Do you know how to put these on?"

"I think so."

I bunched one up like Seedy had shown me to do last year at Halloween, pointed my toe and slid the stocking over my foot. I then worked it up my leg, again, like Seedy had instructed and fastened it with the clips on the girdle. I did the same with the second stocking.

"Bon, Good job."

She sounded as if she was amazed, I could accomplish the task. For the second time, she worked me into the dress and arranged the massive strands of pearls. I slipped on the shoes and she pronounced me dressed.

Even though we had just gotten me dressed for the evening, I suddenly felt dog tired. It dawned on me that I had been up and running since almost three o'clock this morning and it was now closing in on nine o'clock in the evening. I simply wanted to get undressed, get out of the restrictive girdle and go to bed. Just then, the telephone rang, and I nearly jumped out of my skin. Claudette reached over and picked up the hand-set.

"Hello, this is the Desmond residence. Claudette speaking," she said calmly into the mouth piece.

Her face went ashen.

"Yes sir, Monsieur Crawford. I will inform her. She will be ready." And she hung up the telephone. "That was Monsieur Crawford. He wants you at his house within the hour. There is a spur-of-the- moment party there for some British investors and he needs the stars of his next production there to sell them on the idea of investing in the studio.

I too, was now turning pale.

"Is this a regular occurrence? Do movie producers often call and demand that actresses appear?" I was miffed.

"Actually, yes, it is. It is part of your contract."

She reached over and picked up the second telephone that sat on the dresser. It had a red cradle. She clicked the cradle five times.

"Randel, you will need to bring Miss Desmond's automobile around in ten minutes. She will be attending a party at Rodrick Crawford's house."

Then she hung up.

"We must tell your father. Let me get you a coat."

"It is unseasonably warm. Why in the world would I want a coat?"

"Two reasons. First, this is Hollywood and every woman who is of any importance wears a fur coat to a party. Second, if for some reason your camouflage fails you," she pointed down to my now well-concealed credentials, "then you will have an alternative means of cover." And winked.

Back into the closet she flew, and when she returned, this time, she had a set of large emerald and diamond ear bobs, a pair of opera length black satin gloves, a diamond and pearl bracelet, a very small handbag and a beautiful leopard skin coat trimmed in black sable. She had the ear bobs clipped on, the gloves snaked up my arms and the bracelet fastened around my wrist over the glove on my left arm in a blink of the eye. She helped me into the coat, instructed me on how to let it rest in the crook of my elbow and not pull it up onto my shoulders unless I actually got cold. She told me there would be a coat check at the door, to fold my gloves and place them in my handbag then check both my fur and the handbag. She turned me towards the bedroom doors, told me to practice my walk and herded me out into the hall. We stopped briefly in the long gallery to explain what had just happened.

"I'm going with you." Father said.

"What will Monsieur Crawford say if you show up uninvited with his star?" She sounded scandalized.

"Theo will tell him that we had dinner plans. She didn't know what else to do and brought me along." Father replied coolly.

"You had both better be on your way then. You only have about twenty minutes before your commanded time."

Claudette was already pushing me towards the door. I was doing my best to be quick, as well as graceful, as we descended the main staircase, but I think the graceful part was falling short. We reached the foyer and I took a deep breath as Father opened the enormous wooden door. Randel was standing at the foot of the steps with the door to the Daimler already open.

Before I could start down the front steps, Claudette grabbed me and hugged me.

"Be careful, Mon Cheri." And she kissed the air above each cheek.

We hurried down the stairs, climbed into the auto and Randel sped away.

8

In ten minutes time, we were pulling up to the gates at the home of Rodrick Crawford, and Randel was speaking to the gateman. The gateman went back to his little house and suddenly the huge gates began to swing open.

An electronic gate opener. I would have to consider one of those for Mr. Truman. After all he was an older gentleman.

I was still pondering the gate opener when the house came into view. I had thought Theodora's house was big, but this made hers look like a cottage. There were lights everywhere and the house had a massive square tower at its center that must have been four or five stories tall. If the tower had been on a city hall, I would have expected it to have a clock facing out to greet visitors. Craning my neck, I could see through the Daimler's windows that, at the top of the tower, was a covered balcony. The entire balcony was filled with people, and it sparkled with electric lanterns that were every color in the rainbow.

What an incredible view that balcony must have.

I made myself a promise that if I could, I would climb to the top to see. Randel pulled to the front of the house after waiting in a queue behind several other grand automobiles where a valet, dressed in a black tuxedo with tails, opened my door.

"It's show time!" Father said. "Get that smile in place."

I had momentarily forgotten who I was supposed to be. I laughed and put on my best Theodora smile. Now I knew why Father always used those lines. Everyone would be watching from the moment I stepped out of the automobile. I fixed my smile as the footman proffered his hand to help me disembark. I placed my gloved hand in his and allowed him to support me as I climbed out. My father slid over in the seat so that he could exit the automobile from the same side. With what I felt was a very disingenuous smile, I mentally checked myself over while my father got out of the auto. My dress was where it should be. My pearls were hanging just the way Claudette had arranged them. And I had the fur coat hung just in the crook of my elbows as I had been instructed. My father stepped up to my side and handed me the little black handbag that completed my ensemble. At that same moment, a volley of flashbulbs began to pop. My first response was to cover my eyes.

"Look towards the flashes, keep smiling and keep your eyes open. You might even give them a wave. But whatever you do, don't try to cover your eyes." Father whispered as he leaned down to my ear.

I fought the impulse and smiled up. I gave the photographers a slight wave. I used the back of my hand, just like I had seen royals do in news reels. With the wave came a new volley of flashes and they began to shout for me to look at them. Each time I turned my head to follow a voice, more flashbulbs popped. After what seemed like forever, my father took me by the elbow and led me towards the house. Even as we walked away, the flashbulbs continued to pop until the next auto pulled up and someone new became their fodder.

There were two doormen, also dressed in tuxedos with tails, that stood on either side of the home's massive doorway.

It must be something of a uniform.

The doors stood open.

"Good evening, Miss Desmond. Good Evening Mr. Standish." Each man greeted in turn, as we passed through the threshold and into the house.

"I must come here often if the doormen know me by name." I whispered up to my father as we walked in.

"They know everyone's names. First, you are Theodora Desmond. Half the known world knows who you are. But most importantly, those considered Hollywood Royalty expect to be known by the servants at every party," he said, again leaning in close and whispering.

"They really are that arrogant?" I queried.

"Most assuredly," he stated emphatically. "We," he pointed the word, "really are that arrogant."

It was then that I took in the room. The foyer was enormous. It had an oriental feel to it. The highly polished dark wood walls had massive canvas panels that were painted with oriental landscapes. Each panel had been inlaid with thousands of polished greenish stones that I thought must be jade. There were two staircases, one on each wall, that curved up to an open gallery on the second floor. The banisters were shiny black enamel. The rise to each step was painted a deep Chinese red and the treads were an equally shiny black. The lip of each tread was brushed with gold-leaf. And right now, the entire cavernous space was overflowing with people.

If this was a spur of the moment party, what might a planned soirée look like. I wondered.

While taking in the room, my father had steered me over to

a coat check. I was stunned to see a coat check built at the front door of a private residence. Then it registered on me that although the check stand matched the colors of the rest of the room and it had been styled to look like an oriental temple complete with a jade green carved Pagoda roof, it was portable. It must hide away somewhere when not in use.

"Did you want to keep your fur, Miss Desmond?" the coat check girl asked.

I was so busy looking around the room, I hadn't noticed the girl until she spoke. She was beautiful, wearing a bright red satin Chinese Zansae. The tight-fitting full-length dress was fully embroidered with gold stitching and was split up her right leg to the top of the girl's thigh. Her costume, for that's what it was, had been finished off with a black wig styled in the fashion of a Geisha with two buns, one atop the other, with a circlet of beads and a large orchid adorning the middle.

"Miss Desmond will check both her coat and purse." My father said, flashing the girl a brilliant toothy smile.

He helped me out of the fur. I slipped off my gloves as gracefully as I could manage, carefully folding them and placing them in my bag. I handed my father the purse, who, in turn handed them to the girl. He winked at her as he took the ticket. He really was a hound. Suddenly I felt a chill. It was the first time I'd had the coat off since I put it on. My attention moved away from the coat-check girl with whom my father was still unabashedly flirting, to trying to take in everything I was seeing.

"Don't gawk, Eddie. And close your mouth. Remember, this is your everyday world. Above all smile. No matter what happens always keep smiling. Cameras love it. And there are an abundance of cameras here tonight," my father hissed in my ear. He was folding a small scrap of paper and slipping it in his jacket pocket as he stepped back up to my side. I wager it had the coat-check girl's name and address.

As we moved farther into the room, I heard the music for the first time. I looked around for a gramophone but didn't see one as we glided towards the stairs.

"Ah, it sounds like Josephine Baker is here and she's performing tonight. I had heard she was in town."

He held up his hand and I put mine on top of his as we began to ascend the stairs. Someone on the other staircase across the room waved. My father waved back.

"That's Mary Pickford. Wave."

I waved.

"Our host will be in the thick of things near the piano and the performers. We must make sure he knows we are here."

Once we reached the top of the stairs, I looked across a vast ballroom. At the far end of the room on a raised platform stood the most beautiful Negro woman I had ever seen. Behind her was a man playing the piano and one playing the stringed bass. The woman's costume was twinkling in the light but was barely there. I could see her dark nipples through the shear top. Her midriff was exposed to below her belly button. Strips of gossamer sequined material hung in odd lengths down her legs and there was only a scant patch that covered her most private areas. Everything from the top of her shoulders to her toes seemed to be on public display.

"The song is *La Vie En Rose*. Some say it is France's unofficial national anthem."

"It's beautiful and she is breathtaking."

"She and Mary run neck and neck for the title of 'Most Photographed Woman in the World'."

As Josephine Baker's song ended, everyone began to clap. It was that polite party clap. With his hands still in front of his face clapping, Father nodded with his head to a small cluster of men standing just to the left of the stage.

"There's our host. And now I see why half of Hollywood

The Reluctant Doppelganger

was called out on short notice. The dark-haired man standing next to him with the cigarette holder is an English Duke. He is one of the few British aristocracy that still has any money. And he not only has money; he has a prodigious sum of it, too. Seems his father, the former Duke, invested highly in sugar. And he, in turn, has invested heavily in rubber. Currently, one of his companies is producing tires for automobiles. In fact, for now, he seems to have somewhat of a monopoly on the market. RC is always looking for investors. And the Duke would be a major catch. The young handsome-ish man standing next to him is his son the Viscount."

I tilted my head at the word HANDSOME-ISH. In my opinion, there was no ISH about it. The young man in question was heart stopping. He was taller than his father, who was taller than the other men standing around them. But he was not as tall as my father. He looked like the illustrations of the fairy-tale prince in children's story books. He had broad shoulders and a slim waist. It was hard to tell with him wearing a jacket, but I would guess his hips were muscular too, and he had strong stout legs. He had dark brown hair that hung in ringlets, certainly not holding to today's modern style of being hair-creamed slick, parted down the middle and plastered flat against the scalp. A full wide mouth surrounded brilliantly white teeth. But it was his eyes that were arresting – heart-stoppingly arresting. They were an icy blue gray and at this moment they were looking at something behind me and actually sparkling.

I wonder what he's looking at?

"We need to work our way over to RC now," Father urged.

As we moved through the throng, we paused to make pleasantries with other guests along the way. Each time we stopped at a gathering, my father made sure to speak first and always to say each person's name. Silently, I said a prayer for his quick thinking. I would have never made it across the room without him. In between knots of party-goers, he rattled off what he thought were the most salient facts about the people in RC's little entourage. First, there was Rodrick Crawford (RC), the owner and head of the studio. Next to him stood the Duke, and next to him was the Viscount. Taking in the Viscount once again, I could tell his eyes were still alight as he gazed out into the room. He was clearly not engaged in the conversation around him. What was he looking at?

I wanted to turn and look over my shoulder, but I was too busy trying to make small talk with a room full of people who knew me, but I didn't know from Adam.

"Will, how nice to see you. You know, I ran into a lady from Oklahoma just the other day. She said everyone there was naming their baby boys after you."

Will Rogers smiled at that.

Great clue, Father.

He tapped the back of my hand twice. I had no idea what he meant but I was hoping that one tap meant I was on a first name basis and two taps meant I should recognize him, but I didn't know him. Mentally, I wished myself good luck.

"Mr. Rogers, what a pleasure to finally meet you. I just love your brand of humor."

I held out my hand and Will Rogers clasped it. I turned the back of my hand upwards while I watched his face to see if this type of hand shake registered on him. It didn't seem to have any effect at all.

"Well, thank you. That is high praise indeed coming from someone as popular with the public as you are, Miss Desmond," Will Rogers smiled broadly.

"Do call me Theo." I tried to say it like Molly had the first time we met.

"Only if you call me Will."

The Reluctant Doppelganger

"Deal!"

I gave his hand a firm shake and released it. With that, my father moved us on through the crowd. It seemed that, with every group we stopped and spoke to, the topic of conversation was all about a new movie that Warner Brothers was about to release. It was called *The Jazz Singer*. It was a motion picture with sound. The actors actually delivered lines!Everyone was calling it a "Talkie." It appeared the room was split about fifty-fifty as to whether it would be a success or a flop.

When we finally reached RC's cluster, my father had not yet finished giving me all the details on everyone in the group. I'd just have to wing it.

"RC, I'm sorry to crash your party. Theo and I were just headed out the door to dinner when you called."

"Well, that's all right. I wouldn't want to snub one of Hollywood's most powerful agents."

And there you have it. The barbs had been exchanged and accepted. To translate:

My father said, "We already had plans. I cannot believe you commanded our presence."

RC replied, "I don't care about your plans. I call the shots, but I'll let you stay because you do have a great deal of sway as to how things play out."

RC then turned to me.

"I was beginning to wonder if you were going to be able to make it. I was expecting you earlier."

As I started to speak, my father interrupted.

"We have been here for quite some time but getting through the crowd was a major task. Of course, Theo had to speak to everyone she knew."

He looked at me and patted my hand as if he were admonishing me.

"And that's just this floor. The mob on the first floor is

even thicker. I see that Josephine is here. She always brightens a party, don't you think?" Father went on.

Everyone in the group nodded in affirmation. RC frowned for a moment. He was reputed to be like a petulant child when he didn't get things just the way he wanted them. But then, being the businessman, he was, he got back to business and his smile returned.

"Duke, this is Miss Theodora Desmond. Theodora will be playing Delilah in my new motion picture adaptation of Samson and Delilah," RC introduced.

"And Theodora, this is the Duke of Kintyre and Lorne. And his son the Viscount."

I inclined my head first to the Duke.

"Your Grace."

And then I extended my hand to the Viscount. For some reason, I just wanted to touch him. I hadn't a clue if this was proper. He clasped mine in return and fixed that sparkling blue-gray gaze on me. At that moment, I thought I might just melt.

"Your Lordship."

I again turned the back of my hand upwards. This time, however, the maneuver didn't go unnoticed. The corners of his mouth quirked up. And when he reversed the move, I smirked back.

"I've been watching you make your way across the room. I was hoping you would stop to speak with us. I am a great fan, Miss Desmond." He kissed the back of my hand lightly.

"Thank you, I'm flattered, your Lordship."

"Now that's something you don't see every day. An American that knows how to properly address members of the peerage." The Duke smiled and nudged RC slightly.

It was then that I noticed that the Viscount and I were still holding hands. When I looked up at him, he smiled and released my hand. The conversation immediately moved to

The Reluctant Doppelganger

business. It seems that RC thought *The Jazz Singer* would be an overnight sensation. It appeared that most of the studio heads agreed with him. Several of the studios were rushing to be the first but Warner Brothers seemed to have been the victor. Everyone was holding their breaths until Wednesday, the scheduled release date.

RC let the group in on a hush-hush secret. He had been converting Studio B into a talking picture studio for the last three months. Even if *The Jazz Singer* flopped, he said he was going to make at least three talking feature-length films. The process had been a huge success with newsreels and selected shorts. It seemed that movie theaters that ran the talking shorts and newsreels had significantly larger audiences. And those theaters already had the equipment to show motion pictures that included sound, talkies. One of the major concerns for studio heads was the ability of their silent motion picture stars to transition to the talkies. When they were not heard, it made no difference what they sounded like; but now it was important that the voice matched the look.

"And now for my big news. *Samson and Delilah* will be Colossal Studio's very first talkie. That's why, instead of starting the shoot for Samson and Delilah on Monday as was scheduled, I'm pushing it off a week so I can audition actors for the role of Samson." RC beamed, rubbing his hands together like a kid in a candy store.

The man standing next to my father, dressed in a white dinner jacket and black bow-tie, holding a martini glass, turned absolutely beet red.

"You're going to do what?" he spewed in a high-pitched British accent.

The very red-faced man was none other than Reginald Montgrieve. He was one of Hollywood's first leading men. Although aging a bit now, he had been one of motion pictures' first heart-throbs. And he was still incredibly handsome for a man in his mid-fifties.

"That is my role!"

"I never actually promised you the role, Reggie." RC's tone was matter-of-fact. "Samson really needs to be a bulkier, more muscular man. I'm thinking he needs to be younger, too. Oh, and he needs to have a deeper, huskier voice. But most of all, he needs to exude animal passion. Your passionate style is a great deal more refined and dignified. But you are free to audition for the part."

"Me? Audition for a role? Me? Reginald Montgrieve? Star of the silver screen!" he bellowed, his voice rising in volume with each supercilious question. It seemed his voice got squeakier and squeakier too as his anger mounted. "I will show you 'audition'."

With that, he pushed my father out of the way, grabbed me around the waist, and pulled me into him. With his martini glass still gripped in his hand, he pressed his lips hard against mine. He smelled of stale cigarettes and his breath reeked of liquor and onions. Without warning, he tried to force his tongue in my mouth.

Feeling threatened, I acted out of an instinct for self-preservation. I raised my right foot and brought my heel down hard on the top of Reggie's foot, having forgotten that I was wearing high heeled shoes. On impact, he instinctively released me. There was a look of surprise on his face. I drew back and, with all my might, slapped him across the face.

"You cad!"

The martini glass dropped to the floor as his shock turned to rage. He lifted both hands as if to choke me.

"You bitch!"

The three men standing closest to us — my father, RC and the Viscount — started for him. But before they could move the short distance, I stepped one leg in, grasped his outstretched arm, turned, moved in next to him and with a balanced controlled pull, hurled him over my shoulder. Finally, that Judo training had found a useful purpose. Several things happened all at once. Every man standing around me froze in place with a look of total amazement on their faces. All but my father, that is. He knew it had been purely a reaction to years of tirelessly practicing the discipline. It was an act of preservation, actions that had been drilled into me until they had become habit.

"I say," said the Duke, "although quite an impressive display, that was hardly lady-like."

Damn, I had forgotten that I was supposed to be the weaker sex. RC hadn't moved and his mouth gaped open. My father was looking stern by now and the Viscount had an amused smile on his face.

"Father, I think women in America are made of much sterner stuff than that of our fairer sex back in jolly old Britain."

The smile had still not left the Viscount's face.

"Rather." The Duke still looked somewhat stunned.

Several people were helping Reggie up off the floor. He now had one very red hand print across his cheek. If looks could have killed, I would have dropped dead on the spot. I looked down and saw the glass on the floor. It hadn't broken. I was guessing that spoke highly of the quality of the Persian rug that now had a very sodden spot where the glass' contents had spilled. Next to the spill lay three small onions on a skewer. Reggie had been drinking a Gibson. I rather like a good Gibson; I wasn't sure I would any longer. But one thing was for sure. I had just learned that if one expected that there might be kissing on a date, one should not drink Gibsons. The taste of onions on one's lips was terribly off-putting.

"Come back and join the party, Reggie." RC called in a

jovial tone. "I think you've learned your lesson about getting too aggressive with our petite starlet. It would seem that she does not need a gentleman to rush to her defense. It would appear she can take care of herself."

There was a hint of amusement combined with reproach aimed towards Reggie. And a glance of admonishment that was most assuredly pointed in my direction. Reggie walked sheepishly back over to the edge of the group. His nostrils still flared slightly but he was trying to appear sufficiently cowed.

Once again, the conversation turned to the topic of the Talkie. The Duke kept sneaking furtive glances at Reggie as if he were trying to place him. Then I saw it, the dawning of recognition, when he finally put the pieces of the puzzle together.

"Good Gawd!" he exclaimed, interrupting RC.

He looked straight at Reggie.

"I've been trying to place you the entire evening. You are Tommy Musgrave, my former valet. So now you are Reginald Montgrieve. I've always wondered what happened to you, after you pinched fifty pounds from my wallet and disappeared while we were in New York City on business."

It was said as merely a statement of recognition, but once again Reggie's face had gone apoplectic with rage. Most people in Hollywood did not come from Hollywood. Everyone had a prior life, who they were before they were famous. And anyone looking at Reggie at this moment knew that his past had just come back to haunt him. And as apparent as it was to everyone within ear shot, it was doubly so for Reggie.

"You should watch your tongue, your Grace!" He hissed. "You forget where you are. You are in Hollywood and here I am a prince, not a mere duke."

If this bothered the Duke in any way at all, you couldn't

tell. You have to hand it to the British aristocracy; they were bred to be unflappable.

"It has been so long; I had forgotten about your issues with respect to your betters. And yes, you are a prince in this realm. An aging one who is never destined to be King," the Duke sounded as if he were almost bored.

"I'll show you respect."

And he spat at the Duke's feet. He turned and pushed his way through the crowd. You could tell that even RC, forever the diplomat, was at a loss for words. I smoothed down my dress.

"Could you excuse me a moment gentleman? I need to visit the powder room to check my makeup,"

"I'll walk you over," Father said. "I'll get you through this horde. I think RC would hate for any more of his guests to go flying across the room."

Everyone chuckled at this, including me.

As we moved out of earshot, my father leaned into me. "I thought you might want some help finding the bath, since you should already know where it is."

"Thank you. I am sorry about the scene; it all took me by surprise. God, is this what women go through all the time?"

"I don't think most women do, no. But men like Montgrieve think that they can just do as they like without any consequences."

"He might think differently from now on," I laughed.

"I doubt it. He has always had a chip on his shoulder. And his arrogance knows no bounds."

"I hope I don't have to deal with him again this evening."

"He has probably gone off somewhere to lick his wounds. And have a few more cocktails to bolster his pride. I do think he will avoid you at all costs for the rest of the evening."

"You're not angry with me for giving him a Judo flip, are you?"

"Not at all; he got what he deserved. The reason I put you in those classes to begin with was because I wanted you to be able to defend yourself. I dare say, tonight you certainly proved you could do that. I'm sorry he kissed you. That had to be disgusting."

"His lips tasted like liquor and cocktail onions," I shivered. "It will be a day or two before I think I will want a Gibson again."

Father laughed.

"There is the door to the bath that is designed for the ladies." He pointed to a door across the room.

I hesitated.

"I never thought about having to use the lady's restrooms."

"You have no choice this evening. Besides, they aren't so bad. They are usually large with comfortable seating areas."

"You've been in a lady's room before?"

"Once or twice," The corners of his mouth turned up.

Obviously, it had been for some tête-á-tête or a possible assignation with some starlet. I shook my head, took a deep breath and headed for the door. Once inside, I discovered that he was right. I found myself standing in a huge sitting room with chairs, sofas and several dressing tables with large mirrors. The room was full. The ladies in the chairs were in between three doors. Behind them must be the toilets and they must be waiting their turn. Others on the sofas and chaise lounges seemed to be in a state of repose. They were chatting, sipping cocktails and smoking their cigarettes in long fashionable holders. The women at the dressing tables were working on their makeup, getting ready to head back into battle. When I came into the room several ladies looked up.

"Theo, darling," a woman in a red sequined flapper's dress dripping in beaded fringe called out. "It's about time someone slapped the hell out of that man. Where in the world did you learn to do that flip-a-man-over-your-head stunt? Can you teach me?"

Another woman gasped as if she were appalled.

And suddenly the room was abuzz. I was peppered with questions. They all began to chat amongst themselves, and all at the same time as well. I could see for the first time why men likened women to hens. They were all clucking and fussing away. I noticed at once that I didn't need to answer their questions. They simply filled in the void and created their own answers.

I sat down at an empty dressing table and began to appraise my appearance. My lips were a bit smudged where Reggie had forced his lips onto mine. I cleaned them up with a tissue from the box on the dressing table, where at least fifteen shades of lip stick were being provided for RC's female guests. I opened and then closed several tubes, looking for a shade that best matched the one I was already wearing. I picked one and then paused. I had worn lipstick a grand total of two times. The first time was last Halloween and the second time, tonight. And on neither occasion had I ever applied it myself.

I looked into the mirror and tried to observe the woman behind me. She just dabbed it over her lips. Then she rubbed her lips together and finally she blotted them on a tissue. Trying to act as if I knew what I was doing and that this was an everyday occurrence, I began to dab the lipstick on my lips. But apparently, I dabbed a bit too hard and I smeared it down towards my chin. I grabbed a tissue and began to rub the lipstick off the offending area but as I did, I rubbed the make-up off as well. For a long moment, I stared into the mirror wondering what I should do.

That's when the woman who had called me 'Darling' came rushing over to me.

"Oh, my dear girl," she said. "That brute must have really

unsettled you. I know he would have unsettled me."

With that she began to pick up different bottles on the table and proceeded to fix my makeup. As women finished up and passed out of the room, they all stopped to give me a pat on the shoulder or a hug.

"There, there dear. Don't let him get to you," they would say in a sympathetic voice or some version thereof.

"There you go, honey. Back to your normal gorgeous self," the woman fixing my makeup said.

She turned me back to face the mirror. She stood behind me now with both hands on my shoulders smiling at me in the mirror. It was then I recognized it was Norma Shearer, the undisputed queen of Hollywood. I smiled back at her and patted her hand.

"Thank you, Norma," I said, praying that we knew each other.

"You're welcome, honey. We've all known men like Reggie before. Hell, most of us have known Reggie." She said with a wink.

She laughed and gave my shoulders a slight squeeze as she walked out the door.

I followed Norma out. I expected to see my father waiting for me. What I found, leaning against the mahogany paneling perusing a copy of *The Lady's Home Journal* that had been placed on a table beside a chair, was the Viscount. He looked up as I came into view. He smiled as he righted himself.

"Are you waiting to use the lady's room or just checking out the latest in kitchen tips?" I smiled and pointed to the magazine in his hand.

He laughed and pitched the magazine back onto the table top.

"You'd better be careful, or you'll find yourself the topic of one of Louella Parson's gossips. I'm sure she is here

The Reluctant Doppelganger

somewhere. "

"I was hoping you would join me in the tower. I hear the view is outstanding."

With everything that had happened, I had forgotten all about the tower. And in a brilliant moment of clarity, I had an eye-popping thought. I was the one who should know how to get to the tower because I was the one who was supposed to have been in this house before.

"I would love to join you. Do you know, I have been to this house many times but have never actually been up to the tower." It was only a little white lie. "I'm not even sure how to get there."

And that was the truth.

"I was told there is a lift just over there."

I got lost in that beautiful voice. It was that oh so sensual British accent combined with a rich baritone. It gave me shivers.

"Lift?"

"I believe you call it an elevator." He grinned.

"Oh—Oh."

First in recognition and then in surprise; surprise in knowing now that I would not have to climb countless flights of stairs. The high heels and narrow toes of these shoes were most uncomfortable.

We made our way through the room until we reached the elevator. It was almost impossible to see because the door was made to match the dark paneling of the wall. There was a large black button surrounded by an equally large brass plate. The Viscount pushed the button and we waited. I had never been very good at small talk, but I gave it a go.

"How long will you be here?"

He cocked an eyebrow. So, he could do it too.

"My father and I are here for several weeks. We are here to watch the filming of a movie. Your new movie, actually."

"Really,"

I was trying not to sound excited, worried, and frightened all at the same time. It hadn't sunk in yet that I was going to be shooting a movie and shooting a talking movie as a famous movie star, not to mention a famous female movie star.

I must surely have lost my mind. Why did I agree to do this?

"Is something wrong? You look worried. Do you have a fear of confined spaces? I'm sure we could find some stairs."

I scrambled to cover.

"No, it's not that. You brought up the filming. I always get nervous before a shoot."

"A shoot? Now it's my turn not to understand." He laughed.

"Filming. We call it a 'shoot.' We are shooting a picture, and this one is to be a talkie, so I'm doubly unsettled."

I sounded embarrassed and found myself looking down. I quickly looked back up. When I did, I immediately wished I hadn't. I was suddenly captured by his warm, concerned yet still piercing gaze. They were such beautiful eyes and they were so, so, so off limits to me.

The elevator door opened. Once it had disgorged its passengers, we entered its elaborately decorated confines. I noticed that the elevator had only one stop. It must be the tower. We rode up in companionable silence. I wondered to myself why no one ever seems to speak while riding in an elevator.

As the doors opened, I got my first glimpse of the spectacular view looking out across the back of the estate.

"Oh, my," I gasped in awe.

I walked up to the railing with its thick polished marble balustrades, and took in the expansive manicured lawns and gardens that rolled out across the back of the estate. Directly below us was the swimming pool with its cabana and bar.

The Reluctant Doppelganger

Everything was lit. Looking down from this angle you could see through the clear water of the pool to an ornately tiled bottom. The water glistened with submerged lights.

The cabana had brightly colored Mediterranean tiled walls as well. There were changing rooms with lavatory facilities at one end and what appeared to be a guest house on the other. A huge bar with seating stood just in front of the guest house portion of the cabana, where a bartender was serving drinks. Music floated in, coming from some unseen piano.

I gazed out onto the grounds. There were two groves of palm trees that must have had electric lights mounted in their tops. The lights shone down and lit two stone pathways that wound their way through the trees. The paths had great urns of flowering plants and benches placed intermittently alongside them. Both paths seemed to lead back to a tennis court. The tennis court was the only thing on the entire estate that wasn't lit with dazzling electric light. The whole scene felt like one of those make-believe fairy woods in a children's story.

I saw movement on the tennis court. It looked like two people standing very close involved in conversation. Then a thought hit me, and I suddenly felt as if I might be blushing. They were probably involved in a secluded assignation. As if to give them some much needed privacy, I began to move on around the tower.

It appeared that many of the tower's guests had come and gone after checking out the view. There didn't seem to be as many people up here now as there were when I was looking up from the automobile's window. From my new position facing south, I was looking out and across to the palatial grounds of the house — mansion — next door to RC's. It was just as brilliantly lit to excess as RC's estate.

"No one in Beverly Hills must be concerned with their utility costs," I gestured to the neighboring estate.

"I would hate to think of the expense. Unless we are entertaining, we never light our Mayfair home up like this. And as far as our castle goes, it would never be possible. When that old pile was built, candles were the best they could do. And even then, old estate accounting books logged many a complaint by long dead Dukes as to the outrageous cost of the candle bills. That estate over there looks as lit as this one, however, its owners don't appear to be entertaining."

"You have a castle?"

"Yes, a rather large one as non-royal residences go. I'm afraid it is not only my father's pride and joy but also the bane of his existence. There is constantly something in need of repair or update, but it is a beautiful old place. And its surrounding stables, villages and farms made it a wonderful place to grow up, and I hope a wonderful place to raise future generations as well."

He was standing right next to me, but as I looked up into his face, I could tell he was far away from here.

"Sounds wonderful."

"It is."

Then he noticed me and gave himself a slight shake as if he were jogging himself back across the ocean.

"Look at me, standing in an American castle on its ramparts with a breathtakingly beautiful girl and I find myself waxing sentimental about home."

I blushed but then that sense of dread knotted in my stomach. Still, I couldn't help but smile up at him.

"The truth is, I am a bit homesick. We've been in America for almost four weeks, and we are to be here six weeks more. Add in travel time, and we will miss Christmas at home. It will be the first Christmas that I've spent anywhere other than at home in Scotland with my family."

"Oh gosh, I am so sorry to hear that. I cannot think what it would be like to have Thanksgiving or Christmas without being near family."

"Thanksgiving?"

"Oh, how thoughtless of me," I said.

I was slightly embarrassed.

"I forgot that you don't celebrate the Thanksgiving holiday. Well, if you are going to be forced to be here because of the making of my motion picture, then it is only fitting that I have you and your father over for Thanksgiving Dinner."

I wasn't sure why I made the invitation on the spur of the moment and I quickly rethought it.

"Again, I'm so sorry. That was very forward and presumptuous of me. I'm sure that RC has already made all the plans for your entire visit. And I would not presume to think that you or your father would ever want to attend a dinner with someone like me. I'm sure I'm not of your class standing."

I rushed to get the words out.

He laughed.

"I think we share an equality in class here in America. We both are of the wealthy class. And as for this Thanksgiving dinner, I cannot speak for my father, but I would love to celebrate the day with you."

I smiled and he put his arm around my waist, and I placed my hand lightly on his chest. He leaned forward. It was then it registered that he was about to kiss me. I pushed back.

"I'm sorry, I didn't mean to mislead you." The words rolled easily off my tongue, but the words were in direct conflict with what I was feeling.

It was his turn to blush. "This time it was me being presumptuous. I do hope you will forgive me."

"What is there to forgive? We are just at the beginning of getting to know each other. I think there are plenty of people in Hollywood who'll tell you I am a Goodie-Two-Shoes."

And again, he laughed.

We had moved as we talked, and we were now overlooking the front of the estate, and the vista below of the city of Los Angeles, and its thousands of lights twinkling like stars in an earthbound heaven.

"Isn't it beautiful? I can see now why RC chose this location and built this tower."

"If you think this is beautiful, some time you must let me take you to the top of the Eiffel Tower in Paris. You can take in the full panorama of the city."

"I would love that. You have yourself a date."

He grinned. "A date it is!"

The fourth and final vista paled in comparison with the other three. This side of the square tower faced the roof tops and past to those of the garages. In front of the garage was an enormous gravel pad and tonight it was filled to overflowing with every type of luxury automobile imaginable.

I laughed. "We should bring up one of the photographers from downstairs to take pictures of all of those autos. It would be great to use in an advertisement for your father's automobile tire enterprise."

He laughed in agreement before turning to me with a quizzical look, cocking that eyebrow again. It made him just that much more handsome.

"I see you've done your homework. What do you know of my father's tire enterprise?"

"Not much, just that he was invested in the rubber industry, which led to the automobile tire industry. And that currently he is believed to have the market cornered, so to speak, your Lordship."

"Your information is quite correct. It would make a great picture for an advertisement. And you have to stop calling me your Lordship."

"I'm sorry, your Lordship. But no one has yet told me your

name."

I fluttered my eyelashes up at him. This would have been the perfect place to pop a fan open and flutter it as well. But alas, fans for the most part were far out of fashion. He looked mortified and raised the back of his hand to his forehead while extending his elbow high into the air.

"Forsooth Milady! Such a grievous error!" He tossed his head from side to side in a very melodramatic gesture and then he laughed. A deep, rich, full laugh.

"Careful, I hear RC is auditioning the leading man for my next movie. If he sees you can do that, he just might cast you as Samson."

"I might enjoy that." He moved in close again. "I would get to have love scenes with you." He ran his finger down my back and I shivered.

I pushed him away again and gave him a mischievous smirk. "Yes, but then you would get your eyes gouged out and taken away to be put to death. Besides, Samson's costume is pretty much a skirt."

"Please, dear lady! I'm Scottish. I own many a kilt."

He grabbed his jacket and stood very straight as if he'd been insulted. Then he relaxed again. We both laughed so hard a tear formed and rolled down my cheek. He reached up to wipe it away, giving me a warm smile

"Charles," he spoke softly. "But everyone who knows me well, except my mother, calls me Charlie."

"Well, Charlie it will be, fore I am most certainly not your mother."

"No M'lady, you are most certainly not." His voice was low and husky.

Breaking the moment again, I stuck out my hand to shake. If he thought it was odd for a girl to thrust out her hand in greeting, he said nothing. He clasped my hand firmly and gave it a hearty shake as we both laughed again.

We had worked our way back to the elevator. Charlie pushed the call button and we stood, taking one last look out across the gardens. The lights to the tennis courts were on now. I hadn't noticed when the lights were off, but the entire perimeter of the tennis court was engulfed in what looked to be a massive cage.

"Isn't that odd." I said.

"Isn't what odd?"

"That looks like a giant cage around the tennis court. Have you ever seen such a thing?'

"Hmm, no I haven't. What do you think that is on the court itself?"

I looked closer. Lying on the playing field appeared to be a man in a white dinner jacket.

"Oh, my God! I think that must be Reggie Montgrieve."

Charlie chuckled.

"It looks like the old boy has passed out."

"Do you think?" I suddenly felt relieved.

Just then, the elevator door opened. Along with another couple, we stepped inside and didn't give the prone figure another thought.

9

When the door opened again, we stepped back into the crush of party-goers. Josephine Baker was singing again. As we moved into the room, I caught sight of my father. The look of shear panic on his face quickly turned to relief as he saw me and began immediately working his way towards us.

"Your father looks to be very concerned." Charlie whispered leaning close to my ear. "I hope he doesn't think that I too, am a cad like my fellow Countryman."

"My father?" I asked with a start.

"Yes, your father. Only a fool wouldn't recognize the likeness."

"All of Hollywood has never recognized the likeness."

"And, I think that's in large part because of your father's well-crafted smoke screen. Everyone is too busy looking at Theodora Desmond the motion picture actress to pay any attention to the most sought-after agent in Hollywood."

"How do you know he's the most sought-after agent in Hollywood?"

"My dear Miss Desmond, surely you don't think you are the only one who does their homework. After all, *my* father is looking to invest."

As Father reached us, Charlie lifted my hand to his mouth and kissed it. He then handed the same just kissed hand to my father.

"Thank you for accompanying me to the top of the tower."

He turned to my father. "I will leave this beautiful young lady in your care, sir."

He gave a bow of his head to us both and slipped back into the crowd. I stared after him for a long moment before my father dragged me from my reverie.

"God, you scared me half to death. I went to talk to a client while you were in the powder room, but then you never seemed to come out of there."

"Charlie was waiting outside the door when I walked out. He asked me if I wanted to see the view from the tower and I did. I'm sorry I didn't see you, so I thought you had left me on my own."

"Charlie? So now you are not only on a first name, but a nickname basis with the Viscount?"

"Yes, I guess I am."

My father looked me sternly in the eyes.

"You know this cannot be." He paused. "Right?"

His proclamation annoyed me. First, because I knew that the Viscount, Charlie, was attracted to Theodora, not me, and secondly, because *I was* without a doubt very attracted to him.

"I do understand that more than a casual acquaintance is impossible. But I think we have a much bigger concern. He has guessed that you are my father. He said he would have to be blind not to notice the family resemblance."

"No one has ever linked Theodora to me before."

"Well, someone has now." I yawned. "It has been a very long day filled with a great deal of angst. Could we please leave? I think I could fall asleep standing upright this very minute. And that just wouldn't do in these shoes."

The Reluctant Doppelganger

"I think we can afford to leave. I'll have the doorman send for Randel, and we'll need to say good-night to our host. Wait here."

My father shot towards the door to speak to the doorman. When he returned, we once again worked our way across the room. RC and the Duke were deep in conversation when we reached them. Charlie had rejoined his father and stood in the cluster along with three other men, none of whom I knew. When we stepped up, RC and the Duke acknowledged us.

This time I took the lead before my father could speak. "RC, I do hope you will excuse us. It has been a trying day in many ways. First, to learn I was about to be in your very first talkie, and then the incident with Reggie."

"Yes, my lovely little starlet, you may go home and rest; and we," RC gestured to the Duke, "will see you bright and early on Thursday morning in Studio B. We want to do a sound test. You will be the first to try it out."

I extended my hand to the Duke. "It was a pleasure meeting you, your Grace."

He kissed the back of my proffered hand.

It must be a European idiosyncrasy. I thought. "Your Lordship." I nodded to Charlie. RC reached over and kissed me on the forehead.

As we turned to depart, I looked over my shoulder.

"You might check on Reggie. The Viscount and I suspect we saw him from the tower down on the tennis courts. I think he might be passed out."

"Then he deserves what he gets," RC laughed. "The irrigation system just might get him if he's there too long."

Everyone sniggered and we departed.

When we returned home, I found that Claudette had waited up to help me undress. I chided her for staying up, but she assured me that was part of her job as a lady's maid. The truth be told, I was very happy for the help. She didn't have to help with the shoes though; they were gone the minute I entered the door. She had me out of all the jewelry, dress, wig and stockings in a flash. All that was left was the girdle. I tried to manage it myself in the bathroom, but in the end, I had to put away my pride and have Claudette help.

"Oh, my God," I blurted out, as the girdle finally came free. "Why in the world would any woman wear such a thing?"

"If a woman can survive the pains of child birth, a girdle is of no consequence in creating and maintaining a beautiful image. And here in Hollywood, it is more important than anywhere else in the world that I have been, and I have been many places."

She disappeared into the closet and came back carrying what looked like a pair of striped satin pajamas.

"I think you will find these most comfortable. I am assuming that you did not wish to wear a negligee."

"You couldn't be more correct there," I said, rolling my eyes.

I slipped on the pajama bottoms, but before allowing me to don the pajama's top, she had me go into the bathroom, and sit at the dressing table in that room.

Just how many dressing tables does one woman require?

She ran the water into the marble basin next to the dressing table until it was warm and then proceeded to remove my make-up. Once that was complete, she used a night cream on my face. I was pronounced ready for bed and donned the pajama top.

The bed had already been turned down and I headed that direction.

"Wait a moment," she said. She walked over to the bed and to my utter surprise, fell onto it herself. She began to thrash and roll around. As quickly as she had started, she stopped. She hopped off the bed, straightened her dress, hair and cap. "Come with me."

The Reluctant Doppelganger

She took me back into the bathroom. We walked across to the other side to a door I suspected to be a linen cabinet. She opened the door and reached for the light switch just inside. When the light came on, the space it illuminated was another bedroom. This room was smaller than Theodora's bedroom, but not by much, and it was definitely a man's room. The furniture was beautiful in deep dark woods and had a massive weightiness to it.

"This originally was the bedroom for the lady of the house, but when Miss Desmond, Molly, moved in, she converted the master's bedroom into her boudoir. She thought the furniture was beautiful. So, she had this room redecorated and moved the furniture into here. I think you might feel more comfortable sleeping in this room. Well, at least at first."

"Thank you for thinking of me, Claudette. I will feel much more comfortable in this room."

"We will need to keep this our little secret. We don't want Mrs. Reid coming in here to clean. She is too nosey. I will keep it clean for you. We can launder the sheets on Sunday, on her day off." She said with a conspiratorial smile. "I will leave you now. Rest well. If you need anything, remember to pull the bell cord three times. But don't use the one in this room. It will alert the staff as to where you are. Bonne nuit."

She turned and walked back through the bathroom, switching off the lights as she went. Finally, I heard the door in the other bedroom click shut and I was alone for the first time since around three o'clock this morning. I closed the door to the bathroom, switched off the light, and stood for a moment allowing my eyes time to adjust. As they did, the room filled with moonlight. Claudette had already turned this bed down too. I made my way over to it and climbed in. I felt sure I would lie awake, my mind unable to rest after everything that had happened today. But I was wrong. I closed my eyes, a vision of Charlie flashed into my mind, and I was lost to sleep.

10

The next morning, I awoke to a soft knock on the bathroom door. I was debating whether or not to acknowledge the knock when the door gently opened. It was Claudette, who was carrying a tray with a silver coffee pot and a beautiful blue china cup.

Molly really did have a penchant for blue.

"I brought you your morning coffee," she said, setting the tray on a low table draped with a beautiful Moroccan cloth that sat between two large tufted chairs. "Do you prefer it in bed or next to the chair?"

"Next to the chair would be perfect."

I started to climb out of bed when I became uncomfortably aware that I needed to go to the restroom and that my body was making that very apparent.

"Claudette, could you excuse me for a moment?"

"Surely," She started for the bathroom door.

"Would you mind closing the far door as you go through?"

Comprehension dawned on her face. She blushed and closed the door on the far side. I scampered into the cavernous room and shut the door on my side. I was all too aware of the thunderous sound. As the noise bounced off all that marble, it sounded as if Niagara Falls had moved into the house along with me. With nature's call having been answered, I grabbed the cup of coffee off the table and walked through to the other room where Claudette was waiting.

"I am so sorry; it is most undignified to enter a lady's sleeping chamber through a lavatory," she said, staring down at the floor.

"Then we don't have a problem." I laughed. "I'm not a lady."

She smiled up at me.

"I do not imagine that it is any more appropriate to enter a gentleman's room that way either." Her face wore a wicked grin.

"Well, we will just have to make do with our unorthodox behavior." I gave her a quick wink.

The telephone rang and Claudette made her way across to the dressing table to answer it.

"Hello, this is the Desmond residence. Claudette speaking." She spoke professionally into the receiver. "May I tell her who is calling?"

There was a long pause as she listened.

"One moment monsieur." She put her hand over the mouth piece. "It is Samuel, the butler from Monsieur Crawford's home. There has been a death and the police are requesting that members of last night's party come back to be questioned this afternoon at two o'clock."

"Ask who died. And tell them I'll be there."

She spoke for a minute more and then hung up.

"It was Reginald Montgrieve who died. The butler took me into his confidence and told me that he wasn't supposed to say anything about it but that Monsieur Montgrieve has been murdered."

The Reluctant Doppelganger

"Oh, my, and the police will think I did it."

"Mon Dieu!" she gasped.

Suddenly, there was the tremendous clomping of heavy footsteps as if someone was hurrying up the stairs; the clomps turned into heavy thuds thundering down the hallway. The door burst open and Seedy bolted into the room.

"Oh, my God! Is he really dead?"

"I take it you've been listening in on the extension again." I set down my cup and crossed my arms.

Seedy loved to listen in on other people's telephone conversations at Mrs. Winter's boardinghouse. She had spent many a night keeping me current on the lives of the other boarders.

"No, actually; I picked up at the same time as Claudette. When I heard what the call was about, then I listened in." There was no shame in her voice. "So, is he?" she asked again, excited.

"You know just as much as we do. Maybe more than me because you actually heard the telephone conversation." I was annoyed.

"Wow! Did someone get up on the wrong side of the bed?"

"I think I really need at least one whole cup of coffee, maybe more, before I can consider being a suspect in a movie star's murder. Claudette, are there any more cups up here?"

She walked over to a large cabinet in the corner, opened the door and produced another cup and saucer.

"Do you drink coffee, Claudette?"

"Oui."

"Then you'd better grab two cups. I'm sure you are going to want to hear all about this too."

"Oui, monsieur," she said smiling.

She produced a second cup. I hopped up and proceeded into the bathroom. Seedy just stood there until she saw

Claudette follow me through the doorway. Not wanting to miss any gossip, she hurried into the bathroom as well and then into the bedroom beyond.

I spent the better part of the next hour telling them about the evening. I told them about Reggie forcing himself on me, the slap, and then the flip.

"The few times I ever met him he was so kind. I can't believe he would do that." Claudette sounded disappointed.

"Well, he wasn't kind last night. He was horrible; but horrible or not, I slapped him and flipped him. And I know the police will think I killed him."

I went on to tell them about the rest of the party: the view from the tower, my eye-opening episode in the lady's powder room and of course, all about the Viscount.

We all three were giggling when the telephone rang once again. This time it didn't sound the same. The rings were fast and short. As if reading my mind, Claudette stood and hurried towards the telephone ringing in the other bedroom.

"This arrangement is very inconvenient. It is someone from inside the house calling your room." She answered the phone with the red cradle. "Hello. Oui. Tell them Miss Desmond will be ready to meet them in an hour. Oh, and Wallace, please be sure to tell Truman at the gates. You know how put-out he gets when we forget. Au Revoir." She placed the telephone receiver back on its red cradle and quickly and efficiently moved back through the bathroom to where Seedy and I were sitting. "Your father and someone called Georgie are on their way. I assume, knowing Mr. Standish as well as I do, that he will arrive within the next forty-five minutes. We must get you ready. You will need to bathe. Naturally, it would be part of my job to help you but…" She trailed off. "Under the circumstances, I am guessing you would prefer to do that yourself. But I will draw your bath on my way back into the boudoir." She turned to head back.

The Reluctant Doppelganger

"Don't bother drawing a bath. I'll use the shower. I prefer it and if I know my father, like you said, he'll be early. My guess is it will be closer to thirty minutes. Seedy, you go and stall them in case I'm not ready when they get here."

"Consider it done." She hopped up, and along with Claudette, vanished.

I picked up my cup and drained the coffee. I was sure I would need the pick-me-up. Just then, I heard the shower.

Dang, having a lady's maid was a damn fine thing. It's a wonder more people don't strive to have them. I presumed it was because you could feed a family of four for nearly a year on their wages. Still I was glad Claudette was here. I headed for the shower.

It seemed that neither Claudette nor I were correct about my father's arrival time. As I was being dressed by Claudette for the day, the red cradled telephone peeled out its short ring. Claudette again answered.

"Oui. Mon Dieu!" She hung up the telephone. "It is your father. He has arrived. It's only been twenty minutes. Miss Seedy has instructed Wallace to put them in the long gallery. And to keep you informed, Wallace is not happy about taking instructions from your new personal secretary."

All the while she spoke, she never faltered in her tasks. My wig was in place, my make-up had been expertly applied and now she brought out a white girdle, this time. I went into the bathroom to struggle into it and when I returned, she had laid out what she called morning pajamas. They were beautiful. They had white pants and a navy-blue top that had giant white polka dots. The top was trimmed all around the low-cut collar with white ostrich feathers. The moment I touched the pajamas, I could tell they were pure silk. Claudette then produced a pair of white mules with a short-spiked silver heel and a tuft of white ostrich feathers on the broad band across each open toe.

Once I was dressed, she pulled out one of the long strands of pearls, the one with the large pearls, and looped them around my neck. The one long loop hung nearly to my waist. She pulled out a multi-strand pearl choker with a deep blue marquee-cut sapphire surrounded by tiny diamonds, set one above the other that connected each strand of pearls to the sapphire and fastened it around my neck. Next came a sapphire and diamond bracelet. Last, but not least, was a ring with a deep blue sapphire as big as a twenty-dollar gold piece, that was surrounded by large white diamonds.

"Good lord!" I exclaimed, looking down at the ring.

"Mademoiselle attended a party at the home of Mr. & Mrs. Edward McLean, when she was in Washington DC last year, promoting her motion picture. Mrs. McLean wore her famous necklace designed by Monsieur Pierre Cartier. It is a large blue diamond. It is so big and rare that it's been named the Hope Diamond. The big blue stone is surrounded by large white diamonds on a diamond choker. Mademoiselle was so taken with the piece that when she returned to California, she commissioned a local jeweler to make this ring."

I allowed her to slip it over my knuckle. It was exceedingly heavy.

She stood me up and had me spin around.

"Parfait!" she pronounced looking pleased.

I turned towards the mirror, and there standing before me, once again, was Theodora Desmond. I still can't believe it's me behind the mask.

Claudette opened the bedroom door. She whisked me out into the hall, and with her on my heels, we made our way quickly to the long gallery.

11

Not knowing who might be in the room along with my father and Georgie, I opened the door and strode in with what I hoped was fluid grace, but most of all confidence.

"Gol-lee," came Georgie's southern drawl.

Claudette had surveyed the room quicker than even I and found that there were only three occupants—Georgie, my father and Seedy. She closed the door behind us and stood in front of it as if to block anyone trying to come into the room.

"That is quite the transformation. I know a lot of female impressionists who would kill to look as much like somebody famous as you do." He chortled on, oblivious to all the faces trying to silence him with stern looks.

"Georgie, if you wouldn't mind refraining from any comments that would lead anyone overhearing our conversation to believe that Miss Desmond is not who she appears to be, it would be greatly appreciated," my father said in hushed tones.

It had been a very tactful and eloquent rebuke and it worked. Georgie fell immediately quiet.

"Theo, I am in the group that is to meet with the police at

two o'clock today along with you. They are interviewing the guests in groups. And let me tell you there is a hell of a lot of hoopla from last night's guests about being summoned anywhere. It's the elite-of-Hollywood's opinion that if they are to be interviewed at all, the police should come to them. None the less, everyone is going to RC's house in groups," Father explained. Then he eyed me up and down. "Seedy, I think that Theo is going to need her lawyer suit this afternoon."

In unison both Claudette and Georgie gasped out, "No!"

My father looked puzzled.

"Why not?" He sounded put out. "She will need to look dignified and professional."

"She slapped the dead man and threw him over her shoulder," trilled Georgie. "Dressed like that she'll look as guilty as hell."

"No matter what you say about the others, Mademoiselle IS one of Hollywood's elite. As the young Monsieur says, she will look as guilty as hell," agreed Claudette. It sounded far less dire with Claudette's tinkling French lilt. "She must appear to be as 'put out' as all the others. And in this circumstance, she will need to adopt the behavior of those British aristocrats in such matters. She must out-dress everyone there and maintain an air of constant boredom."

"She's a hundred percent right there, Bertie." Georgie chimed in.

"Okay, then. But could you find something with fewer feathers for her to wear? Something a tad bit more conservative?"

"I think she looks exquisite." Georgie was giving me that appraising look.

With all the verbal crossfire that had been going on about me, but not including me, I was just noticing Georgie. He, too, had made an amazing transformation. Yesterday he'd been dressed in a sequined and beaded evening gown with a head band sporting a spiky plume. And today, standing before me was a handsome man now clean shaven. His hair was slicked down and parted in the middle. He wore a double-breasted navy-blue pin-striped suit, a starched white shirt with a high collar and a very conservative red and blue striped tie. The look was finished off with black wing-tip shoes so shiny you could see yourself.

"You look pretty exquisite yourself, Georgie." I think it might have been the first time I had spoken since entering the room.

He smiled, showing two rows of dazzling white teeth. His eyes crinkled when he smiled. His crinkled eyes assured me that my compliment had been taken sincerely.

"Alright, I'll be back at one o'clock to pick you up," my father said.

"No, you will not." Claudette had her arms crossed with an emphatic look on her face.

My father looked taken aback.

"Miss Desmond has not yet eaten. And we will need to start from the beginning if this look does not meet with your approval. And contrary to your views that being thirty minutes early is being 'on time,'" she waved one hand in the air as if dismissing the thought. "That concept is not shared by your Hollywood elite. You may pick up both Miss Desmond and her secretary no earlier than 1:30, preferably 1:45."

He started to speak, and Claudette raised her finger on the hand she'd been waving and now pointed it directly at my father.

"1:45 will allow her to be five to ten minutes late. This is your Hollywood elite's definition of 'on time'." Her tone brooked no argument.

"That's fine," he snipped. "But why in the world would

we take Seedy?"

Claudette crossed her arms again. I doubt Father was used to anyone taking him on like that.

"You know, Mr. Bertram Standish, to be such a high and mighty Hollywood agent and a lady's man to boot, you seem to have no clue about how a real 'Professional Lady' behaves and thinks." Her voice had dropped low and her accent had gotten thick.

My father looked downright testy now.

"Theodora Desmond is a business commodity; even more so now, with this change. As you already know, her image and marketability are paramount. I have always been after Miss Desmond to obtain a personal secretary to handle her business affairs. It would allow her to focus on what generates her income, that of being an actress and public figure. Now, Miss Desmond has found a very professional personal secretary, one, who through a long-held friendship, will most assuredly have her best interests at heart. Miss Desmond will want a close friend along to give her a sense of security. You will not be able to do that because you are just as much a suspect as she is."

I could tell by the look on my father's face that he had never considered himself a suspect. Claudette too, could tell.

"You should take care, Bertie." Her voice was light and gentle now. "I can tell that you too are among those Hollywood elite who think they would never be suspected of murder." And she gave him a warm smile.

"You know Claudette, the day I convinced you to become Molly's maid, I was looking for someone to keep her safe. I was expecting you to be more of a second mother to her. I never expected behind that pretty face and endearing French accent, was a savvy business woman, too." He smiled. "1:45 it is then."

Instantly, the entire mood of the room lifted. I walked over to Seedy to say good morning when Georgie gasped, pointing to my backside.

"You are wearing a girdle under an Elsa Schiapparelli silk pajama. Good God, that is sacrilege."

Claudette was nodding her head. "I agree, but there was not anything else that could be done. There is just so much of it."

And here we go again, back to talking about my credentials.

"You must find something for him to wear that is not so...so defining." Georgie said, looking like he'd just smelled something sour, and waving one hand up and down while the other was perched just above his cocked-out hip.

The posture did not work with the suit at all, and I was guessing he was thinking the same thing about me and the girdle right now. I was so confused; one moment I was a him, the next moment I was a her. I had been hoping this would simply just take some getting used to, but it might be just the way it was from here on out, I feared.

"How about we look through her closet and see what between the two of us, we can find or put together that might work?" Georgie asked Claudette.

"That is a good idea!" And they were off.

Seedy walked over to the red cradled telephone and pushed the connection switch up and down four times.

"Good Morning Mrs. Reid." She paused. "There will be three for breakfast. Will twenty minutes be enough time?" Seedy listened. "Thank you," she said pleasantly and then she looked over at us and grimaced. Immediately switching from the grimace back to a smile she went on, "And please have Wallace bring coffee up to the long gallery." She replaced the receiver in its cradle and turned back to us. "That woman does not like me in charge."

12

Seedy, my father and I had our breakfast downstairs in the bright cheery morning room. Then my father left, promising not to be back until 1:45. Seedy and I had thanked Mrs. Reid for a superb meal and made our way back upstairs to my bed chamber.

The room looked as if it had been struck by a tornado. Clothes were everywhere and some of them were in pieces. I wasn't sure where they had gotten it, but a large sewing machine had been pulled into the room and Georgie sat behind it sewing away.

They both looked up as we entered.

"Good, I'm glad you are here. We need to build this dress onto you," Georgie said. "Go stand on the fitting pedestal in the closet. And you," he nodded to Seedy, "go help him undress."

"No," came Claudette's voice, halting. She pointed to me. "Sit down at the dressing table. I will help you get undressed. I like to have my mistress' closet tidy and organized, unlike this disaster of a man throwing everything he touches just anywhere it lands." The barb rolled off

The Reluctant Doppelganger

Georgie like water off a duck's back.

I sat and Claudette began. Everything came off a piece at a time and was put away where it belonged. Seedy had taken up a position seated on the bed, simply watching everything in awe. When I was down to the girdle, she laughed.

"That's what we needed last Halloween."

She saw the confusion on everyone's face but mine. So, she went on to explain.

"Eddie went to the Film Guild's masked ball as Theodora. We had a devil of a time trying to hide the same thing that you have apparently hidden with a girdle."

"This afternoon we are going to hide it with a corset, I am trying to alter. One that I'm finishing up right now," Georgie drawled looking up from behind the sewing machine. With an audible zip, he pulled the two threads away from the sewing machine's foot far enough to snip them. When he held it up, the garment was one odd looking creation. For one thing, it appeared to already have small breasts; and where normally it was open at the bottom, he had attached a piece of fabric in a triangle shape, point side down. At the point was attached a long thin flat cord. On the back of the corset he had attached two small rings, one slightly above the other. "Into the closet," he ordered.

I complied. Once we were inside, he started to close the door. Then he stuck his head out just before it shut. He grinned widely at the girls. "No peeking!" and he winked.

Once the door had clicked shut, he turned to me standing on the pedestal still in the girdle. "Spread your feet about six inches apart and brace yourself."

I moved my feet in until they were approximately the desired distance apart and grabbed hold of each side of the surrounding mirrors. Georgie walked up to me, slipped his fingers into the waistband at my sides and, with a great grunt, he gave it an almighty tug downward. He dropped his entire body down to the ground. What I felt first was a rush of cool air and then I felt my credentials slap Georgie in the face. He popped immediately back to his feet.

"Guess I got too close. Sorry about that." He gave me a shy grin.

I couldn't believe it, but he actually blushed. He moved right to the next task at hand—getting the new garment on.

"You are going to have to give me a minute." I began to scratch the offending area so vigorously that I almost purred. "Dang, I've been needing to do that since I got that blasted thing on."

"You might want to shave that area. It would make being battened down a lot easier. But if you do, you'll need to do it daily because stubble itches even worse," He sounded almost apologetic.

"Are you kidding me? It is one of four places on my body I actually have hair and I've already shaved two of those." I shot my arms into the air to show my bare pits.

"It's up to you; I'm just making you aware."

"Oh, I'm aware." I gave everything one last good scratch.

He stepped on the pedestal and held the garment low so that I could step in. Then he jerked the corset away before I could.

"I forgot; with this you need to put on a garter belt first." He moved over to a set of narrow drawers and began opening them, rummaging through their contents and then closing them again.

"Claudette will kill you if you get those out of order." I admonished in a sing-song voice.

"I think her bark is worse than her bite." He held up a beige garter belt. "But then again, I might be wrong about that."

He handed it to me, and I slipped it on. Once again, he was back on the pedestal holding the garment low for me to step into. I did. He began to gently work it up my body, unlike the process of removing the girdle. I was uncertain as to whether he wanted to make sure he didn't catch my credentials in his face again or he thought the maneuver required more finesse. Once it was in place, he began to cinch the laces. Unlike the corsets of twenty years ago that were designed to make the waist smaller and therefore both the breast and hips fuller, today's corset was designed to bind the bust in an effort to make the hips, waist and bust appear to be the same. In other words, women today wanted to look like boys— ironic, huh? Once everything was properly cinched, Georgie took hold of the cord attached to the point of the triangular shaped fabric.

"The time has come my friend. I need the balls to go up and your manhood to go back."

Following Georgie's instructions proved to be more difficult than I expected. The corset impeded my movement. I could not bend down that far.

"I could use some help, I think."

"We need to clear something up first." Georgie stood back and lifted a finger in the air.

"And that would be?" I asked sardonically.

"I am spoken for."

"Spoken for?"

"I am taken."

"Are you telling me that you have a lover?" I snipped out.

"Yes, that is precisely what I'm telling you."

"I am standing here in a corset unable to bend at the waist. You are wanting me to tuck my credentials so that you can bind them down. And you pick now to tell me that you have a lover? Now? Really? Do you think now would be the time I would choose to make sexual advances towards you? Have you been smoking reefer?"

Georgie looked up and smiled sheepishly.

"I guess you are right. The timing would be awkward. I just wanted you to know." I rolled my eyes. He moved in towards me.

In a flash, the huevos went up and Georgie pulled me backwards as he pulled the triangle tight against me. The cord went between my hips and its end was woven back and forth through the two small rings, then cinched.

"Damn, that's tight." I complained.

"Don't move." He patted my bare bottom.

"Now who's getting fresh," I admonished.

He grinned. He hopped off the pedestal and opened the door. Both Seedy and Claudette were standing there looking in. Suddenly I felt naked, even though I was more clothed than when I was in the girdle. Georgie grabbed a tailor's belt off the dressing table and in just moments was back at my side. He knelt down. He took a pair of scissors from the belt and cut off all but a few inches of the excess cord. He then slipped a thimble on his index finger and pulled out a needle and thread. He pushed two fingers between me and the fabric.

"If you stick my credentials with that thing, I'm going to use a Judo flip on you too," I warned.

Georgie smiled up at me with the scissors now clamped in his mouth. "I'm really good at what I do," he mumbled through a mouth full of scissors.

It didn't take him but a minute to stitch me in. Next came the silk stockings. Once all the under garments were in place, he showed me the dress. The frock that Georgie and Claudette had chosen was a very straight line beaded beige dress. It fell to just below the knee, and except for an elaborate pattern of monochromatic bead work, the dress was very nondescript. And suddenly I saw why the dress was so plain. Claudette had disappeared into the other bedroom and returned with something that reminded me of a hijab attached to a modern hat. I only knew about a hijab because I had read the script for Samson and Delilah and I was to wear one in the movie.

"Sit down." Georgie patted the dressing table bench.

Once I was seated, he and Claudette began to get me into the unusual new fashion accessory. The low riding hat left only the two ends of the bobbed wig exposed, and with the help of Claudette, those ends curled up on my cheeks. The hijab was already attached. It came around my right ear and draped down like a small cape to about my elbow and then curved its way back up under my chin, and attached back to the hat, at a single point on the other side. The fabric of the hijab looked very familiar. Then recognition dawned. What was now my new striking hijab had just this morning been the Moroccan tablecloth between the two chairs in the other bedroom where I had taken my morning coffee.

"I had really liked that tablecloth." I looked up at Georgie in the mirror and smiled.

"You will make heads turn wearing it. It would have gone unnoticed as a tablecloth in an unused bedroom," he retorted, focused completely on his task.

Beige kid leather shoes with four-inch heels were slipped on my feet and the thin leather band was buckled across my arch. I was handed matching wrist length leather gloves. Claudette added a large multicolored topaz brooch on my right side, pinning the hijab to the dress to avoid any hat crisis if by chance, there was a sudden gust of wind. The look was completed with a pair of yellow diamond and topaz earrings. Only one earring could be seen because the other one was hidden by the hijab.

It was nearly 1:40 in the afternoon when Claudette and Georgie had finished working their magic. Claudette had not exaggerated at all when she told my father that we would have to start all over. But everyone in the room agreed that the finished product was absolute perfection. It would achieve the height of fashion while maintaining a modicum of conservatism for the seriousness of a murder investigation.

The red cradled telephone rang. My father was here, and for maybe the first time in his life, he wasn't early. I led the way down the stairs, pulling on my gloves at the landing. Wallace was in the foyer standing next to my father; he moved to the bottom of the staircase and held out his hand to take mine. I never understood assisting a lady off the last step. To me, she had accomplished the hard part already; but it was a courtesy extended to women and I, being Theodora Desmond, accepted the proffered hand graciously.

"You are always beautiful, Ma'am, but you look exquisitely stunning this afternoon," Wallace said, smiling.

I didn't need to turn around to know that Claudette and Georgie were beaming at the compliment. Wallace offered my hand to my father and he took it. The door was opened, and the three of us walked out into a sunny California afternoon to the waiting automobile where Randel was already holding the door open. He helped us in and moments later we were off.

13

The gates to RC's home stood open, but we still were stopped by the gatekeeper. As we motored down the length of the driveway, I noticed the gravel parking area in front of the garages. It was almost full again this afternoon. We pulled to the front of the house. The automobile door was opened for us. Today the footman's tux was gone. He was clad in a simple black suit and tie. He extended his hand into the automobile and I placed mine in his. As I climbed out, I caught sight of Seedy's face. She was slack jawed just like I had been the night before. Fortunately for us, my father had noticed Seedy's look of awe and reminded her, before getting out of the auto, that she was supposed to be accustomed to this lifestyle and to please neutralize her expression. In other words, to close her mouth. With Seedy falling in behind us, I put my arm through my father's. We meandered up the sidewalk with an expression of utter boredom mixed with annoyance plastered on our faces.

When we reached the front doors, the two doormen once again greeted us by name, and we passed through into the massive oriental foyer. The coat check girl, along with her oriental pagoda, were gone. I guess Hollywood royalty didn't wear furs in the afternoon. The room, although still very opulent, looked harsher in the light of day. There was no Josephine Baker singing *La Vie En Rose*, but from the landing above that led to the mammoth ballroom came the thunderous murmur of a great many voices.

The butler, Samuel, met us at the door.

"You look absolutely stunning today, Miss Desmond. I will show you upstairs. That is where everyone is gathering to be interviewed. The police are using the stage as their headquarters. They seem to be calling everyone over in small groups. I am not sure how they have been determining who is in what group."

He had been moving us ever closer to the staircase as he talked. Instead of motioning us up and departing, however, he led the way up. As we crested the top and could see into the ballroom, I heard Seedy give an audible gasp. My father looked sternly back at her.

"Excuse me, Sir. I caught my heel on the stair." She gave him a wink.

What Seedy had caught sight of was the huge chunk of Hollywood's royalty, some moving around the room mingling and others sitting in small clusters deep in conversation. Chairs had been brought in, but they were not the comfortable kind. They appeared to be rented ballroom chairs that I was sure were gold painted wrought iron with cushioned seats.

I strode into the room first with Father behind me and Seedy behind him. I did just as Claudette had instructed. I had arranged my face to look extremely put out and totally bored. As I looked around at the others huddled together in their cliquish clutches, I knew her instructions had been sound indeed. They all wore the same expression.

A middle-aged woman dressed in a business suit, sitting

across the room, looked at me, said something to another woman wearing a large hat, then stood up and made her way towards me. Two steps behind the woman, the lady in the large hat was hot on her heels.

"Careful what you say," Father whispered. "The first woman is Luella Parsons and the rather attractive woman behind her is her arch rival, Hedda Hopper. You don't want to be all over the newspapers and radio tomorrow. They were here last night and saw the altercation between you and Reggie. They will try to sensationalize it. Don't let them."

"Oh, my dear," Louella spoke with high drama and a saddened expression on her face. "What an awful thing to have happen to poor dear Reggie."

"It was! Wasn't it?" I said, gushing right back at her with a mock look of shock.

"Especially after the brawl you two had last evening," chimed in Hedda.

"Brawl?"

"Everyone saw you slap him then throw him over your shoulder."

I laughed, in what I hoped was a dismissive tone. "Oh, that? We weren't angry. We were talking about a new movie idea with RC. It's about an older zany aristocrat detective and his young socialite wife. Reggie was talking about doing his own stunts for the movie. We were simply giving RC a sample. I am afraid I did get a bit overzealous in the flip though, and I might have bruised Reggie's pride as well as maybe a couple of spots on his bum." I giggled as if I had just made the funniest of quips.

The two women smiled and chortled, but I wasn't fooled a bit. They weren't buying it. Well, at least not one hundred percent anyway. Out of the corner of my eye I could see a woman making a beeline straight for Louella, Hedda and me. It was Regina Banks. She was known in Hollywood for her roles as a siren. In the movies, she cunningly lured many a man to his downfall and in real-life too. She had laid waste to five husbands at current count.

"Darling," Regina drawled out in a voice colored with sultry sensuality, albeit a little gravelly. "Don't you look just divine. I loved that Persian look with the head dress and veil when I saw it this past summer in Coco Chanel's salon in Paris. I just didn't think it would ever go over well in American society."

It seemed that Regina was trying to get my fashion sense slighted in the gossip columns. I wasn't sure why, but I could not let it slip by unchallenged. After all, it wouldn't be my fashion sense brought into question but that of Georgie and Claudette's. And with the care they had taken thus far in my appearance it just wouldn't be fair. I knew that being purported to be on the worst dressed list was akin to being socially ostracized. I felt a surge of anger rise up. I hoped it wasn't showing on my face.

"I can certainly understand your concern for an overly tall lanky woman such as yourself. It is a fashion best carried on a petite frame such as mine. And of course, Coco is my designer of choice. Her designs are so well suited for me. Just like this one." I boldly implied that it was a Chanel original. Well, it was original and that was a fact. I raised my wrist and arranged my fingers in the style you see so many models take in today's fashion magazines. Then I slowly turned, as gracefully as I could, allowing everyone around to take in the entire effect of my ensemble. "Mrs. McLean thought it was tres chic. You do know Mrs. McLean, don't you? Mrs. Edward McLean, whose husband is the publisher of the Washington Post." Of course, it was a lie, but they had no way of knowing that. And I was sure that Theodora Desmond's visit to the publisher's home was common knowledge to the two journalists and most likely to Regina as well. Inwardly I said a silent prayer of thanks to Claudette for telling me the story of the ring last night and about Theodora's visit to the powerful socialite's home. Daggers flew from Regina's eyes. It was just then that Charlie came into view. He had crossed the room when he saw me modeling.

"My dear Miss Desmond, you look simply breathtaking. I didn't think you could look more beautiful than you did last evening, but you have proven me incorrect in my assumption."

"You flatter me, your Lordship."

He took my hand and pressed the back of it to his lips.

I could tell the two journalists were dying for an introduction.

"Ladies let me introduce you. This is His Lordship, the Honorable Charles Pennington, Viscount of Kintyre and Lorne. Your Lordship, these are Louella Parsons and Hedda Hopper, both noted newspaper columnists and radio hosts. And this is Miss Regina Banks, who I'm sure needs no introduction being a famous star of the silver screen."

Charlie nodded to all three ladies.

"Would all of you be so kind as to let me steal Miss Desmond away?"

He didn't wait for an answer. He lifted my hand onto the back of his and escorted me away from the viper's nest and out onto the terrace. As soon as we were out of sight of everyone, he let go of my hand and turned to me with a laugh.

"I thought you might have had enough of those three. I had been eavesdropping on your conversation ever since I saw the gossip sharks put you in their crosshairs. I hope I wasn't being presumptuous."

"Most assuredly you were not," I smiled at him and sighed. "Some days this keeping up appearances can be quite tedious."

"I am all too aware of it. Being in the public eye all the time does get tiresome. I'm so glad to see you again. I feared that I was going to have to invent a reason to see you prior to our Thanksgiving date." He was smiling and his icy eyes sparkled.

"You don't need a reason." Then I thought about him just popping by and how much work it took to get me ready to receive guests. "It just takes a little notice," I amended, returning his smile.

He lifted that damned eyebrow again. This time I noticed that the corner of his mouth curled up along with it. I answered the unspoken question.

"If men were only aware of just how much effort goes into looking like this," I twirled around, "they would never question the time a lady takes."

He laughed out loud.

Just then, a man in a rumpled gray suit stuck his head out the French doors.

"There you are. The detective is ready to talk with you both."

He stepped all the way through the doorway onto the terrace and then gestured for us to go back into the house. We were led to the stage where, last evening, Josephine Baker had wowed party goers as she sang. The piano had been pushed against the back wall and in its place, there were several chairs. These were not the banquet style chairs that now littered the ballroom floor. These were mismatched overstuffed comfortable chairs. The fact that they were mismatched told me that these chairs had been brought from other rooms within the house. They were arranged in a semi-circle around an ornate card playing table. It too had come from another room. The gaming table was being used as a makeshift desk. Behind the makeshift desk sat a large muscular man. The best description would be to say he looked ruggedly handsome and tough.

His large size and strong masculine features were made even more imposing by his chair. He was seated in what must have been an old movie prop. It was a formidable gilded throne that had been pavéd with paste pearls and gems in every color, size and shape. The throne had a royal blue tufted velvet cushion with gargantuan gold tassels at each corner. If the chair had come complete with a costume change, the man seated in it might easily had been mistaken for Zeus. Alas, in his rumpled black suit, he looked more like the butt of someone's attempt at a joke. If it bothered him that someone had tried to be humorous at his expense, it didn't show.

He stood as we approached. That was when I noticed that two other policemen had their charges in tow as well. Headed towards the same location were RC with one officer and the Duke and my father with the other. RC arrived first. He stepped up on the platform and shot out his hand. "How is my Throne of Power working out for you?" RC clasped the policeman's hand.

"Actually, quite well. It does work like you said it would." the rumpled suited man replied.

"That has always been my experience ever since I discovered its unusual power."

"What unusual power?" the Duke inquired. He had taken in the new surroundings and was as much intrigued as I. In fact, he had asked the very question I had been about to voice myself.

"Anytime I need to have a difficult conversation with someone or must discern which parts of a two-sided argument are the true facts, I use the throne. It is the damnedest thing; it automatically imposes fear. People tend not to be able to pull the wool over my eyes when I'm sitting in it." RC could hardly contain his pride at owning such a magnificent magical tool.

"I dare say my good man, I find that hard to swallow." the Duke said questioningly.

"I did too," said the rumpled suited man as he motioned for us all to sit. "That is until I found Mr. Crawford to be correct. It really does seem to have a great deal of sway."

I filed that away, just in case I was ever summoned, and I found RC seated upon his throne. Once everyone except for the rumpled suited man was seated, he spoke again. His voice was hearty, robust and radiated power and authority. To my thinking, his commanding presence and imposing physique as he stood towering over everyone now seated before him, held a great deal more sway than the glittering throne. And I would wager he knew that too, but he went along with the ruse out of deference to his very powerful host.

"I am Detective John Lister with the Los Angeles police department, Beverly Hills division. I want to thank each one of you for coming today. I appreciate you taking time out of your busy schedules to meet with me. As I am sure each of you already knows, Mr. Reginald Montgrieve died last evening. His death has been classified as one with suspicious circumstances. Therefore, an investigation is being conducted. I have asked you here today so that the police department can obtain any information regarding the circumstances revolving around his death. Conducting these interviews in groups like we are doing today is highly irregular. However, being that the deceased was considered to be a public figure, as is everyone that was at last evening's party, we have received a special dispensation so that we will not be required to have everyone come separately to police headquarters. It was decided that, due to the amount of attention Mr. Montgrieve's passing has generated, having each person that attended last night's soiree come to be interviewed at the police station would most likely create utter chaos, and a good deal of unwanted exposure to the press.

"We all thank you Detective. That is a wise precaution," my father said, smiling.

"I can assure you, Mr. Standish, it was not my idea. I don't feel that the wealthy and famous deserve any special kid gloves treatment," the detective said flatly.

If you were very observant, you would have seen my father's smile falter just the slightest, but in the blink of an eye it was back in place.

"First, I would like to go through each of your names to verify that the people sitting in front of me are the people I have on my list. I have already identified Mr. Standish. Mr. Crawford and I met earlier."

RC nodded his confirmation.

He looked at the Duke.

"You are Mr.," he paused for a second. "Is it Mr. Kintyre or Mr. Lorne or is it hyphenated?" he said with a puzzled look on his face.

"I am afraid, my dear detective, I am going to increase that frown you are currently wearing instead of lessening it." The corners of the Duke's mouth turned up slightly.

The detective looked at him expectantly.

"I am Sir George Pennington, the Earl of Groftenshire and the Duke of Kintyre and Lorne. My proper address is Your Grace but since I know that titles are not part of American culture, you may simply address me as Mr. Pennington."

"Thank you, Your Grace," said the detective. "I think I find your proper address the easiest."

"As you wish." The Duke smiled.

Detective Lister looked at Charlie. "And you are his son?"

He had made the query half wavering between a question

and a statement. Charlie took the cue. "Yes, I am His Grace's son. I am the Honorable Charles Pennington, Viscount of Kintyre and Lorne. My proper address is Your Lordship. But please, just call me Charlie."

"Thank you, Charlie," said the detective as he scribbled in his notebook.

"Although I'm a huge fan, Miss Desmond, I still need you to verify that you are Theodora Desmond."

The inspector's voice was much softer and gentler than it had been with the men. And now he wore a huge smile on his face and his eyes sparkled with what I could only assume was adoration.

"I am indeed Theodora Desmond." I answered nodding my head and returning his smile.

In the next moment, I felt as if he was trying to catch me off guard with his flattery. His smile dimmed slightly, and his eyes became intense.

"Miss Desmond, it was reported by several of the guests in attendance last night, well actually all of the guests we have interviewed so far, that you and the deceased had a verbal and physical altercation that ended by you hurling Mr. Montgrieve over your shoulder and throwing him to the ground." He chuckled slightly at this. "As hard as I find it to believe that a woman of your diminutive size and delicate features could possibly pitch a man the size of Reginald Montgrieve to the floor, so many sources have confirmed it I must ask you if this truly was the case."

I'm not sure what bothered me more, the fact that I had hurled Reggie Montgrieve to the floor in a room full of people or the fact the detective was now laughing at me.

"I can assure you, Detective, that I did flip Reggie, Mr. Montgrieve, to the floor last evening. The man was a cad. When he learned that the role of Samson in Mr. Crawford's upcoming film might not be his, in a drunken rage, he forced himself upon me supposedly to offer proof to Mr. Crawford that he was the man for the part. I slapped him. He became infuriated and tried to choke me. He caught me by surprise. I have trained in Judo since I was seven years old and I hold a tenth-degree black belt in the discipline. It was more out of instinct than that of any kind of self-defense."

At this the detective stifled a smile.

"I would be more than happy to demonstrate with you, if you wish." My offer was delivered pleasantly and followed with an exaggerated smile. Sarcasm dripped from each word. In a heartbeat, this man had roused my ire and filled me with indignation. I could tell my cheeks were flushing.

"That won't be necessary, Miss Desmond." His voice still sounded amused. He coughed, covering his mouth in a gesture meant to hide his efforts to regain his composure.

"The man truly was being a cad, Detective." RC interjected, leaning back in his tufted arm chair, crossing his legs and steepling his fingers.

"We all were there when Mr. Montgrieve forced his intentions upon Miss Desmond. Her recounting of the events is quite accurate." The Duke spoke matter-of-factly.

The detective looked down at the notes he'd just made. "Merely to clarify, Miss Desmond, you hold the tenth-degree black belt in the Judo discipline?"

"Yes Detective, I have been studying Judo since I was seven years old. I also hold the distinction of being one of the youngest ever to hold a tenth-degree black belt."

"I study Judo myself, Miss Desmond. And I, too, am a black belt, but I only hold the second-degree. However, I have only studied the discipline since I joined the police force. Mr. Montgrieve was lucky you only flipped him to the ground," he bore a knowing smile. "Any black belt practitioner could offer up lethal force. You have my utmost respect for your accomplishment." His warm smile was back now.

"Detective, why do you think Reggie's death was murder?"

"At this point, Miss Desmond, it is not considered to be a murder. Currently it is classified as *death with suspicious circumstances.*" The detective was looking at me very seriously.

He proceeded to ask everyone about their movements during and after the party.

"Your Grace, are you and Charlie staying at the Beverly Hills Hotel while you're here?"

"We are indeed. We each have our own bungalows there."

"And you each went back to your bungalows after the party? Is there anyone who can vouch for your presence?"

Charlie looked uneasy.

"My personal valet helped me undress. He will be more than happy to assure you of my location last evening."

The detective had noticed Charlie's unease as well.

"And you, sir? Can your valet vouch for you as well?" He looked hard at Charlie.

Charlie stammered a bit before he answered. "My valet was not there. I had dismissed him before I returned. I was with a young lady," he smiled sheepishly, looking directly at the detective and then moving his gaze to me.

"And who was this young lady?"

Again, Charlie looked over at me. His eyes seemed to implore my forgiveness. "It was Regina Banks." He now looked directly at the detective and purposely did not look in my direction.

Now I knew why the woman had verbally accosted me out of the blue. She thought I had designs on what she now considered to be her Viscount. Charlie dropped his eyes to his lap. I'm sure a hurt look had crossed my face. I'm not sure why, however. I had no right to look hurt. I had no designs on him, and I could not have any designs on him. Besides, I had rebuked his advances. This was the nineteen twenties, for God's sake, not the Dark Ages. He just wanted to have some fun, and any girl except for the so called 'good girls' would, too. That wasn't the problem at all. The problem was and is, I'm not a girl.

The detective kept asking questions, but I was lost in my own thoughts and his words were like a buzzing in the background. I sat back in the tufted wing-back chair. It was then I became aware that my toes weren't touching the floor. I hated the fact that I was a grown man and that I could not sit in a chair, lean back, cross my legs and get comfortable without my feet dangling in the air.

Did petite women hate that too?

I was sure they did. As my mind rambled on, my gaze moved to the massive throne. The jewels sparkled as they caught the light. But these jewels weren't real, they were only paste. Something niggled at the back of my mind but try as I might I could not pull it into focus. My father reached over and touched my hand and I was jolted back into the conversation.

The Duke was explaining his altercation with Reggie. He was telling the detective about Reggie having been his valet before he became a successful movie actor.

"The man took fifty pounds from my wallet and disappeared while we were in New York City on business many years ago. Funny thing was, about five years after the fact, I received an anonymous letter that I was sure was from him. It said, 'Thanks for the loan.' And the letter was accompanied by a fifty-pound note. Damnedest thing. Then, when I recognized him last night, he flew into a rage."

I looked over at the detective. He was writing furiously. When he looked up, he said, "I think I have everything that I need from each of you currently. If I have any further questions, I will be in contact." He stood, and with that, we were excused.

I turned to see Seedy perched on the edge of one of those uncomfortable ballroom chairs. *Oh my*, I thought, *she must be bored out of her mind and uncomfortable as well.* I walked over to her, prepared to apologize, but when I got there, I could tell she was brimming over with excitement. "Whatever in the world has you so positively charged? Come on spill."

"I overheard that policeman there." She pointed to a policeman now deep in a whispered conversation with Detective Lister, still seated upon the Throne of Power. "He was telling that other officer by the stairs that now they know it was murder. Seems they found drugs in Montgrieve's stomach and there were traces of the same drug on the glass they found on the tennis court. But they don't think it was the cause of death. There were scorch marks on his dinner jacket. They think he was electrocuted somehow."

"Electrocuted," I gasped.

"Shh, not so loud. We are not supposed to know."

Charlie walked over to us. "I'm terribly sorry, Miss Desmond."

"Sorry about what?" I said, with a great deal more aplomb than I felt. "If you are talking about your tryst with Regina Banks, all I have to say on that matter is, don't give it a second thought. It is the nineteen twenties after all. We are not living in the Dark Ages." It hadn't sounded any better coming out of my mouth than it had in my head. "And if you are talking about her lighting into me today, then you have redeemed yourself already by getting me away from her. Lord Charles Pennington, I would like to introduce my personal secretary, Miss Cecelia Schofield." I said it a bit snippier than I had intended. I gestured to Seedy. He gave a polite nod in her direction. "Cecelia, this is His Lordship, the Honorable Charles Pennington." Seedy actually curtsied. "If you will excuse us your Lordship, we have another engagement this afternoon. Come Cecilia," I motioned for her to follow me as I began to stroll away from the Viscount.

Charlie nodded and wished us good day. I was aiming for the front door. I wanted out of here. I found a footman on my way across the room and asked him to order my car around. I searched for my father only to find him back on the stage with RC deep in an animated conversation with Detective Lister. They were both sitting on the same side of the table. They had pulled their chairs out of the semi-circle and were now seated side by side facing the inspector. It was 'the ole one-two punch.' I wondered what in the world they could want from the man. Whatever it was, with those two sharks circling him, the poor guy didn't stand a chance.

Standing there, I made a decision. Seedy and I would take the car back to the house. I would have a footman tell Father that I would send Randel and the car back for him. I turned to tell Seedy my plans, but she wasn't there. I looked across the room and saw her hanging up the telephone. In moments, she was back at my side. "Something wrong?"

"Not at all. I was just telephoning Mrs. Reid to let her know we were on our way and we were requesting an early supper."

I smiled at her. I think Seedy was liking her new role and she was good at it too. With me in the lead, we headed for the door and home.

14

When we arrived back home, Mrs. Reid had prepared a cold supper of roast beef, pickled onions, freshly whipped mayonnaise, and several cheeses with warm fresh bread and cold beer. And all of that was topped off with a fresh fruit compote floating in apricot liqueur served with a dollop of freshly whipped cream. I had been so hungry upon our return that I hadn't even taken time to change clothes. Towards the end of the meal, Father had come and gone. Seems he and RC had some business to conduct. He only stopped long enough to fix himself a sandwich and to tell me there was another party tomorrow night that I would need to attend. This party was at the home of a German industrialist who was new to Beverly Hills. RC smelled money; and again, he was hauling out his treasure chest of curiosities, Theodora Desmond being one of the major curiosities in his collection. Seedy had her appointment book out and we were scheduled. She assured my father she would find the correct address and answer any RSVP that might be required. Then he was gone.

It was going to be the first time in the last seventy-four

hours that I was going to be able to relax. I was going to have an entire evening to myself. Seedy and I had discussed playing Gin Rummy on our way back from this afternoon's inquisition. Claudette had snipped the threads that held me bound into the corset device Georgie had built and I was now dressed in loose tweed pants and a simple white silk blouse. I was not wearing any foundation garment and the freedom I was experiencing was divine.

Seedy and I were in the long gallery playing cards when there was a knock at the door and it softly opened. It was Wallace.

"Miss Desmond, would you have a moment to speak to us?"

"Us?"

"Randel and me, Ma'am."

"Most certainly." I wondered what they could possibly want. I could tell by the look on her face Seedy was thinking the same thing.

The door opened wider and Randel stepped through holding the gray hat from his uniform in his hands in front of him. He was staring down at the floor. Wallace closed the door behind them as quietly as he could, then moved to stand alongside Randel.

"Go on, tell her." he said to Randel.

Randel looked up for the first time. It was also the first time I had really noticed the man's face. I knew he always wore a smile, and he was quiet and professional. But I had never really looked at him before, seen him as a person, not just the chauffeur, I mean. He was tall and slender with broad shoulders. He had neatly cut brown hair parted on the side but not slicked down. His eyes were a deep emerald green shot through with flecks of gold. His skin was smooth and fair, and he had a wide, full, pleasant-looking mouth.

"What is it Randel?" I coaxed in a soft, even tone, the one

you would use with a child. I'm not sure why, but he was emanating a childlike sensation.

He looked down again, as if he were thinking. When he looked back up, those childlike green eyes were filled with unshed tears.

"What is it, Randel?" I implored.

"It's Georgie, ma'am. They've arrested him for the murder of Reginald Montgrieve."

"They've what?" both Seedy and I said in unison, as we jumped to our feet. "Why in the world would they do that?"

"It's a really long story ma'am. He couldn't have done it. I know he couldn't have done it."

If there was one thing that my father and the disciplines of Judo had drilled into me, it was to always keep calm. And right now, it was exactly what I needed to do. Seedy ran over and put her arm around Randel. She led him to a chair by the fireplace. She had him sit in the chair. He started to protest, but Seedy insisted. I motioned for Wallace to do the same. He too, wanted to protest as well but his concern for Randel's welfare caused him to acquiesce. By now, Randel was openly sobbing. Tears dripped down onto the dusky gray uniform, leaving dark gray spots where they fell.

"It may be a long story," I laid a hand on Randel's shoulder, "but I'm afraid that's where we need to start. Do you think you can get control of yourself long enough to tell me?"

Randel nodded and Seedy handed him her handkerchief. He started to dab at his eyes and take deep breaths.

"Perhaps ma'am, I should start." Wallace's voice was solemn.

I nodded for him to go ahead.

"You are aware that we work for the studio?" He asked it as a question, but I felt all he sought was a simple confirmation.

The Reluctant Doppelganger

I nodded my head yes.

"The studio has strict rules about family members working together in the same household."

I must have looked confused.

"You see, ma'am."

There was a struggle going on inside the man. I could tell that whatever he was about to divulge had been a closely guarded secret for a long time.

"Well, ma'am. Randel and I are brothers." Suddenly it was like a great burden had been lifted off Wallace's shoulders.

"Brothers?" I'm sure I looked quizzical. They could easily be father and son. Wallace must have read my expression.

"Yes ma'am, half-brothers actually. We shared the same father. I was a grown man when my father married Randel's mother. Our father died shortly after Randel's birth. He was five years old when his ma too died, of scarlet fever. There was no one to take him, so I did. I've raised him. I went to work for the studio about twelve years ago. I have worked in several different motion picture actor's homes over that time. Four years ago, when you moved into this house, the driver that had been assigned to you was hired away from the studio by an oil man in Texas. Randy had just lost his job at a factory that had closed. He had been a driver for the factory. I knew he could do the job, so I had him apply to the studio using his middle name as his surname, which was his ma's maiden name. He got the job and I hope you think he's done well. But the studio will fire us both if they ever find out.

The burden that had been lifted from this man's shoulders had now been placed squarely onto mine. I couldn't even imagine the kind of courage it had taken for him to divulge his confidences to me.

Randel looked up. His eyes still brimmed but the flow had been stanched.

I could tell, taking in Randel's expression, that this was just the tip of the iceberg as far as confessions go.

"Georgie is not like you, ma'am. He's not strong and confident. He's very talented and he is a loving and kind soul, but he's not strong." Randel sputtered and then sniffed, holding Seedy's handkerchief to his nose.

"What do you mean 'strong like me'?'"

"He can't take care of himself, ma'am, like you can. In jail that is. He was arrested once. They held him in the drunk tank. A couple of the drunks forced themselves on Georgie and the police wouldn't do anything to stop it. They told him to quit complaining since that's what he liked anyway. He's terrified of jail. Now he's there again." He'd said all he could, and he broke down once again.

Wallace picked up the tale. "Georgie and Randel have been seeing each other for almost as long as he has worked for Miss Desmond — I mean 'you.'" There was a quick but noticeable stutter in his amendment.

Suddenly, it dawned on me. "You know, don't you?"

Both men nodded their heads in the affirmative.

"Georgie told you?"

Again, their nods confirmed.

"Please, ma'am, we have to help Georgie." Randel begged.

"Why do the police suspect Georgie?" I asked.

It was Randel who answered. "Georgie is a fine tailor and dress designer. He is very successful in what he does."

"And exactly what does he do?"

"You are familiar with couture?" he answered my question with a question.

I nodded yes.

"Most of the European designers create their fashions for small skinny women. But a good many of the wealthiest American women are neither small nor are they skinny. Georgie re-creates the latest fashions in sizes that fit a more matronly shape."

Then I remembered the sewing room at the Drakestone Hotel. There were racks and racks of clothes, some in very large sizes.

"Is his studio at the Drakestone Hotel?"

"It is. That's how he got mixed up with Reginald Montgrieve."

"Montgrieve dressed in women's clothes?"

"Lord no," and he chuckled. "Montgrieve wanted a couple of custom-made suits. One of Georgie's female clients suggested to Montgrieve that he should hire Georgie. He did. Montgrieve was impatient and kept hounding Georgie to finish his suits quickly. Montgrieve found out the location of Georgie's studio somehow and just showed up. If you have been to Georgie's studio you know how he works. He always wears a dress there. About six months ago, Montgrieve contacted Georgie and wanted to meet.

"It turned out Montgrieve was addicted to Veronal. He regularly purchased the drug and even used several different drug stores to supply his needs. Only the larger drug stores carry Veronal because it is highly taxed, and those shops are members of an organization called the California Society of Pharmacy."

"I know of the Society. Among other things, it maintains records of those who use highly taxed pharmaceuticals that are considered dangerous. They also maintain a list of those who are considered abusers of those same types of drugs. Both lists are updated monthly and are mailed out to each member of the Society."

"That's right," Randel said, giving me a look of astonishment.

"My grandfather owns McPherson Drugs and I use to work there every summer," I said, answering the puzzled look on his face.

"Montgrieve's own doctor wrote the Society and had him placed on the abusers list when the doctor deduced that he was addicted. The pharmacists at all the larger stores refused to sell Veronal to him any longer. Montgrieve was desperate so he blackmailed Georgie. He wanted Georgie to pose as his ex-wife and purchase the drugs using her name. He told Georgie that his ex-wife was on the known user's list so there would be no problem obtaining the drug.

"Georgie asked him why he simply didn't purchase the drugs from a smaller drug store that wasn't a member of the Society, because those shops wouldn't have a copy of either list. Montgrieve said that the tax was so high on Veronal the smaller mom and pop stores couldn't afford to carry it. And if they were to start, it would raise eyebrows of suspicion. He threatened Georgie with the police, saying he would inform them that Georgie was a homosexual and that he had made sexual advances towards him, if Georgie didn't buy the drugs for him. Georgie was terrified, so he did as Montgrieve demanded.

The police found an almost empty bottle of Veronal in Montgrieve's jacket pocket and the bottle had Georgie's fingerprints on it. They already had his fingerprints from last year when the police raided the club at the Drakestone Hotel for serving Prohibition alcohol. Georgie wasn't even in the club at the time, but the police like raiding the Drakestone and arresting everyone they find on the ground floor for being a possible sodomite. That's how Georgie ended up in jail, his fingerprints being taken, and being accosted. He had been in his workshop. Thank heavens he wasn't in a dress that night. He had just stopped by to pick up and deliver a garment to a client." He paused and then looked at me pleadingly. "Please, ma'am, I'm afraid he might try to kill himself."

My mind was racing. I couldn't think of anything to do

but I had to try something. "Seedy, get on the telephone and see if Detective Lister is in his office. Then call my father. Oh, and grab a check book if you can find one. When all else fails, throw money at it."

"Huh?" Seedy said.

"It's one of my father's favorite sayings. 'When all else fails, throw money at it.'" As I barked out orders, I pulled the bell cord three times. I was going to need Claudette's expertise as well. "Randel, get the car ready to go in thirty minutes." Claudette opened the door, took in everyone there, and looked confused. I grabbed her by the arm and pulled her out of the room. "No time to explain now. I need something to wear to jail."

15

Claudette had my make-up and hair refreshed in a flash. I was girdled and dressed in record time. I was wearing another Chanel black dress. This one was belted at the waist with a full skirt. What made it truly eye-catching was the oversized, turned out, bobbing in the air, solid white collar, that made me feel as if I were wearing angel wings on my shoulders. Around my neck went a choker that had six rows of equally sized perfectly round black pearls with a massive fiery black opal at their center, which was surrounded by pea sized white diamonds. The opal itself was the size of a silver dollar. My black felt hat had a wide brim that was white pleated satin on the underside. The shoes were shiny high-heeled black and white patent leather t-straps. My hands were clad in black leather gloves with a white leather ruffle at the wrist. On the left arm between the ruffle and the glove was placed a black opal and diamond eternity bracelet.

Claudette flew into the closet to select a fur. We were pulling out all the stops tonight. While she was in the closet, I looked down and spotted the massive sapphire and diamond ring I had worn this morning.

The Reluctant Doppelganger

Had that been just this morning? It seemed like a lifetime ago.

The ring had been a discarded choice for tonight's ensemble. Suddenly I had an idea. I picked up the ring and shoved it into the tiny black beaded handbag I'd been issued. Claudette returned holding a breathtaking black diamond mink stole. She draped it just below my shoulders.

"Good," she pronounced.

I didn't even look in the mirror. If it was good enough for Claudette, it was good enough for me. I hurried through the bedroom door.

"I've got the sapphire ring so don't panic when you can't find it," I yelled back to her.

Everyone was downstairs in the foyer waiting on me.

The minute my foot hit the last tread; Wallace was there to help me step off. Instantly, Seedy started reading down her list. "I found your father as is evidenced by his presence," she said, not looking up but pointing her pencil at Father. "Detective Lister was not in his office and no one knew where to find him. But oddly enough, he just telephoned and said he would meet us at the station. Wallace located the checkbook for us. We will need to add me as a signatory, off the subject. And Randel has the car waiting outside. I have informed your father the jig is up and everyone in the household knows the score. And I believe that is it." She took a deep breath and looked up, giving me a quick smile.

"Not quite," I announced, walking over to Seedy. "Hold out your left hand," I commanded.

Seedy, looking puzzled, did as I asked. I pulled the huge ring out of my purse and slipped it on her fourth finger.

"You are now officially the fiancée of George…. What's Georgie's last name?"

"Herndon, ma'am," answered Wallace. "Titus George Herndon, ma'am."

"Well then, Cecelia June Schofield, you are now the official fiancée of one Titus George Herndon," I pushed the ring onto her finger.

Seedy smiled. "Dang, this thing is heavy. He better be ready to make me the most beautiful clothes in all the world," she grinned, still mesmerized with the huge sapphire ring.

"I'm glad that's all you want. Because you won't be having his babies." I gave her a quick wink.

Everyone laughed nervously.

Wallace opened the door and we thundered through. Randel was standing next to the automobile with the door to the Daimler open and ready. Wallace started to close the door behind us when I called back to him. "Hop in and come with us. I'm going to need you to look after Randel once he discovers that the love of his life has just gotten engaged to someone else. And that someone else is a woman." Wallace smiled, and in minutes he was climbing into the front seat next to Randel. By the time he had gotten his door closed, Randel was already pulling away.

16

It had taken nearly forty minutes to reach the police station. All the while, everyone in the car had been throwing out thoughts as to how best to exonerate Georgie of the charge of murder. Now the large automobile was beginning to slow. We were nearing the station house. From my position in the backseat I could see all the way through the front windshield. There was a crowd of people gathered in front of the station. Suddenly the car was picking up speed again and Randel was steering it back out into the street.

"Pull the privacy blinds and put up the privacy shield. Do it now and hurry!" shouted Randel.

Everyone moved at once. No one questioned Randel's command. As we flew past the police station there were flashes of light blinking all around the closed window shades. The car kept moving as my father, Seedy and I stared wide-eyed at each other without moving. I discovered I was holding my breath when I gasped for air. My father grabbed the speaking tube.

"What the devil just happened back there?" he shouted into it.

It was Randel who replied, "It was the press, sir. They had gathered outside the station. My guess is they know the police have a suspect in Mr. Montgrieve's murder."

"Why should that bother us?"

"I will tell you in just a moment. But let me do something first. Keep the privacy shades drawn and shield up for a moment."

The big car again started to slow. I could tell Randel was pulling over and then we came to a stop. I heard a door open and felt it shut. We waited and waited. Then I heard Wallace's voice coming through the tube this time. "Please be patient. Randel has stopped to call the station house."

My father looked somewhat confused while Seedy looked frightened, and I'm sure my face displayed a mixture of both. The door opened and shut again. The big car moved once more onto the road.

"You can put down the privacy shield now but leave the shades drawn," came Randel's voice through the speaking tube once again.

As my father cranked the shield back down, Randel turned into an alley and brought the big car to a stop.

"What the devil is going on?" my father exclaimed again.

Randel turned in his seat. "I'm sorry for the rough ride, but the front of the police station was mobbed with reporters."

"What do we care? We are used to dealing with photographers and reporters." Father's voice sounded agitated.

"I know, sir, but there was one reporter in particular you didn't want to run into. Her name is Fredonia Crocker and she works for a paper called the *Moral Monitor*. She and her paper were the ones responsible for the ruination of that Judge, Phineas Edwards. Fredonia tried to connect him to the mob, but the Judge wasn't part of the mob and there wasn't any proof to be found. So, she hired a guy that looked like the Judge to dress up like a garter boy, and she had her photographer take pictures."

"What is a garter boy?" asked Seedy.

"A garter boy is a slang name for a female impressionist. He wasn't, of course, but when the pictures hit the papers, his wife left him and took their children, and he ended up resigning his position. For a time, he was under investigation by the police for possibly being a homosexual. That's why I know how to get us inside without going through the front door. Miss Desmond used to have me drive the Judge to the police station for his formal interviews in her auto to throw off the reporters.

The press was always waiting, so we would call from a coin operated telephone and have them open the back door to the station house. That's what I did when we stopped back there. I called the station. They will meet us at the alley door. You will want to crank up the privacy shield.

When we get to the station, Wallace and I will get out of the automobile and block any line of sight past the door of the auto to the door of the station. You three just need to keep your heads low and move as quickly as you can into the building." Without another word, he turned back around and drove all the way through the alley onto the street behind. Then he began to circle back to the police station.

Father raised the privacy shield and sat quietly with an anxious look on his face. No one said a word during the short drive back. The auto turned once more. I could tell we were in another alley by the way the automobile engine echoed off the confined space between the buildings. The Daimler came to a stop. Two doors opened and quickly closed again. We braced ourselves.

When the door opened on the auto, the door to the police station already stood open and an officer had stepped through and next to Wallace who stood next to Randel who stood even with the open door. Together, along with the auto door, they created a wall, blocking the sight of anyone looking down the alley from the other side. The car itself blocked the view from this side.

My father climbed out, standing stooped. He first helped Seedy and then me out of the car. We hurried, bent low, past our human shield and quickly moved inside the building and out of view. The door closed behind us, but not before Randel assured me that he would be waiting for our return.

We were led down a hall and then up a staircase. Every wall in this place seemed to be painted an institutional mintish green. Several of the officers asked for my autograph as we passed through, and I scribbled a quick signature and gave them my best Theodora smile. When we reached the second floor, we were led down another hallway lined with offices. We were almost at the end of the corridor when our guide stopped at a nondescript door. He knocked lightly.

"Enter." I recognized the low tones as those of Detective Lister. The young officer pushed open the door. The room was small and painted the same shade of institutional green as the rest of the building. It did have a window, but I could tell it looked out onto the alley where we had entered the building. It was not exactly a stellar view.

The detective sat behind his metal desk, his bulky muscular frame too large for both the desk and the chair. He looked as if he had been squashed into the spot. He was still wearing his rumpled black suit. He extricated himself from the chair and welcomed us into the tiny room with an extension of his arm and an open palm. There were only two chairs. My father motioned for Seedy and me to sit.

"Would you bring us another chair, Willard?" Lister asked the younger officer.

"Sure thing," Willard answered back with a quick salute.

The Reluctant Doppelganger

Minutes later he returned with the chair. He slipped it into the already cramped office and my father sat. Willard closed the door on his way out. With pleasantries having been exchanged, and privacy assured; it was time to get down to business.

"I've come about the man you've arrested for Reggie's murder, Titus George Herndon." I lifted my chin. I was hoping I was displaying a great deal more confidence than I felt. In turn, Detective Lister raised his chin. I wondered if he was mirroring me. I had read somewhere that mirroring the actions of the person you were talking with instilled confidence and was a way to build quick rapport. Either that or he was making fun of me again. I was sure the next few minutes would reveal which.

"And exactly how do you know Mr. Herndon?" He looked me straight in the eyes. His eyes were piercing. They cut through me and my heart began to race. I was sure this was a skill he had honed to a razor's edge as a police detective.

"Mr. Herndon is, among other things, my haute couture," I said, rather haughtily.

Detective Lister cocked his head and smirked. "In other words, he's your dress maker."

"A dress, my dear detective, is a garment one purchases at Woolworth's. My ensembles are considered works of art." And with that my chin rose even higher. The collar on my dress seemed to want to echo the sentiment and it bobbed in the air like unruly angel's wings. I noticed the detective's smirk turned into a smile. I made a mental note not to wear this frock to any other serious business meetings.

"Detective Lister," my father said. "Putting Miss Desmond's wardrobe aside." He gave me that look he always did when he thought I had gotten off the subject. "I've known Georgie Herndon for years. He is a very talented tailor as well as couture. He works for some of the most influential people in Los Angeles. Have you discovered a motive as to why he would risk his professional standing by murdering Reggie Montgrieve?"

"We think it is drug related. We found Mr. Herndon's fingerprints on a bottle of Veronal that was in the deceased's dinner jacket pocket." The detectives voice was very solemn, and he sounded grave.

As my father and Detective Lister continued to discuss information of which I was already aware, my attention waned. I looked down at the detective's desk top. It was well organized. Everything seemed to have a place. The file closest to his right elbow must have been the one he was working on when we arrived. It was filled with photos. The photos were all stacked neatly inside so I couldn't see them. However, the corner of the top photo was askew and protruded slightly outside the folder. I recognized what I was seeing immediately. It was a section of the huge cage that surrounded RC's tennis court.

It seemed that the conversation between my father and the detective had lagged. He had learned nothing new. "Detective, I couldn't help but notice your file filled with photos. Are those the photos of Reggie's murder scene?"

"They are." He placed a protective hand on top of the folder.

"Could I ask you a question? It doesn't relate to the murder at all. I noticed the picture that was sticking out was of the cage that surrounds RC's tennis court. I'm never seen a cage like that before. Have you by chance asked Mr. Crawford about it?"

The detective laughed. "As a matter of fact, I did. Like you Miss Desmond, I found it very odd because I'm a tennis player myself. It seems that Mr. Crawford is rather a poor tennis player, and he spent a great deal of time chasing tennis balls.

The Reluctant Doppelganger

He was at the Orange County Fair last year and saw a product they have been using on ranches and farms for about twenty years now. It's called chain-link fence. It can be made in any size. Ranchers and farmers use four, eight- or ten-foot heights for their land, but Mr. Crawford had an idea. He asked the company's representative if he could make one twenty feet high. The man said yes and so, two weeks ago, they installed the new custom-made tennis court enclosure.

Mr. Crawford and the fence company are going to start marketing them to the Beverly Hills set. Seems there are a lot of wealthy tennis enthusiasts who chase a great many balls." He smiled as he slipped the photo out and slid it in front of me.

"Oh my," Seedy gasped.

Detective Lister had gotten so caught up in his story about the enclosure, which he obviously thought was a good idea, that he had slid the photo out of the folder to show me the chain link enclosure, momentarily forgetting that Reginald Montgrieve's body was propped up against that same chain-link fencing, dead. He started to pull it away, but I placed my hand on top of his and stopped him.

"Wait!" I had just noticed something in the shiny gray shades of the photograph. "Is this where and how you found Reggie's body?" I removed my hand from atop his and pointed to Reggie in the photograph as I leaned forward to inspect it.

"Yes."

"That is not where he was lying passed out when Charlie and I — the Viscount," I amended, "saw him. He was lying here," I pointed to the other side of the court. "He was sprawled on the ground, not sitting up or slumped over, as the case may be, against the fence," I said. In the picture, I could make out scorch marks on the back of his white dinner jacket in the same pattern as the chain-link fence. "Is the fence electrified?"

"No, and that's a huge missing piece of the puzzle."

"He looks like he is soaking wet."

"He is. The gardeners turned on the lawn watering systems around five in the morning."

"Would it be asking too much to look at the other photos?"

Detective Lister didn't even hesitate. He opened the folder and laid out the pictures one by one and side by side. We were all scanning the photos now. Most of them were just different angles of the same thing. Reginald Montgrieve slumped forward with scorch marks on the back of his jacket. The portion of the tennis court directly in front of him had gotten wet and pooled water. The chalk lines on the clay court surface seemed to have swirled in a circular pattern from the force of the water current created by the pressurized water coming from the watering system. In the center of the swirling muck was a muddy high-ball glass.

Another photo had been taken after they had moved Reggie's body on to a stretcher and covered it from view. This photo was of Reggie's personal effects, I was guessing. There was a cigarette case. I knew from seeing it earlier in the evening that it was made of gold inlaid with mother of pearl, as was the cigarette lighter that lay next to it in the picture. There was a monogramed handkerchief with the letter M, a pair of monogramed cuff links, and a signet ring that also bore the letter M. There was his wallet and four one hundred-dollar bills laid out side by side for the photo along with a small square bottle with a label that read Veronal.

That label was pink. I knew that from working summers in my grandfather's drug stores. Veronal came packaged two ways. The most often seen was in pre-measured pink envelopes. The bottles were usually issued to physicians who generally kept them in locked cabinets in their offices because Veronal was a highly taxed and monitored drug. It was used as a sedative and most often used in mental asylums. It was a first of its kind pharmaceutical. Its classification is called a barbiturate. Looking closer at the picture, it appeared the bottle was almost empty, just like Randel had described.

"I know with Reggie being soaked this might be impossible to know, but were there any of the Veronal crystals loose in his pocket? The pink label doesn't appear to have gotten wet. They tend to peel off if any moisture gets near them and the crystals tend to clump before dissolving. Was this the bottle that had Georgie's fingerprints on it?"

The detective looked bemused. "To answer your first question, there was none of the Veronal loose in his pocket. The bottle was in his inside jacket pocket along with his wallet, so it didn't get wet. I think that was because he was slumped over, and his body protected the contents from the watering system. I removed the contents of his pockets myself and checked the jacket for any hidden pockets. I would have noticed if the pocket had any of the Veronal crystals in it."

"I'm guessing you found that incredible wad of cash in a hidden pocket?" I was stunned that Reggie was carrying around that much money.

"No actually. It was in one of his side jacket pockets."

"Doesn't it strike you as strange that he was carrying a fortune in cash all in large bills in his jacket pocket?"

"It does indeed, Miss Desmond." His voice became inquisitive as he leaned back in his chair and crossed his arms.

I was so caught up in my investigation of the photographs, that at first, I didn't notice him looking hard at me. "Is there something wrong, Detective?"

"I am waiting for you to enlighten me as to how you know so much about Veronal and how you knew from a monochromatic photograph that the label on the Veronal bottle was pink." And with that, he cocked his head to one side.

The tension in the room was palpable. All eyes were on me. I had learned a long time ago when dealing with anyone as sharp as my father, and I was betting the man sitting across from me was, to stick as closely to the truth as possible. I quickly ran through what I was going to say in my head. The only thing I had to lie about was who my grandfather was. I considered those to be good enough odds, so I started in.

"Almost every question I have asked thus far is simple deduction. However, regarding the Veronal, my grandfather owns a drug store. I used to work for him during the summers when I was not in school. He is not a supporter of Veronal because of its addictive properties. It is currently in a class by itself called barbiturate and it is packaged two different ways. The first is in the glass cruet with a pink label and white letters, like it appears in your picture. The other form of packaging is in individual paper envelopes just like most headache remedies except that the Veronal envelopes are a very distinct pink.

The reason I asked if you found any loose barbiturate crystals is because the bottle in the photograph appears to be almost empty. I find it very strange that Reggie would be carrying the cruet in a jacket pocket to begin with. The top could have easily fallen out and spilled its very valuable contents.

Besides, no individual could afford the tax on such an amount. Well, perhaps Reggie could have afforded it, but I seriously doubt any pharmacist would have filled such an order. The cruets are reserved for physicians and institutions.

"Where is your grandfather's drug store?" The tone of his question was merely conversational.

I knew that Molly was from Oklahoma, but I had never been there, and I knew nothing about the place, except it had oil wells, cowboys, and Indians. Then it came to me. The only town I knew of in Oklahoma was the one that laid claim to Will Rogers, Claremore. Or at least I hoped that was it. "Claremore, Oklahoma, the same as Will Rogers," I said as brightly as I could manage.

He nodded his head in the affirmative. I was hoping I had pulled the wool over his eyes.

"Why did you ask if that was the bottle where we found Mr. Herndon's fingerprints?"

I weighed my options. I liked the detective. I thought he was an honest straight shooter. I read people well and this guy was on the up and up. "I'm going to put my cards on the table, Detective." I looked him straight in the eye. I nearly jumped when my father placed his hand on my shoulder and gave it a slight squeeze. He knew what I was up to and he was warning me to be careful.

"Reggie was addicted to Veronal. When his own doctor discovered his addiction, he had him placed on the abuser's list that is distributed by The California Society of Pharmacy to all of its drug store members. They wouldn't sell it to him anymore. I know that Georgie was being blackmailed by Reggie to purchase Veronal. I'll bet you ten dollars the Veronal that Georgie has been purchasing is in the pink envelopes and not the cruet."

"How was he blackmailing Mr. Herndon?" the detective asked.

Here goes nothing, I thought. I was about to gamble with Georgie's life. I hoped like the devil I was right about this guy.

"Like I told you earlier, Georgie is a designer. He has a studio."

"His studio is in one of the old ballrooms at the Drakestone Hotel. We already know that."

Then the police already knew about the homosexual connection.

"When Georgie is working, he tends to wear a dress for creative purposes."

"We know he wears dresses."

"Well then, you seem to know a lot."

"Miss Desmond, we *are* the police. Investigation is a large part of our job. We tend to be quite good at it. And while we are on the subject of investigations, you might also know that, along with the abuser's list compiled by the California Society of Pharmacy, there is also a user's list of drugs that are highly taxed. Mr. Herndon's name appears nowhere on either list."

"Reggie had him impersonate his ex-wife, Zelda Rossi, an actress wanna-be. Check your list. I'm sure you'll find her name on it. Reggie had Georgie make a couple of suits for him. Reggie discovered the location of Georgie's studio, went there, and found him wearing a dress. After Reggie was placed on the abuser's list, he threatened to turn Georgie in to the police for being a homosexual if he didn't pretend to be Zelda and buy the Veronal. Georgie is terrified of the police. It seems he was sexually assaulted while being held in a drunk tank after being falsely charged some time ago and the officer on duty did nothing. Out of pure fear, Georgie did as Reggie demanded. Reggie would then come to Georgie's studio and retrieve the drugs. Let's cut to the chase, Detective. Georgie is no murderer nor is he a homosexual. He's engaged to my personal secretary."

Seedy placed her hand on the detective's desk. The mammoth ring shimmered in the dingy light of the office.

"Miss Schofield, is it? That is one very impressive ring." Lister glared at her with a look of disbelief. "He must be a very, very good designer to afford such an expensive engagement ring."

"I don't think the stones are real," Seedy whined with a sad pout. "But I would never ask dear Georgie." Then she smiled warmly.

Again, a slight smirk crossed the detective's face.

"I want to pay his bail, Detective. I want to take him with us this evening."

"Miss Desmond, his bail has been set. But…" he trailed off.

"But what?"

"It's two thousand dollars."

I did my best not to react. After all you could buy a house for half that. "Will you take a check?"

He nodded yes.

"Seedy, write the detective a check," I commanded flatly, my eyes never leaving his.

Seedy pulled out the checkbook and wrote a check to the City of Beverly Hills for two thousand dollars. She slid the checkbook over to me to sign. I tried to mimic Molly's signature as best I could. I was sure a two-thousand-dollar check would raise eyebrows at the bank. I would have Seedy call them first thing in the morning. I removed the check from the book and handed it to the detective.

He chuckled. "That must be nice," he said as he stood. "I'll take this down to processing and get the paperwork started. I'll be back in about fifteen minutes."

He walked out of the room, closing the door behind him. I nearly collapsed. I gasped and started to speak, but my father calmly put a finger to his lips. We all three sat without saying a word for what was closer to thirty minutes. In the silence, I fingered through the pictures that the detective had left lying on the desk. As I leaned in to closely inspect them, I noticed an open notepad on the far corner of the detective's desk. It had the same name written over and over filling almost every square inch of the page. The name was Hugo Wainwright.

The door opened and the detective once again filled the

room. He spoke as soon as he was fully back in his office with the door closed. "They are processing Mr. Herndon now and the duty officer will bring him to my office once he is done."

"Detective, I was looking at the photos while you were away. A couple of things stood out. I know the enclosure is new, about two weeks, isn't that what you said earlier?"

"Yes, ma'am."

"And the landscaping appears to be new as well."

"It is. They had to pull out all of the landscaping in order to install the new chain-link enclosure."

"But these lampposts don't appear to be new. Look here. The paint seems to be peeling. See the gray surface in that spot compared to the blacker surface of most of the post," I said, pointing to the spot on the picture.

"Yes. The court lighting was already there and did not need to be replaced. Mr. Crawford was most displeased that the workers had chipped the paint in so many places. According to Mr. Crawford, all fourteen poles will need to be repainted."

The door opened. There was Georgie standing just in front of the duty officer. Seedy jumped up and flew to Georgie. She flung her arms around him and kissed the stunned man square on his lips.

"Oh Darling! I've been so so worried about you. Have they treated you okay?"

I thought she was overdoing it a bit, but who was I to say how a woman would react if her lover had been ripped away from her and arrested on false charges, only to be returned after his time spent in jail. I was amused to see Georgie hug Seedy back. He looked so relieved to see us that it didn't matter that he didn't understand why Seedy was gushing so. We all stood.

"Detective, I will have my attorney get in touch."

The Reluctant Doppelganger

"No need to get in touch with me. Mr. Herndon has all the paperwork. That is what you will need to give to his attorney." Lister smiled.

My father shook his hand as did Seedy and Georgie. I was bringing up the rear. I extended my hand. The detective clasped it with both of his massive ones. "You are truly a special lady, Miss Desmond. I've been a fan of your films since the beginning, but, I have to say that in silent movies, no one can truly get the full measure of you. We will talk again soon, I hope. Officer Densmore will see you back down to your automobile. Have a good evening."

With that, we departed. He watched us until we reached the stairs. I looked back and he gave me a wave. Then he stepped back in his office, closed the door and was gone.

Our little party was quiet until we reached the door.

"The press has discovered your limousine in the alley. Detective Lister had us block off both entrances, but they are standing in front of our men with their cameras at the ready. We will block them on both sides as you get into your auto." Officer Densmore said with a serious smile.

The door opened and two rows of policemen piled out once again creating a human shield. Georgie and I raced the six or so feet to the automobile's open door. Seedy and my father climbed in behind us. Officer Densmore waved as he shut the door. The motor was already running. All the shades were pulled down and the privacy shield between the front and back seats was up. The minute the door latched, and he was sure the officers were clear, Randel put the big machine in reverse, and it shot backwards out of the alley. I could hear cursing as members of the press literally jumped to get out of the huge automobile's way. The Daimler V-12 was the largest production automobile that has ever been produced so far, and it cut a wide swath.

There was little talking, and it wasn't until we were close

to home that we lowered the privacy shield. We kept the shades drawn. When we arrived back at the house, Mr. Truman had gone for the evening. Wallace climbed out of the auto and opened the gates. He closed and locked them behind us. I was seriously going to see about getting one of those electric gate openers.

Once inside the house, we found that Mrs. Reid had prepared a huge supper with cold roasted meats, fresh bread, roasted vegetables and two pies, one apple and one coconut cream. There was wine and beer as well. Mrs. Reid was going to seat Seedy, Father and me in the dining room, but I insisted we would all eat in the kitchen together. We called Claudette down from upstairs and had a marvelous meal, laughing and talking. Seedy told Georgie about their engagement. The way she told the story had everyone in stitches. Wallace couldn't believe she had kissed Georgie in front of the police detective. Georgie assured him that he couldn't believe it either. There was no talk of the future. It was all light fun, banter and stories.

"Georgie," I said. "There are two apartments over the garage. One belongs to Randel. The other one is empty and furnished. You will need to stay close. Until all this is sorted out, you cannot go back to the Drakestone. Tomorrow I will hire movers to pack up your studio and move it here into the ballroom. It is about the same size and I'm sure it will do for the time being. I'm not throwing any balls that I know of in the foreseeable future."

Georgie happily agreed.

When dinner was done, I coaxed my father into staying the night. Claudette helped me change out of, what I now called, the angel-wing dress. I went back down and told Mrs. Reid and Wallace that they were finished for the night and should retire. Mrs. Reid protested saying that she needed to clean up after supper. But I told her that Seedy and I would do it.

The Reluctant Doppelganger

Randel and Georgie helped us put away what little leftovers there were. They cleaned the dishes of all the scraps and said they would take out the trash on their way out. Seedy and I were at the kitchen sink. I was washing and she was drying.

As Randel and Georgie stepped out the kitchen door and closed it behind them, Randel caught Georgie up into his arms. Georgie pushed up to his tiptoes, and their lips met. The kiss was one of those warm, sweet kind of kisses, the ones you usually see from older couples who have been married half their lives. It simply said, 'I love you'. He released Georgie and put his arm around his neck, pulled him close, and they walked towards the garage.

"You think Georgie will make it to the empty apartment?" I asked Seedy.

"Oh, I'm pretty sure he won't."

"I wonder what it feels like to be that kind of in love?"

"You're asking the wrong person, my boy," came her dreamy reply.

She dried the last dish, we flipped off the electric light and we both headed upstairs to bed.

17

The next morning, I awoke once again to a soft knock at the door. As I opened my eyes, I looked towards the bathroom, but both doors stood open and no one was there. The knock came again and from as close as it sounded, I knew that it was coming from the actual door to the bedroom. I jumped out of bed and headed into the bath.

Just before closing the door, I yelled, "Come in." in a voice, still low and gruff with sleep.

I finished up and started back into the bedroom when I saw a man's bathrobe hanging on the back of the door. There was a note jutting out from the pocket. It said, *I thought you might could use one of these.* The note was signed Wallace. I slipped the robe on, pulled it together and cinched the tie around my waist.

When I entered the room, both Claudette and Seedy were there. A coffee pot with three blue cups and saucers sat on the now bare table between the two wing-backed chairs. Both ladies were standing behind the chairs.

"Have a seat, ladies," I said gesturing to the chairs.

Claudette moved around the chair she had been standing

behind and filled the three cups with steaming coffee. She handed me my cup and then, along with Seedy, she sat. Since there were only two chairs in the room, I perched myself on the corner of the bed. I sipped my coffee waiting to see which lady would speak first. It was as I expected. Seedy opened the notebook she had brought with her and proceeded to fill the silence.

"First, you will be attending a party this evening at the home of the German industrialist, Herr Heinrich Von Müller and his wife Hazel. He speaks fluent English and his wife is British."

"How on earth do you know that?"

"I called their home and spoke with Frau Von Müller's personal secretary to RSVP and I told her I wanted to make sure you were prepared, so I asked and she told me.

"Next, I arranged for a moving company to move Georgie's studio from the Drakestone to here this morning. In fact, they already have him out of the Drakestone and are headed back here. Georgie insisted on being there when they loaded everything up, so I sent Randel to keep an eye on him."

My mouth fell open, I think. "Where did you find someone to move him so quickly?"

"Yesterday when we were at Mr. Crawford's house, while you were being interviewed."

"Interrogated," I interjected.

"Whatever. I went up to the top of the tower to check out that view you were going on about. I noticed while I was looking over towards the garages that the moving truck that had brought all of those ballroom chairs had had a flat. The name on the side of the truck was F. C. Cecilia and Sons Moving Company. You can see why I would remember it. When I went to call Mrs. Reid about our supper, Mr. Crawford's personal secretary, Clayton Foster, was on the phone to the moving company changing the date of the pickup. Seems Mr. Crawford originally wanted the chairs picked up this morning at 7:00 am, but then wanted that time moved to tomorrow morning at 7:00 am, just in case the police weren't finished with their *interrogations*. So, I knew they would have this morning open. I called them last night after we finished with the dishes and before I went to bed."

"How do you know RC's personal secretary? And please don't tell me you eavesdropped on him during his telephone conversation."

"Not really; he was just telling the movers who he was when I picked up. And besides, how else was I supposed to know when he was finished so I could call Mrs. Reid?" she asked it, as if eavesdropping was simply the natural order of things.

I noticed that Seedy was still wearing the giant sapphire ring.

"Did you sleep in that thing?" I pointed to the ring.

"Yes." She held up her hand and turned the ring from side to side watching it sparkle in the light. "It might be the only time I ever get engaged and the only time I'll ever get to wear something so absolutely awe inspiring."

I had been so busy playing a role, I had failed to notice that the role I was playing was that of a very wealthy woman. And that my friend, Seedy, had come from much more humble beginnings. I had no clue how it would feel to have something so beautiful and valuable as that ring thrust on me, knowing full well I would have to give it back.

"You will need to wear it until Mademoiselle Desmond proves that Georgie didn't kill Reginald Montgrieve." Claudette said.

"Until I prove it? What makes you think I can figure out who killed Reggie?"

"You got Georgie out of jail."

The Reluctant Doppelganger

"I got Georgie out of jail by throwing money at the problem, not by any sleuthing attributes."

"But you did know all about the Veronal. And you did notice the chipping paint on the lampposts," Seedy added.

"I knew about the Veronal because of my grandfather and it's not important about the lampposts. They got chipped when they were digging up the landscaping."

The red cradled telephone rang. It rang in this room.

"I guess everyone in the house knows where I am now."

Seedy moved to the telephone to answer it.

She listened for a moment before speaking, "Tell them not to come through the front door. Have them pull around to the garage and come in the ballroom doors. The movers can bring the studio furnishings through just one set of double doors that way and not run the risk of nicking any woodwork or plaster in the rest of the house. I am on my way down now." With that she hung up the telephone. "I've got to go. The movers are here with Georgie and Randel in tow." She turned and shot out of the room.

Claudette stood up and placed her coffee cup back on the tray. She filled my cup one last time. "You take your shower and I will take the coffee things back to the kitchen. By the time you are finished, I will be back to dress you."

This time when Claudette left, she went through the bathroom. I was finishing my coffee when I heard the water to the shower come on. I smiled.

An hour later Claudette was putting on the finishing touches. I was back in another Elsa Schiapparelli silk pajama, this one with pale pink pants and a shocking pink and white striped top. This top was a halter, and I was wearing yet another undergarment created by Georgie which gave me small breasts in front while leaving my back fully exposed. Today, I was bedecked in a turban. It was tall and had an even longer ostrich plume held in its center with a large jade brooch. My arms were bare, so my bicep was adorned with a light green jade slave bracelet and of course my neck simply dripped with pearls that hung all the way down to my waist. I was wearing the same mules with the silver heel and tufts of white ostrich feathers as I wore with the last silk pajama.

I left Claudette to clean up and headed downstairs, hoping to find some breakfast. I really wasn't sure what time it was. I would have thought it early, but after Seedy had run down her list of everything she had already accomplished, I felt it must be closer to noon. When I reached the ground floor there was a cacophony of noise coming from the direction of the ballroom. I made up my mind not to go in that direction if I could avoid it. I made my way to the morning room, closing the doors as silence filled the room. On the sideboard, chafing dishes were filled with bacon, eggs, a tray of fresh cinnamon rolls, biscuits and sausage gravy. I filled my plate, poured another cup of coffee and sat down to eat. The peace and quiet were certainly a luxury I could grow accustom to. Looking out the window to the back lawn, I could see Mrs. Reid picking herbs from the little herb garden she had next to the garages. Wallace, Randel and Georgie passed by the window with each hand loaded down with dresses on hangers. Seedy had her notebook and was giving, what I was sure were detailed instructions to the movers carrying a large fabric table.

The red cradled telephone rang. I knew everyone was outside and that Claudette would not answer the telephone unless I was upstairs, so I walked to the sideboard and picked up the receiver.

"Good morning, Mr. Truman. This is Theodora."

"Good Morning, Miss Desmond. I hope you are well this morning."

"I am indeed."

"Mr. Crawford, along with two other gentlemen, would

The Reluctant Doppelganger

like to come up to the house."

"By all means let them in."

"Will do. Thank you, Ma'am." And he hung up.

I ran to the ballroom. When I opened the door, it appeared that Georgie's studio was not only almost in; it was almost set up and organized too. I was going to give Seedy credit for that. Wallace stepped in from the terrace door carrying another load of dresses.

"Mr. Truman just called; RC is at the gate and headed up to the house." My voice sounded a bit panicked.

A look of horror crossed Wallace's face. He put his load of dresses on the fabric table then shot past me, grabbing his jacket off a hanger as he went. Seedy was the next to appear in the open doorway.

"RC, and I'm guessing the Duke and the Viscount, are driving up to the house right now. Is my father still here?"

"I don't think so. He said he had a few errands to run but he did say he would be back. You take the backstairs up to the long gallery. I'll have Wallace deliver your guests there."

I did as Seedy instructed, but when I got to the long gallery, I wasn't sure what I should be doing. The morning paper lay folded on the sofa where my father had been reading it. I grabbed it and sat in the chair Randel had used the night before, the one in front of the fireplace. Damn, my feet didn't touch the floor. Hearing footsteps on the stairs, I hurried to the card table and spread the paper out just in time to hear a quick knock before the door opened.

Wallace ushered in not three men but four. I had been somewhat off, however, when it came to the cast of characters now pushing past Wallace. Rushing towards me with a huge smile on his face and his arms outstretched was RC. Behind him was my father, and standing side by side just inside the doorway were the Viscount and Detective Lister. I put both arms out to meet RC's embrace. He kissed me on the forehead, then stepped back to look at me. His face bore a huge Cheshire Cat grin that boldly displayed his slightly yellowing teeth. His brown eyes were alight, and suddenly he reminded me more of a predatory wolf than a smiling tabby cat. My gut reaction was that he was here to sell me something. I was soon to learn my gut was once again right on target.

"How are you this lovely morning, my beautiful little star?"

He didn't wait for an answer.

"Bertie and I have some very exciting news. I was going to wait and let you be surprised this evening at the Von Müller party along with everybody else, but Bertie," he motioned for my father to step up beside him, "thought with everything that has been happening with Reggie's death and all, that it might not be the best idea to surprise you with this news."

I cocked my eyebrow as if to say, *Well then go on, out with it.*

RC interpreted my expression and continued. "I have cast the role of Samson in our new film *Samson and Delilah*."

If he considered it to be OUR new film, I wasn't sure why he felt the need to give me the title of the movie. I had received the new script with actual lines by messenger the morning after RC's impromptu party. I remember thinking it was very strange because it was being delivered on a Sunday morning. Come to think of it, Wallace had answered the door that morning. It was supposed to be his and Mrs. Reid's day off. Yet they had both worked last Sunday. I made a mental note to talk with them about it.

"Well?" RC was saying.

I had gotten so lost in my thoughts that I missed what RC had been saying. Now I was totally clueless.

"Well what do you think about our new Hugo Wainwright?"

Suddenly I was putting two and two together. I had seen

The Reluctant Doppelganger

that name written over and over on the pad that had been on the Detective's desk. He was writing the new name over and over trying to get used to it, just like a new bride would do. Hugo Wainwright was Detective John Lister, and he was about to be playing the role of Samson to my Delilah.

Oh, my God, could the news be any worse?

But the answer to that question always seems to be yes it could, and in this case, yes it did.

"Since it might give our little secret away early, I have asked his Lordship here to escort you to tonight's party at Mr. & Mrs. Von Müller's home," RC announced cheerily.

I started to ask, *what am I, some sort of commodity?* But Claudette had made the answer to that question very clear yesterday, when she was lecturing my father. I was indeed a commodity. Theodora Desmond was currently the most valuable treasure in Rodrick Crawford's treasure chest of curiosities. And I was Theodora Desmond, head curiosity.

When I snapped out of my reverie, I was guessing the expression on my face had unsettled the room. Every man in the room seemed to have some version of disappointment on his face, including my father.

"Are you unhappy with our selection? You must admit, he has the robust physique that Samson requires. He's quite handsome, and he has a marvelous speaking voice." RC was building up the Detective's attributes just like a slick-talking carnie peddling snake-oil.

All I could think of was how hard it was to maintain this illusion of me being a woman, and now it was going to be doubly hard because the man I would be working with every day, sometimes in intimate settings, was a trained police detective.

Instead of collapsing to the floor in despair, I plastered Theodora's beaming smile on my face. I started spouting empty platitudes about how wonderful it would be to work with him, how excited I was that he had gotten the role, and the biggest of my lies, how much I was looking forward to getting to know him. I was out of control and I had to regain it and quickly.

I found the only set of eyes in the room that weren't seeking my approval: Charlie's. I looked deep into those icy gray-blue eyes and started taking deep breaths. It only took me a moment to gain control again. Exhaling one last deep breath, I spoke. "RC, it could not be better news. Detective Lister, or should I say Hugo, I know firsthand the absolute joy associated with being discovered. I wish you well and may movie goers everywhere fall in love with you."

"Thank you, Miss Desmond," Detective Lister said humbly. "I'm not so sure right this minute why I agreed to do it."

"There is an easy answer to that one, Hugo; fame and fortune, in that order." I gave him a beaming smile.

"Yes ma'am," he said, once again humbly. I wondered how long the humility would last. Now there was a commodity of which Hollywood was sorely lacking.

I turned my attention to Charlie. As I did, I found he was smiling broadly. My guess was that, when I had chosen his eyes to look into, it hadn't gone unnoticed and I feared that it might have been misinterpreted. But I would worry about that later. Tonight, he was to be my escort or date as the case may be and I needed him to be amenable, not that he had ever been anything less than the perfect gentleman.

"Well then, my dear Viscount, it would seem that we have an engagement for this evening. Since you and your father are guests, I'll have Randel pick you both up around 6:45 this evening. Then he can stop back by here and collect me. My house is in between your hotel and Herr and Frau Müller's home. We should arrive at the party around 7:15; that allows us to be fashionably late. Are those acceptable arrangements?"

"Those are very acceptable arrangements with one exception. I believe my father is having dinner with RC and was planning on going to the Von Müller's with him. Would you allow me to escort you alone?"

"I would absolutely have no issue with that. Our plans for the evening are set then."

There was a knock at the door.

"Come in," I called.

The door opened slightly and Seedy pushed her head through.

"I am so sorry to bother you, Miss Desmond. Could I speak with you privately for a moment?"

"As you can see, I'm in a meeting, Cecelia."

"I know ma'am, but…It's your new house guest. Seems he has found some of his things in disarray."

"I will be down to check on him momentarily. I think we are almost finished here."

She nodded and quietly slipped out of the room, closing the door. I wondered what the problem with Georgie could be. If Seedy thought it was important enough to interrupt, then it must be serious.

"Well, gentlemen, I think that really does conclude our business." I walked to RC holding out my arms, slipped them around him and kissed him on the cheek.

I moved to my father next.

"You didn't have much to say today, Bertie. My guess is you are representing Hugo here." As I shook my father's hand, I gripped it a little harder than I should. I could tell by the look in his eyes he was Hugo's new agent.

"Hugo, welcome to the motion picture world." I moved to shake the detective's hand. "You *are* going to have that suit pressed before tonight, I'm hoping." When we clasped hands, I turned the back of mine up just to see what would happen. As we started to shake, he turned our hands back to side by side again. So, we were fifty-fifty, equal partners. That frightened me even more.

When I got to Charlie, I put both hands lightly on his biceps, leaned in and kissed him on each cheek. I pulled away and looked him square in the eyes. "I can't wait until tonight. We will have a marvelous time."

I moved to his side where the bell-cord hung and pulled it once. In moments, Wallace was opening the door. "You rang, Miss?"

"Wallace, would you see our guests to the door, please?"

Wallace stepped completely into the room and opened the door wide. He extended his hand towards the hall and bade my guests exit. I was getting the evil eye from my father, but he too left the room. I followed everyone to the bottom of the stairs. No sooner had I reached the bottom step, there came a resounding crash from the direction of the ballroom.

"If you will excuse me, gentlemen, I must see to my new house guest. Wallace will finish seeing you out." I nodded to the small party, turned and moved back down the hallway.

When I reached the ballroom, Georgie looked panic-stricken. The room Seedy had worked to ensure was meticulously arranged was now in total disarray. Georgie was on his knees searching through the drawers of an eight-foot long fabric cutting table, muttering curses.

"What on earth is wrong?" I asked, stepping into the room.

Georgie looked up. Tears of frustration glittered on his cheeks.

"I'm missing a bead."

He sounded utterly defeated. He stood and pointed to a matchbox that was brimming with tiny gold beads.

I sensed someone behind me. I turned to see Detective Lister standing in the door. Suddenly he seemed like a much bigger man than I had realized.

The Reluctant Doppelganger

"I thought something might be wrong and perhaps you could use some assistance."

He had both arms stretched above his head, propped in each corner of the door frame, casually leaning as his muscled body completely filled the opening.

"But if it's just a lost bead then I'll wager you can manage," he grinned. He pushed himself upright and made to leave.

"Just a bead?" Georgie called out mockingly. "That bead is part of a set of one hundred beads. They were created specifically to attach a jeweled brooch being designed by the French jewelers, Cartier," he drawled. "The brooch will be featured on the bosom of the wedding gown of Estelle McCarney."

We both were looking at Georgie now.

"Aloysius McCarney's daughter, the owner of the Happy Scotsman's gold mine?" came Lister's stunned retort.

"The very same. And more importantly for me, husband of Florence McCarney, the bride's mother and demon from hell. These beads are all twenty-four-carat gold." He clasped the matchbox and turned it so that the precious metal glinted in the light filled room. "They are worth nearly ten dollars and fifty cents each. Mrs. McCarney has told me that each bead will be counted, and she will expect any unused beads to be returned. She made it quite clear that I would be responsible for the cost of any of the beads that go missing. There are ninety-nine beads here. I am missing one. Ten dollars and fifty cents is a lot of money!"

"Why were you keeping something so valuable in a matchbox?" I asked him, somewhat disgusted with his lack of forethought.

"I wasn't keeping them in a matchbox." He snapped back, annoyed with my tone. "I had them in a little glass-stoppered bottle. Now the bottle is gone, and the beads were all just rolling around in the drawer." He pointed to the offending open drawer on his work table. "I had to have something to put them in and the matchbox was the first thing I found."

Detective Lister stepped fully into the room. His casual manner was gone, and he wore a frown on his face.

"What kind of bottle was it?"

"It was just an old bottle I found at the Drakestone. Back when it was a proper hotel, there was a doctor that use to office in one of its shops. Now it's just filled with mostly junk, but there are lots of small bottles just perfect for holding the little bits and bobs of my trade."

Detective Lister slipped his hand into his jacket pocket and produced a small glass bottle. The top had been sealed with red wax. He tipped the little bottle up slightly, and there, almost hidden from view by a white crystalline powder, was a single gold bead.

"I'm pretty sure I've found your missing bead."

He righted the bottle once again and began to slowly turn it between his fingers until it revealed a faded pink label with large white letters — VERONAL.

Georgie went very pale and gave an audible gulp. My heart sank.

Lister moved to the counter. He placed the bottle on the edge. He was looking down at it. I was looking at it too, and so was Georgie. Georgie began to back away. Lister's head snapped up.

"Don't be a fool, Herndon," he bit out. "If you run, I'll just have to catch you. And you know I will, so just don't." This time, his tone was if he were merely stating a fact, that it would be causing both men more trouble than it was worth.

His focus shifted once again back to the bottle. He was quiet for a long moment. No one in the room moved. Georgie now looked terrified. The detective looked up at Georgie again. He placed both of his massive hands on the counter flanking the Veronal bottle and leaned in towards the man.

"First, I do not think you are stupid enough to have stood here and told me about this Veronal bottle if you had been the one to put it into Reginald Montgrieve's jacket pocket." His eyes never left Georgie's. "Because if you had placed it there, you would know that I had it now."

Then he turned his head towards me. The corner of his mouth turned up in a lopsided smile.

"What are your thoughts?" he asked me.

His query took me by surprise. Maybe Detective Lister was asking for my thoughts as a way of building rapport between us, as my new co-star, Hugo Wainwright? Or maybe, he was just including me in the conversation since I was there.

"May I?" I gestured to the little bottle.

He stood up, stepped back and extended his open palm in consent. I moved over to the bottle and inspected it from all sides before I lifted it for a closer look. There was only a smattering of Veronal in the bottle. As I turned the bottle, the long gold tubular bead, known to any seamstress as a bugle bead, winked at me from beneath the snowy crystals held within its glass prison.

"Have you measured the amount of Veronal in the bottle?"

"Measured it?" he answered my question with a question, sounding quizzical.

"Yes, measured it." I held the little bottle up. I turned to Georgie. "When you purchased Veronal for Reggie, how did it come?"

"I'm not right sure I take your meaning."

"I mean, did it come in a bottle like this?"

"Nah, it comes in pink envelopes, just like you get with headache powder, only pink not white."

"How many envelopes did you get with each purchase?"

"It always had thirty envelopes. I think it was supposed to be enough for a month. But Montgrieve had me buying it at two different drug stores each month. It was awfully expensive, but he always gave me cash. And he told me the last time, I needed to find a third store."

"And when was the last time you purchased it?"

"The day before he died."

I turned back to the detective now. "My guess is that you will find exactly one dose in this bottle," I shook the bottle slightly to emphasize my point. "I think this was just for show. I'm not quite sure why, but I think it was meant to be found. I don't think Reggie was supposed to die."

"Are you saying you think that Reginald Montgrieve was dosed?" Lister sounded astonished at my declaration.

"Yes, detective, I am saying he was dosed and that only by misfortune was Georgie implicated. Have you found the rest of the other twenty-nine-day supply? I would wager it would be at his house."

"If, Miss Desmond, you don't think Mr. Montgrieve was supposed to die, what was the point of all of this?"

"How did you find out that Reggie was dead?" I answered his question with a question this time. "Did Mr. Crawford or one of his staff telephone the police? Did the person who reported the murder say Reggie was dead?"

"We could not find anyone at the Crawford residence that admitted to having placed the call. I questioned the officer on duty who took the call. He said that the caller told him that someone was passed out on the lawns of the Crawford estate. Passed out drunk on illegal booze."

"Drunk on illegal booze? Who in the world would think that ridiculous law would apply to the wealthy, and especially the wealthy of Hollywood?"

"Silly law or not Miss Desmond," the detective's face was reddening, "it is the law, and NO ONE is above the law."

The Reluctant Doppelganger

"Oh, come on Detective, when was the last time you raided any private parties in Hollywood? The liquor at Hollywood parties isn't bathtub gin. They are the finest imported wines, beers and liquors from around the world. Prohibition doesn't exist when it comes to Hollywood's wealthy and famous. It may not be fair, but it is the truth. When your men arrived at Mr. Crawford's home, what did they actually think they were going there to do?"

Detective Lister's face had gone from red with anger to the pinker shade of embarrassment. "Out of courtesy to Mr. Crawford, they had gone to notify him that there had been a complaint."

"So, now what do we know?" I set the bottle down and held up my right index finger. "Number one, we know the Veronal bottle was stolen from Georgie."

"Stolen? Really Miss Desmond. Why in the world would you think someone stole what now appears to be a discarded pharmaceutical bottle?" Lister folded his massive arms across his chest.

"It's a simple deduction, detective. As you could tell from Georgie's behavior," I now used my index finger as a pointer, "he had no idea the bottle was missing. Yet you have it. Meaning someone took it without Georgie's knowledge or permission. Isn't that the definition of stealing?"

"Why yes, but…"

"Number two, someone called the police station to report a public drunk, not a murder."

The detective had begun to follow along and appeared to be listening.

"Our villain knew that no one in RC's circle of friends and associates feared imprisonment over prohibition. They wanted to get the police to investigate a public drunk. When they did, they would find Reggie passed out, the Veronal in his pocket, and detain him and possibly commit him to an asylum for his drug addiction. We also know that whoever it was had access to Veronal. Most likely Reggie's own supply."

"Villain?" the Detective laughed as he visibly relaxed. He unfolded his arms and crossed back to the work counter. He placed both hands on the table again and leaned in. "Miss Desmond, you have been in Hollywood too long."

He bent down close to my face. I expected him to smell of stale cigarette smoke and old coffee, but I was wrong. He smelled lightly of sandalwood and his breath had a minty freshness. He had come prepared to be close.

"The police would call this person a suspect or a perpetrator but not *the villain*."

And there was that lopsided grin again. I couldn't help but smile back. He pushed himself back to standing.

"Alright, what else do we know?"

"We know we need to find the rest of Reggie's Veronal. Have you searched for it at his house?"

"No," was his sheepish reply. "We...as Mr. Crawford requested...we didn't feel it was necessary since Mr. Montgrieve was not found at home."

"Come on then, we need to run down RC. The studio owns the house, so I'm sure he has a key."

The detective and I started for the door. We were almost out of the room when it hit me.

"Georgie, in all those racks of clothes do you think you might have a nice suit the detective could possibly wear this evening. He will be attending the party at the Von Müller home tonight and he needs to look like a million dollars."

"I could find something for him, I'm sure. Can you come back to be fitted around two o'clock this afternoon?"

"I'm pretty sure I'll be busy," the Detective started to object.

"Nonsense," I said, flapping my hand in the air the way I'd seen Gertie do when she was being dismissive. "He'll be here." And I exited the room, pulling the detective behind me by his tie.

18

Once we were outside the ballroom walking in the direction of the front foyer, I let go of the detective's tie. He immediately started to protest again. I stopped and turned on him. "I have never seen you in anything other than a rumpled suit. If you are bound for stardom on the silver screen, you need to look the part. Not to mention the fact that once the introduction is made tonight, you and I will be standing side by side under siege by photographers and their nasty little flash bulbs. I want you looking like you belong at my side. So, we'll hear no more about it. Be back here at two."

"Well said, my little starlet." boomed RC as he clapped loudly. "I was going to take the delicate approach in speaking with your new leading man. But I dare say, I like your tactics much better."

When I turned, I saw both RC and my father standing in the doorway of the dining room. Charlie was seated in one of the chairs at the dining table. Obviously, they had been waiting. "I didn't expect you to still be here," I blushed a bit with embarrassment over my tirade.

The Reluctant Doppelganger

"We did bring Hugo with us. I thought it only polite to wait on my newest actor," RC grinned.

"Actually, I'm glad you are still here. We need to visit Reggie's villa."

"Wh-what?" RC blustered.

"The detective here was going to get a search a warrant, but I told him the studio owned the villa and that if he got a search warrant, he would have to name the studio, and ultimately you, RC, in that warrant. I knew you wouldn't want that, so I told the Detective that you had a key and that if you came with us, I mean him, to search through what is rightfully yours, then no warrant would be needed. We could do it right now and no one would be any the wiser."

"See here, Wainwright!" RC bellowed.

In a calm steady voice, Detective Lister cut in, "It is still Detective Lister at this point, Mr. Crawford. And it is until I solve this murder case, as we agreed."

My father stepped up next to RC and placed his hand on his shoulder. "I think, RC, Theo does have a point. This way you could be there to oversee the process, and neither you nor I would have to spend our valuable time correcting any issues that might arise if anything leaked out."

RC pondered for a long moment. Then he walked over to the telephone on the hall table, lifted the receiver and clicked the cradle up and down. "Give me Clearbrook 9-2-1." There was a pause as the call was connected.

"Edwina, collect the file on Montgrieve's villa and meet me there in twenty minutes with the keys." He didn't wait for an answer. He just hung up.

I pitied Edwina. I hoped that she was paid well for having to put up with RC's demanding nature. He had told her twenty minutes, knowing that it would take us at least thirty minutes to get there from here. If someone was going to stand around waiting, it wasn't going to be RC Crawford.

"My Rolls Royce won't hold five without one of you sitting up front with the driver. And that just won't do at all."

"RC, why don't you, Father, and Charlie take your Rolls, and Detective Lister and I will follow in the Daimler. That way, I can make sure Detective Lister is back at the house by two o'clock for his fitting with Georgie."

I could tell Charlie looked a little hurt. I was sure he'd rather ride with us, but I wanted to talk with the detective in private.

In a matter of moments, we were all out the door and the two big cars were in route to Reginald Montgrieve's villa, known to most of the women in Hollywood, but not to Reggie, as 'Casa Culo Arrogante,' House of the Arrogant Ass, another nugget of information I had gleaned that night in the lady's room.

"Where do you think he would keep the Veronal?" I asked the detective, as we sped along the street.

He motioned with his eyes towards the driver's seat and Randel.

"Oh, don't worry, Detective; Randel is completely trustworthy. I trust him to keep my biggest secrets." I said, rather too loudly. "You are trustworthy, aren't you Randel?"

"That I am, Ma'am." Randel answered, winking at me in the rearview mirror.

The detective still looked uncomfortable, even with our assurances, but he continued, "I would think it would be somewhere in his private bed chamber or bathroom."

"Those were my thoughts, too. So then, we are on the same page. It would be to our advantage to encourage RC and Bertie to help us as much as possible. It will make dealing with their need to be in control so much easier."

As the car slowed, I saw that we had reached our destination. Before us was a twelve-foot stucco wall. Along its peaked ridge, it had been roofed with red tile shingles.

The Reluctant Doppelganger

The massive gates stood open as we drove through. The front of the home was invisible as the driveway turned sharply then followed a course close to the wall on one side and a thickly wooded park-like knoll on the other. We had nearly reached the flanking wall when the driveway made another sharp turn and we were headed back the same direction we had come, only this time, the thick woods were on both sides of the car. On one side the woods gave way to lawn, and suddenly there it was. Unlike Theodora's and RC's home, this house was all on one level. It was a sprawling hacienda made of stucco and it, too, had a red tile roof. There was a covered porch that wrapped three sides of the mammoth house. There were several seating areas, all with rustic furnishings, and at the far end where the porch connected to the house, was a massive outdoor stone fireplace.

As both cars pulled up to the main entrance, I could see Edwina standing next to the front doors. Randel opened my door and helped me out. The detective followed in my wake. As I looked up at the house, I noticed that in the seating area closest to the door, a rustic rocker was still in motion. Edwina had been sitting, waiting on us to arrive. She had hopped up when she heard the cars pass through the gates, I was guessing. The other three gentlemen met us at the bottom of the short set of steps up to the front porch.

"That driveway is the damnedest thing. The house sits on twenty acres, but the original owner wanted the property to look like it was part of a natural setting, like the redwood forest that lines the driveway is natural to this part of California. Anyway, he wanted most of the property to be to the back of the home, so he built the house very close to the front of the property and then put in that twisty driveway through the man-made forest to give the illusion that the house sits back further than it really does. But the house is splendid." RC sounded more like a real estate agent than a movie studio owner.

"We should get on with what we came here to do." Detective Lister encouraged.

Suddenly, he had become very task oriented. A get-down-to-business type of man. I admired that in him, most likely because those were the qualities, I admired in myself. RC led the way up the steps. Edwina must have already unlocked the door because she simply turned the knob, pushed it open and stepped back.

RC led the way inside. "Where would you like to start, Detective?" RC asked as we all filed into the foyer. The room was huge with hallways running off it in every direction. The ceiling was vaulted with rough, hewn timber that had been stained and varnished. The floor was made of Saltillo terra cotta tiles laid on the diagonal making the room appear even larger than it was. Three giant chandeliers made of deer horns sporting stained glass cylinder globes lit the room. It made me think of some old Spanish mission.

"I think I would like to start in Mr. Montgrieve's bed chamber. Would you be so kind as to direct us?"

"Certainly, right this way." RC started down one of the hallways that led towards the back of the house. The hallway was long and paneled in heavy rustic wood stained a burnished redwood. It was lit with horned wall sconces, smaller versions of the chandeliers in the foyer with their stained-glass globes. At the very end of the hall, we came to a wooden door. It was like everything else. It was made of heavy roughhewn lumber. It was banded in black hammered metal straps. Instead of a door knob, there was a thick black metal lever RC lifted to unlatch the door before pushing it open.

When the door opened, the contents of the room was of little consequence. The back wall was comprised of the largest single pane of glass I'd ever seen, which brought the spectacular vistas of the property beyond right into the room. It was a tropical forest where every imaginable flower was in full bloom. The spell-binding gardens were all nestled in a palm grove that had palm trees the size of buildings and the whole of it all swayed in what I could only imagine was a soft California breeze.

The detective's voice brought me back to reality. "Gentlemen," he said to everyone in the party, "If you would stay as close to the center of the room as possible, Miss Desmond and I will give the room as thorough a search as we can. Miss Desmond, if you would start with the bedside tables, I will start in Mr. Montgrieve's personal bathroom."

I began with the bedside table that had a closed book, *The Great Gatsby*, with a marker sticking out of it. I assumed, that, although he lived alone, this was Reggie's side of the bed. I opened each of the two drawers and found them empty. I thought that odd. I moved to the other side of the bed and opened the drawers of that bedside table. Its drawers were empty as well.

Detective Lister came out of the bathroom shaking his head. "There were only six personal items in the entire room. A toothbrush and toothpaste, a razor and a shaving cup, a bottle of Scotch and a bar of soap. Does that strike anyone as odd?"

"That is odd, but just as strange is the fact that, other than a lamp on both bedside tables and a copy of *The Great Gatsby*, marked where he'd been reading it, each drawer is empty."

With that pronouncement, everyone in the room began to search. But we all came quickly to the conclusion that there was nothing in this room that was in the least bit personal. A movie set was more personalized than Reginald Montgrieve's bedroom.

"Well then, Detective, it would appear that there is nothing

here to find. Shall we proceed to your next area of interest?"
RC gestured towards the door.   "That would be Mr.
Montgrieve's study, I think." Lister was nodding his head in
agreement.

RC was standing at the door ushering everyone through.
The detective and I were just about to exit when I noticed
what I assumed was the closet door. If Reggie's closet was
anything like Theodora's, then it would be a room unto itself.
I walked over to the door and opened it. I switched on the
electric light. I jumped when the light came on. I was staring
at a reflection of the detective and me in a floor to ceiling
mirror. The room was nearly twice the size of Theodora's
closet.   The first thing I noticed was an entire section
dedicated to nothing but white dinner jackets like the one
Reggie was wearing the night he died. Below the jackets was
a full row of dark trousers ranging from dark blue to black.
Running down the center of the space was an enormous
built-in cabinet with rows and rows of tiny glass drawers. I
stepped into the closet and turned on a switch that was on the
end of the built-in cabinet. Instantly all the drawers were
illuminated.   There seemed to be only one item in each
drawer. Some drawers held ties, others sported gloves and
still others were filled with undergarments. Two rows of
racks on both sides of the closet were filled with clothes. I
wasn't sure, but I would wager Reggie had more clothes than
Theodora.

On the back wall, was the bigger-than-life portrait of
Reginald Montgrieve. It was stunning. It was the portrait
that Claudette had told me about the day I had arrived at
Theodora's house. It had been painted by the same artist
who had painted the one of Theodora that hung in her
bedroom. The picture was of a much younger Reggie. He
had been an incredibly handsome man. He stood looking
royally out at the viewer. From my vantage point I could see

he was dressed in a short waisted white dinner jacket with two rows of brass buttons. He wore a deep blue bow tie and a white shirt. Pinned to the jacket with a large golden brooch was a plaid scarf that started at his breast pocket and disappeared over his shoulder. His elbow rested on a high-backed chair that was gilded. I was drawn towards the picture. As I moved closer, the rest of the portrait came into view.

Reggie was wearing a tartan plaid kilt that matched the scarf that hung over his shoulder; a fur sporran, white knee socks and laced black dress shoes completed his ensemble. In the large gilded chair, that I now took to be a throne, sat a simple unadorned gold crown. At the crown's crest was a huge ruby the size of a large egg that glinted at the viewer. It wasn't faceted like today's gems, but it burned with inner fire. By now all six members of our little band had gathered in Reggie's closet.

"That bastard!" The Viscount exclaimed. The Viscount was standing on the other side of the center cabinet staring at the portrait as well.

Lister and I, standing opposite him, looked over in surprise.

The Viscount noticed us. "He's wearing our family's tartan. The crown is that of a medieval Scottish king and the ruby is the legendary Rose of Kintyre."

"Legendary?" both Lister and I said in unison.

"The story goes that the ruby was part of a dowry paid to the king by his queen's family. The king had it mounted in his crown and dubbed the ruby The Rose of Kintyre. The king wore the crown into war with the Irish, where he fell in battle. His loyal knight, our ancestor, spirited the crown away so it wouldn't fall into the hands of their enemies. Legend has it that he brought the crown back to our castle and hid it. He then returned to the battle where he, too, was killed. He never told anyone were he had hidden the crown with its precious ruby." The Viscount told the tale as if he were telling a child's bedtime story.

"Has anyone ever searched for it?" asked Detective Lister, excited.

"Oh, only off and on for about the last eight centuries now," laughed Charlie. "Every new generation has a go at it. You must understand, Detective, the old pile is huge. It has, at last count, sixty-three bedrooms. One entire three-story wing has never been renovated other than adding glass pane windows instead of wooden shutters. That wing has no electricity or indoor plumbing. In fact, each of its floors still has their original medieval privy. The privies each have three seats that, once upon a time, dropped sewage straight down into the castle's moat. They are staggered so that the ones above didn't drop sewage down on the one below it," Charlie mused.

The detective frowned in disgust.

"Surely you've used an outhouse or have gone camping, Detective," I said, smiling at him.

"I haven't been in an outhouse since I was a child and I have never been camping," he said, not at all pleased that I found his reaction amusing. "There does not appear to be anything in Mr. Montgrieve's closet that has any relevance to his murder." He began to herd everyone from the room. He and I were bringing up the rear again, walking side by side in the cavernous space. "I cannot believe any one man has so many clothes," he ran his finger down a rack of what looked to be golfing pants.

I gazed at the seemingly endless stacks of individually lit glass drawers. The top of the massive cabinet was gleaming white marble. Its surface was totally devoid of anything personal – with two exceptions. The first displayed time pieces. A round glass cylinder perched horizontally atop a wooden base. The bands of eight different Swiss wrist watches encircled the glass cylinder. Next to that was a wooden box about four inches tall made of the same wood as the base of the wrist watch tower. The box was about six inches long and four inches deep. The top of the box was open. It was about an inch deep and was lined with deep blue velvet. In it, nestled side by side, were three pocket watches, two gold and one silver. My guess was that the tray that held the pocket watches lifted off and the box below would hold watch bob and chains. As I passed, I tested my theory. The tray did indeed lift off, but the box beneath, also lined with deep blue velvet, was empty.

I went to replace the lid when I noticed a few small white crystals that resembled salt.

"Look here, Detective, I think I may have found where Reginald Montgrieve kept his Veronal."

"If those are Veronal crystals, it would appear that someone has absconded with the rest of the pink packets."

"It would appear so."

The rest of the home's search revealed nothing. The house gave the distinct impression that it was merely a furnished dwelling ready for its new occupants to move in and add their personal touches.

We had just stepped back outside onto the porch and Edwina was locking up the house when a thought occurred to me. "RC, doesn't Reggie have any servants?"

It was Edwina who answered, never looking up from her task of locking the front door. "He did have staff. Last week he gave his valet two weeks off to go visit his ailing mother in Chicago. He also called me and had me remove his housekeeper and butler. He said he wanted some time to himself since his valet would be gone. He was sure he could manage the house for two weeks. I found it quite odd, myself." The massive lock clicked into place and she looked up at us, after removing the key.

Judging from the expressions on everyone's faces, it would appear that we all thought it odd.

"That is curious," RC said quizzically.

"Yes, it is," Lister echoed.

Randel had the door already open when Detective Lister and I stepped off the porch. We climbed into the backseat and he closed the door. Once we were headed for the gate, Randel asked, "Begging your pardon, Ma'am. But did you and the detective find the bootlegger's hold?"

It was Lister, who got the words out first, "The what?"

Randel had our full attention. "Yes sir. The man who built the property was, among other things, a bootlegger. Everyone used to say that he had a keep on the property where he used to store hooch before shipping it out to speakeasies. When I used to drive a truck for the factory, I worked at night. I used to drive by the back wall of the property and there would be trucks lined up like they were unloading. But when I would drive by during the day it just looked like a blank wall. So, I was wondering if you found any secret doors or anything like that inside the house."

"Would you mind driving us around to where you used to see the trucks parked?" Lister asked.

"I would be happy to, Sir."

"We don't have time. It is a quarter to two, and you are supposed to be meeting with Georgie. You have to look sharp tonight. We'll look first thing tomorrow."

19

When we arrived back at the house, we both flew up the front steps. By the time we reached the front doors, they were swinging open. Claudette and Seedy stood at the bottom of the stairs. Wallace was pushing the massive doors shut behind us.

"Georgie is waiting on you, Detective," Wallace said, now directing the big man towards the ballroom.

Seedy and Claudette were hurrying me up the stairs. "We only have four hours to get you ready," Claudette was saying. I looked down and noticed Lister looking uncomfortably back up at me. I smiled. At least for a little while, he would know what I had been going through for the last several days.

When we reached my room, Claudette took control. She had Seedy head to the bathroom and start my shower. She told me to sit at the vanity and she began removing my jewelry. I had my back to the mirrors and found myself looking up to the portrait of Theodora. The artist was truly amazing with his attention to life-like detail. The picture was huge. I had thought of it as life-size, but it was bigger than life. The dang thing was as big as one of my bedroom doors.

"Door!" I cried out and I shot to my feet.

"Mon Dieu!" Claudette screamed and jumped backwards.

I looked over my shoulder into the mirror. I had on no jewelry, but my hair was straight, and my make-up looked fine. I bolted through the door and down the hall. As I reached the bottom of the stairs, I realized I was barefoot. I grabbed the newel post and swung around it and let the momentum hurtle me down the hallway towards the ballroom. When I reached the door, I flung it open.

There, standing on a raised alterations platform, stood Detective John Lister. He was shirtless and wore black tuxedo pants on which Georgie was busy pinning the hem. I smiled as I took him in. His arms were comprised of thickly corded muscles, his chest had sculpted pectorals and his abdomen had very defined ridges rippling all the way down past his belt line. I pursed my lips. He grabbed his shirt and covered himself as he blushed.

"My dear Detective Lister, I have seen a man in his bathing costume before." My grin grew wider at his modesty.

"That may be, my dear Miss Desmond. However, I am wearing less than a bathing costume. And with that said, you have never seen ME in a bathing costume."

I made a mental note that Detective Lister in a bathing costume was a must see. We both turned our backs to each other.

In a decidedly casual tone, he asked, "Could I inquire as to the reason for your sudden visit?"

Good Lord! I had gotten so distracted by the detective's reaction to me seeing his chest bare, and my reaction to that bare chest, that I had gotten side tracked.

"Didn't you think it odd that Reggie had hung that splendid painting of himself in the closet?"

"Yes, it was a bit unusual. But eccentric people do odd

things."

"I think it covers a doorway. The doorway to the bootlegger's hold."

"Why do you think that?"

"Because that bedroom is the only room in the house where you can see all the way to the back wall. If there is an opening somewhere on that back wall into the hold, it would be a prime spot to supervise the loading and unloading of the trucks Randel was talking about."

"Why is finding this bootlegger's hold important to the case?"

"I'm not sure but my gut tells me it is."

"I know you are not looking at each other, but we are all right in the same room. There is no need for y'all to keep yelling." Georgie said, standing and walking over to his work table.

"Oh, Georgie," I said, turning around again. Detective Lister had regained his shirt and had it buttoned all the way to the top. "Well, we should look at it, first thing in the morning."

"Yes, we should."

"I'll head back upstairs to finish dressing for the evening. I will leave instructions for Wallace to put you in one of the extra bedrooms. That way you can change here. There is no need to run across town to your accommodations simply to dress for the party. I will let RC know he can pick you up here.

"Since RC and the Duke are dining before they come to collect you, I will have Mrs. Reid make sure you are properly fed. She is an excellent cook. In fact, if you don't mind, I will dine with you. That way neither of us will be starving or get so drunk we can't stand before the evening is out." With that I left the ballroom and made my way back upstairs.

Claudette had insisted that Detective Lister and I eat at

4:45. She wanted to make sure she and Georgie had plenty of time to get us both dressed for the evening. I was fairly certain I was the one who needed the most dressing time.

Georgie had taken the Detective's tuxedo up to the guest room. He had also taken the dress that I was to wear up to my room. Once finished with dinner, we both retired to our separate quarters.

At 6:30, Wallace rang up to say that Randel had left to fetch the Viscount. Claudette was almost finished. Tonight, I was dressed in royal blue satin. The wig was not my usual blond bob but one set into a Marcel wave with a jeweled headband of seed pearls, sapphires, aquamarines and diamonds encircling my head. In the center of my forehead, just above my eyes, was a quarter sized sapphire tear-drop that sparkled wickedly in the light.

The barely-there royal blue satin hugged my body. It had one long sleeve that slunk its way down my left arm. Starting at the shoulder, there was a stripe of silver bugle beads running all the way down the sleeve until it reached the tip of the pointed cuff that ended over the knuckle just above my middle finger. There was a loop that slipped over my finger to hold the point in place. The other shoulder was bare. The dress itself poured down my body like cascading blue water, only to puddle into a train behind me. The dress was split just to the right of center, scandalously high on my thigh just above the garter line of my black silk hose. The shoes were royal blue satin with a T-strap beaded with silver bugle beads. They sported a thick five-inch heel. Georgie had left instructions that there was to be no jewelry hanging down onto the dress and nothing pinned to the satin bodice. This last commandment came with the threat of violence. The ensemble was completed with a white fox stole draped once again in the crook of my arms. The red cradled telephone rang again. It was Wallace. Randel and the Viscount had just passed the gates and were on their way up to the house. I moved to the stairs. Claudette advised me to go half way down and wait for the Viscount there. It was always better for a man to gaze up on a beautiful woman than to look down at her. I complied.

When the door opened admitting the Viscount, I broke into a smile. Dressed almost identically to the portrait of Reginald Montgrieve stood the Viscount in his dress kilt. The tartan plaid was the same, but instead of white, the Viscount's jacket was dark blue matching the blue in the tartan.

"Nice legs." I said, grinning.

"Ever wonder what a Scotsman wears under his kilt?"

He raised the kilt scandalously high on his thighs and gave me a wicked grin before dropping it back in place with a slight swish of his hips.

"Astonishingly, you seem to look more beautiful every time we meet." His wicked grin turned to a smile of appreciation.

"Thank you," I said, as I started down the stairs to meet him.

I had to admit; Georgie had out done himself. The garment made it appear as if I were wearing nothing underneath. When, in actuality, every inch of me was squeezed into something. As I descended the stairs, the dress created the sensation of water flowing behind me. Charlie's hand was there when I reached the last step. I slipped my arm through his and we were off.

Just like Cinderella and her fairytale Prince. Well, not a prince. Could one substitute a kilt-wearing Viscount for a Prince? Surely one could. After all I was a substitution, too.

20

When we pulled up to the Von Müller home, as usual the press and their cameras were cordoned off behind velvet ropes. This time there was a red carpet leading from the drop-off point, up the stairs and directly to the front door of a neoclassical mansion that was every bit as opulent as RC's. The massive pillars that supported the front façade were lighted both from the top and the bottom. When looking up at it, I got the feeling that the man who lived here was one of immense power.

As the door to the big Daimler opened and a hand thrust inside to help me out, I looked over at Charlie and said, "It's show time. Get that smile in place and don't close your eyes when the flashbulbs go off."

He smiled. "You sound just like your father."

"Sssh! Mums the word about that." I chided. I slipped my hand into that of the footman and exited the auto. Flashbulbs popped everywhere as I waved to the photographers.

As Charlie stepped onto the red carpet, there was a loud whistle. "Those are some sexy gams you got there, Viscount." Everyone in the crowd laughed as did Charlie,

The Reluctant Doppelganger

giving his kilt another swish and the flashbulbs popped. As we walked towards the door, my bare thigh slipped in and out of view. Each time it was exposed, flashbulbs popped. Once inside the house, I checked my fur at the door. Then the Viscount and I blended into the throng.

The Von Müller's home was every bit as big as RC's, but RC's home was designed as a place to entertain first, then a place to live. This house was a big home that was used for entertaining, which made most of the rooms very crowded. We worked our way to the ballroom. The entire back wall of the house, which I assumed must have been glass panels, had been removed. Now the ballroom opened onto the terrace, and the terrace stepped down to the pool and cabana, and past that were formal gardens. People thickly dotted all the landscapes. There was a full orchestra on a raised platform off to the side of the terrace and they were playing, *Someone to Watch Over Me*. One minute we were working our way through the crowd, the next Charlie slipped his arm from mine and, clasping my hand, he twirled me into his arms; and suddenly we were on the ballroom dance floor.

I was a good dancer; however, there were two distinct problems. First was that I know how to lead, not follow. And secondly, I had never danced in a dress before, especially one with a long, flowing train. I bent back and pulled the train into my arms. The moment I relaxed into the dance, I found there was no issue with him leading at all. He swept me across the dance floor through three consecutive songs.

"Oh, Charlie, I must stop. I would like something to drink and I need to look fresh when RC introduces Hugo and me."

Charlie once again took my arm and we moved out onto the terrace to get some fresh air. "I will get us a drink. What would you like?"

"I think I'll have a glass of champagne."

He nodded to me and headed off in the direction of the bar

next to the swimming pool. I became enamored with the band. They introduced Josephine Baker. When she reached the microphone, the band began to play *La Vie En Rose*. A flute of champagne appeared at my right hand and I felt a soft touch on my bare shoulder. My eyes were fixed on Josephine. As she sang the beautiful French tune, I sighed, "I wish I understood French."

Then softly in a deep rich baritone the words were being sung into my ear.

"And when you speak, angels sing from above
Everyday words seem to turn into love songs
Give your heart and soul to me
And life will always be ... a life in pink.

If you are being literal. Sounds much nicer in French."

I looked up to thank Charlie, and to my surprise it was Detective Lister. "You speak French?"

"I spoke French before I spoke English. My parents are French Canadian. My parents moved to California because they both hated the cold Canadian winters. My father is a carpenter by trade and my mother is a seamstress. Hence, the reason I knew that a *haute couture* was a dressmaker."

I laughed. It was at that moment Charlie returned drinking a pink gin and holding a flute of champagne.

"Good Evening, Viscount. You seem to have forgotten your pants." Lister gave a rare laugh. "You look just like Reginald Montgrieve."

"With one exception, my good man. This is truly *my* family's tartan."

"That and you don't have a gold crown with a big fat ruby in it," Lister laughed again.

"You are spot on there." And instantly Charlie was laughing too.

A waiter passed near, and Lister called to him, "Are you collecting empties, too?" The waiter nodded. Lister whisked the champagne glass out of my hand and set it gently on the man's tray. I look puzzled. I had barely taken two sips from it.

"It wouldn't be too gentlemanly of me to horn in on another man's date." He smiled, gave us both a quick salute, and slipped into the crowd.

Charlie handed me the flute of champagne he was carrying, and we moved out of the crush and into the formal garden where we had a wonderful conversation about Scotland, his family, and most of all, the family castle. Ever since he started telling us about it this afternoon I had wanted to know more. I had a hundred questions to ask and Charlie seemed to enjoy talking about it. We were lost in conversation when my father found us. On his arm was his date. My mouth dropped open. Dressed in a beautiful lavender beaded dress was Gertrude Myers.

"Miss Desmond, Your Lordship, might I introduce my companion, Miss Gertrude Myers. Gertie, this is Theodora Desmond and her escort for this evening, his Lordship the Viscount of Kintyre and Lorne."

"Charlie," the Viscount nodded and took Gertie's hand and pressed the back of it to his lips.

So, I guess I wasn't supposed to know Gertie and she wasn't officially here as my father's secretary. "Good evening, Gertie. I'm Theo.

"Nice to meet you Charlie," Gertie said. "And I know just who you are, Miss Desmond." She smiled and patted me on the shoulder. I grinned.

"Theo, RC is making his big announcement in fifteen minutes. I've already caught up with Hugo and he's making his way to the bandstand. You and Charlie should as well."

As the four of us made our way back up to the band, Gertie said, "You look stunning this evening, *leo meum*."

I smiled.

My father and Gertie moved a little ahead of us as the crowd undulated. Charlie leaned into me. "My lion?"

I shrugged.

When we reached the edge of the stage, Detective Lister was already there. RC was mid-speech. When he looked down and saw that I had arrived, he began the buildup for the introduction.

"And starring as Delilah will be one of Hollywood's most acclaimed actresses, Miss Theodora Desmond." He held out his arm and the spot light shifted to me. As I mounted the stage the band played, Yes *Sir, That's My Baby*. I clasped RC's hand and he pulled in close and kissed me on the forehead. "And her co-star for the film is a newcomer to the silver screen. I would like to introduce Mr. Hugo Wainwright." Hugo mounted the stage to the tune, *The Sheik of Araby*. He shook RC's hand, and we stood together as flashbulbs popped furiously.

RC moved out of the shot. Hugo slid his arm around my waist and when he pulled me close the crowd went wild and we were blinded by the brilliance of the flashes. I slipped from his grasp and slid down the stage until Hugo and I were holding on to each other by just our fingertips, then we bowed to the crowd and the roar went up again. I looked down at Hugo and for the first time noticed his tuxedo. The pants were black, but the jacket was a burgundy so deep it was almost black itself. His bow tie was just a few shades lighter and gold cuff links glittered in the spotlights. He had made a transformation almost as amazing as my own. Gone was the frumpy detective. He had been replaced by the suave and debonair leading man, Hugo Wainwright. As we moved towards the steps leading off the stage, hordes of well-wishers clustered at the bottom.

In a moment, we'd been rerouted and were being escorted down a back flight of stairs, reserved for the band's use, away from the crowd. We stepped off into the grass. "Hang on a minute," Hugo called to me. I stopped. He gathered up my train and handed it to me. "You don't want grass stains on your dress," he said. We tromped around to a side door where we were ushered into the Müller study. An elegantly dressed middle-aged couple were seated close to each other on a long brown leather tufted Chesterfield sofa. They looked cozy even though the room was massive with its twelve-foot ceiling where book shelves covered every inch of wall from top to bottom. I could only assume that the couple was our host and hostess, Herr und Frau Von Müller.

"Guten Abend, Herr und Frau Von Müller." I said, thankful for Seedy's last minute lesson.

"Guten Abend," Herr Von Müller replied, standing and giving me a sharp nod of his head.

"We are both great admirers of yours, Miss Desmond. And we were very proud when Mr. Crawford asked us to host a party to announce his next movie and its stars," Frau Von Müller said with a sophisticated British accent.

"I do have to admit, it is much louder and a great deal more gregarious than we intended," said Herr Von Müller, smiling. There were only traces of his German ancestry when he spoke.

RC came through the side door just as he spoke. "I am pretty sure you mean out of control," he said, laughing. "Welcome to Hollywood, Mr. and Mrs. Von Müller, where a party is only considered successful by how far out of control it gets. The further out of control it gets the more talked about it is afterwards, and the more talked about it is afterwards means the more people will try to crash your next one." He was still laughing heartily as he moved to shake both their hands. Then he turned to Hugo and me. "I wanted to get some good publicity shots. This is Max Green," he said, introducing the man who had just followed him through the door. "He's the studio photographer. The Von Müllers wanted to meet you and I thought their study would be a good place to get you away from your adoring public. Let's get the shots and then you both can get some peace and quiet and visit with our hosts."

Fifteen minutes later, I was seeing spots before my eyes and would have bet Hugo was too.

"What about the Viscount, RC? He is my escort this evening."

"Leave the Viscount to me. I'll see he gets back to where he belongs and that his feelings are in no way injured. In fact, I think I have just the thing. I saw Regina earlier. I'm sure she can ease his distress over losing his date to another man." He winked as he and Max headed towards the side door.

"Sir?" Hugo asked. "Would it be possible for Miss Desmond and me to look through Mr. Montgrieve's home again tomorrow? Some new information has come to light."

"Oh?"

"Yes sir. I doubt it will pan out, but if we could meet you or your secretary there in the morning it would be greatly appreciated. I am so sorry for any inconvenience it might cause." Hugo spoke both respectfully and solemnly.

"This is becoming a damned nuisance. I have appointments all day tomorrow and I will need Edwina the entire time." RC began to fish in his vest pocket. He produced a key and tossed it to Hugo. "I'll be glad when you're on my payroll detective. Be sure to return that," RC commented, pointing to the key now in Hugo's hand. He gave another wink and was gone.

Hugo looked at me, puzzled, as we made our way over to two chairs to sit across from our hosts. I wasn't sure how I felt about RC arranging for Charlie to run into Regina Banks again. The logical part of me knew it was the best thing that could ever happen, but for some reason I was jealous. Hugo pocketed the key and we sat.

"Whatever did Mr. Crawford mean when he called you Detective?" Frau Von Müller, asked, looking perplexed. "Is it another role you are preparing for?"

"No Ma'am. I am a police detective with the Beverly Hills police department. That is how I met Mr. Crawford and Miss Desmond. Mr. Crawford wanted me to be in his film, but I told him I couldn't do it until we solved Mr. Reginald Montgrieve's murder," Hugo explained politely.

The Von Müller's looked horrified. "Murder?" They both asked at the same time.

Hugo went on to explain.

"That poor man," sighed Frau Von Müller. "I've known him since he was a boy and I was a young girl. His father designed several pieces of jewelry for my father as gifts for my mother. I knew both Thomas and his twin brother Martin." Frau Von Müller seemed saddened by her long-ago memory.

"His brother is a twin? I had heard he had a brother. I heard his brother designs costume jewelry for many of the top fashion houses. And that he was quite successful. But I had no idea they were twins." I said, amazed at the news.

"Yes, they are identical twins, both very handsome men. And they used to be inseparable, always creating mischief. But several years ago, Reggie came to the United States. When he did not return home to England, a rift in their relationship opened and bad blood developed. No one was ever sure why. Martin refused to speak of it or anything about his brother at all. I was looking forward to seeing him again now that Heinrich and I have built a home here in Beverly Hills."

"Where does his brother, Martin, live? The police have not been able to contact him," Hugo said, all business now.

"The last time I knew, he was living in Paris. He moved to

be close to the French fashion houses." Frau Von Müller explained.

The Von Müllers looked tired, so we allowed our conversation to draw to a close. The Von Müller's butler arranged for Randel to pick us up at the side of the house, thereby avoiding the herd of press stalking the grounds. As we stepped outside the side door, once again Hugo lifted my train and handed it to me. With his arm around me for support, we made a mad dash for the Daimler.

21

The drive back to the house was quiet. We were both tired, a bit overwhelmed and lost in our own thoughts. As we approached Theodora's house, Randel's voice came through the voice tube. "Pull the shades and crank up the privacy screen." I looked through the front windshield and saw, surrounding the front gate, was a horde of reporters and photographers. We hurried to comply with Randel's instructions. The big auto slowed to a stop and sat for what seemed like forever outside the gates. Reporters were yelling their questions at the car. I wondered what was taking Mr. Truman so long to open the gates, then the big car began to move. Hugo and I sat as still as startled deer in the backseat. We pulled to a stop and Hugo made to open the door. I placed my hand on his, stopping him.

"Let Randel open it. He'll know if everything is safe and when we are alone."

It took a few moments from the time I heard Randel exit the car until he opened my door. As he helped me out, I could see that Wallace had the front door open and was waiting at the top of the steps. I gathered my dress and allowed him to help me out. Hugo was right behind me as we hurried up the steps and into the foyer. Wallace closed the door behind us.

"They've been outside the gates for the last two hours," Wallace informed us.

"That's about the time RC announced the new movie and us as its stars," I said, as I reached the bottom step.

I was on the third step when Hugo spoke. "I had a wonderful time, Theodora. I hope you sleep well. I was hoping Randel would take me home, but if I need to get a cab, I can do that instead."

My mind was racing down so many paths I hadn't even considered Hugo. Then it struck me. It was the first time he'd ever called me anything other than Miss Desmond. I turned back to him. "Won't you stay here, John? Your things are already in the guest room. You see that mob at the gate, it will be the same way at your place, and I doubt you have a wall, a gate, a guard and an entire staff trying to protect you from them."

"I'm sure I'll be okay," He said, smiling.

"I'm not so sure you will, John. After tonight, your life will never be the same. Your life will never belong to just you ever again. I can assure you of that." My tone was serious. Then I brightened. "Besides, if you stay here, we can head to Reggie's house first thing in the morning."

"W-e-l-l?" He was stalling.

"Great! Then it's settled. Wallace, would you please make sure Mr. Wainwright has everything he needs?"

"Yes, Ma'am," Wallace replied as I turned and started back up the stairs.

"But what about propriety?" Hugo called up to me.

Again, I turned. "Propriety? My dear boy, this is Hollywood. The word "propriety" is not even in the Hollywood dictionary." I smiled at him, shot up the stairs and disappeared down the hall to my room.

When I reached my bed chamber, Claudette was there ready to undress me and Seedy was lying on the bed thumbing through the latest addition of "Vogue Magazine." I knew that both ladies wanted to hear the details of the party but there was no time for that now.

"Good, I'm glad you are both here. Seedy, please telephone Randel and Georgie. Tell them to meet us in the long gallery in ten minutes. Claudette, could you make coffee for everyone; I don't want to wake Mrs. Reid. But first get me out of this damnable dress. And find me something comfortable to wear." I lifted my bare arm and the short zipper under the arm went down and the dress became loose enough to wriggle out. It crashed to the floor. I gathered it up, wadded it into a ball, and pitched it on the bed. Claudette unbuckled my shoes and I stepped back down to the ground flexing my sore toes. I really don't see how women manage heels for long periods of time. I shot into the closet and had my magic foundation garment off in a heartbeat. The cool air hit my body and I sighed. My striped pajamas hung on a hook at the back of the closet. I snatched them off and had them on in a flash. I opened the door to find that Claudette had gone to make the coffee.

"Randel and Georgie are on their way. I'd better hang that dress up if I can figure out how." Seedy was holding the dress, turning it every which way.

"No! I'm taking it with me to show Georgie." I found my robe, tied it around my waist, snatched up the blue dress and proceeded to the long gallery barefooted.

When Seedy and I arrived, Claudette was pouring coffee for Randel and Georgie.

"That was quick," I said to Claudette.

"Mrs. Reid was still awake and had thought you might be wanting coffee." Claudette never looked up from her task as she spoke. She handed the cups to both men first, then to Seedy and finally to me.

"Why would she think I might want coffee at two in the morning?"

"The truth is she always puts a fresh pot on just before she goes to bed. That way it can be ready at a moment's notice."

"What a clever woman!" I sipped from my blue cup gratefully. "Randel, isn't there a second car in the garage?"

"Yes Ma'am!" he said enthusiastically. "It is a Mercedes-Benz Armbruster Cabriolet. She's brand spanking new, a 1927 model Miss Desmond got about two months ago. She might just be the fastest car in Beverly Hills. She's one of those European right-hand drives."

"Good! Tomorrow morning, we need a smoke screen. Seedy, I want you dressed as me. Georgie, I want pants tomorrow. Something like tweeds that are durable.

"That's not a problem. Coco Chanel has introduced an entire line of lady's wear based on men's dress clothes. I've created a couple of copies already."

"Have them in my room by seven in the morning. Oh. And NO more trains, unless it's a photo shoot. I had a devil of a time getting around in this tonight." I threw the beautiful royal blue satin creation, now crumpled into a tight ball, directly at him. He merely grinned.

"Randel, I want you to have the Daimler at the front door at nine o'clock sharp. Have the Mercedes-Benz running in the garage but leave the door down so it can't be seen from the road." I went on to explain my scheme. It took less than ten minutes and we were all headed to our beds.

22

There was a knock at my door the next morning. "Rise and shine," came a cheery French voice as Claudette let herself in. "I have brought coffee. I will be back in thirty minutes to start dressing you. Georgie has already brought up your clothes. I think you are going to enjoy them. He set out your brown and white wing-tips, the ones you wore the day you arrived," she said as she set the coffee tray on the bare little table between the two chairs. "Have your coffee and get your morning bath. I will be back soon." She exited this time through the bathroom, and I heard the water come on.

I hopped out of bed, poured my coffee and took it with me as I headed into bathe. I had my morning ablutions finished and sat down at Theodora's dressing table just before Claudette walked back in the door, twenty minutes later.

"I want to wear the blond wig with the Marcel wave."

"Oui, mademoiselle." Her tone was patronizing, and she gave me a slight curtsy.

By eight o'clock I was dressed. The look was very masculine, but it felt wonderful to be back in trousers again and in my own shoes. The suit reminded me a great deal of the navy-blue pin striped suit that Georgie had been wearing the first time I saw him dressed as a man. It was a looser cut and the jacket was designed to stand open rather than be buttoned. The shirt was silk instead of cotton and I wore my own undershirt beneath it. The hat was an exaggerated version of a man's hat, slightly taller and the brim just a bit wider. Unlike men's hats, it had combs inside to help hold it in place. At first, I wondered why someone hadn't thought to put them in men's hats. Then I remembered that men had a propensity to lose their hair and I understood why it would be pointless.

"You need the ring that Seedy is wearing to finish off this ensemble, but…" she trailed off.

"But right now, it is serving a better purpose where it is. Especially since Detective Lister is in the house," I said, as I made my way to the door. "I should have just enough time to grab some breakfast before we go."

I bounded down the hall and stairs. It was the first time I hadn't had to act like a lady in nearly a week. I gathered my composure before entering the dining room. Hugo was seated at the table reading one of the three morning newspapers scattered over the table-top and Seedy was filling her plate from the chafing dishes on the sideboard. She was dressed in my night table hijab ensemble.

"Good morning, all," I said brightly.

Hugo looked up over his paper and smiled. "Good Morning."

"Well aren't you the pair," Seedy said, in a rather sing-songy tone.

"Excuse me?" I asked, as I began to fill my plate.

Seedy carried her plate to the table, set it down and picked up one of the newspapers. She folded it in half and then into quarters.

"Nice picture," she said, holding it up so I could see. It

was the picture with Hugo's arm around my waist as we smiled and waved to last night's cheering crowd. She began to read. "Rodrick Crawford announced last evening, at a party hosted by German industrialist Heinrich Von Müller and his wife, that Hollywood's hottest movie star, Theodora Desmond, would co-star with a dashing Hollywood newcomer, Hugo Wainwright, in his upcoming talkie, *Samson and Delilah*. Sources report that Mr. Wainwright spent the night at Miss Desmond's home last evening. Will it be love songs and movie reels for the young Hollywood couple?" She slapped the paper down on the table and sat giving me a mischievous smirk.

Hugo sprayed the coffee he was drinking halfway across the table, just as the telephone rang. A moment later, Wallace entered the room. "It is Mr. Crawford on the telephone. He wishes to speak with you, Miss Desmond."

Hugo looked worried as I lifted the extension at the end of the sideboard. You could hear RC's screams from across the room the moment I said, "Hello." I held the telephone away from my ear. When I heard RC pause to take a breath, I interjected, "We will be there in thirty minutes." He began to protest, wanting us there quicker. "Are the press at your gates?" I asked.

Everyone could hear him scream, "NO," almost to the front door.

"They are at mine so we will have to slip away from them. It will take every bit of a half hour. See you then." And I hung up.

"Oh my," Hugo said, still dabbing at the table cloth in a futile attempt to remove the coffee spots. "This isn't good."

"On the contrary my dear, Hugo. Things couldn't be better."

Seedy laughed at the confusion on Hugo's face.

The clock began to strike nine.

"Battle stations," I said, as I finished my toast and took a quick sip of coffee. Again, Hugo looked confused. Seedy headed towards the front door.

"Come on," I said to Hugo, as I bounded towards the kitchen door. Hugo was hot on my heels. It felt grand striding across the side lawn towards the garage. When I reached the first garage door, I could hear the motor running behind it. Seconds later, Hugo was standing beside me, breathing hard.

"You move fast."

I didn't answer. I was watching the front of the house. Randel had the door to the Daimler open. The front door to the house opened and Seedy stepped out onto the porch. At the front gate, a crowd of photographers tried to get pictures. Seedy waved to the crowd and a roar rose up. She marched down the steps and Randel helped her in.

I turned to Hugo, "Help me get this door up."

When the door was fully open, Hugo let out a long whistle of approval. "That is one beautiful automobile."

"Get in!" I aimed for the driver's seat. The top was down, so I placed one hand on the low-slung door and vaulted into the cockpit. Following my lead, Hugo did the same.

"Those clothes really have changed your personality. I've never seen a woman leap over a door before."

I chose to ignore the comment. Truth was I was so excited to drive the car, that I hadn't even thought about how a woman would have gotten into the seat. The motor hummed as I goosed the throttle. The Daimler was moving now. I could see Mr. Truman opening the gates. The press was snapping pictures and shouting questions towards the big car. But all anyone could see was Randel as he looked ahead. All the shades were drawn, and the privacy shield was up. Randel paused longer than necessary to make sure he had everyone's attention. Then he turned left, pulling the big car

The Reluctant Doppelganger

out into the street.

"What's going on?"

"It's our diversion." I looked over at him with a smile and gave him a quick wink.

Suddenly the members of the press were disappearing from the front gates, running down the street in the direction Randel had driven. Mr. Truman stood in the middle of the opening. He pulled out a red bandana and waved it furiously up and down.

"That's our cue."

I released the brake, put the car in gear, and gunned the throttle. Instantly we were a bright red blur roaring out of the garage and down the driveway. Mr. Truman jumped into his gate house, moving fast for an older gent. We shot through the gates and turned right onto the street. I made the corner without either braking or hitting the curb. The right-hand drive took a bit of getting used to, so I was doubly glad when we didn't hit the curb on the turn. The Mercedes' big engine purred like a kitten as it picked up speed.

In no time, we were out of sight of the house, flying down the motorway. The gauge read seventy. I wasn't sure if that was miles or kilometers per hour, but whatever it was, it was fast. I looked over at Hugo and there was a huge joyous grin on his face.

"Oh, you are just going to have to let me give it a try some time," Hugo shouted over the wind and the motor.

Even with the very circuitous route we had taken, at the speed we'd been traveling, we made it to RC's house in record time. I could see the massive gates looming before us. I'm guessing the gatekeeper figured out who was headed for the house at break neck speed and pushed the lever on the electronic gate opener. Now it was a race. Could the gates open before we got there, or would I have to stop and wait on them. As I was hoping, the gates would win the race. The

Mercedes shot through the opening and gravel flew as we bolted up the driveway towards the house, past a crew of grounds-keepers hard at work on the front lawn. I pulled up in front of the house and came to a rather sudden stop.

Hugo bounded out of the car just the way he'd gotten in. He was almost to the front door when he looked back and realized I was still seated behind the wheel. "Something wrong?"

"Answer a question for me," I called out. "Is it Hugo or John who has forgotten his manners?"

Hugo laughed. He walked quickly back to the car, still smiling. He opened the door and extended his hand. "So now you've decided to get dainty on me," he smirked.

I turned my legs out of the car. He took my hand and gave my arm an almighty tug. I flew out of the car landing on my feet.

"You cad!" I was laughing now. "What do you bet he is sitting on his Throne of Power."

We were both still laughing when we reached the front door. It opened the moment we stepped in front of it.

23

We were ushered into RC's study on the first floor opposite the spot where the coat-check stand appears when needed. The room was cozy with an immense window that looked out onto the front lawn where a swimming pool-sized water fountain stood at its heart. There, seated behind a heavy carved wooden desk, sat RC, and yes, he was perched upon his golden, jewel-encrusted Throne of Power. Anger radiated off him. He stood as I entered.

"What the devil are you wearing, Theo!" he bellowed. "You look like a man."

"I am wearing Coco Chanel. She has an entire new line of women's versions of men's clothes. They worked perfectly this morning when I wished not to be mobbed by the press."

"And that is precisely what I wanted to talk to you both about. Why in the world would you allow Hugo here to be seen staying at your house last night?"

RC didn't care that he stayed. He cared that he had been seen. Hugo squeezed my hand in concern. I hadn't been aware until that moment that we were still holding hands and had been since he helped me out of the car. I let go.

"I did it because there was a mob of press at my front gate when we arrived back at the house. I knew that they would be at the Detective's residence, too. I assumed that Detective Lister lives in an apartment and not a high-rise with a doorman. Since he has never had to deal with the press on this level, I thought that he might be caught off guard and say something that those vultures could misconstrue. Have you arranged for a new place for him to live?" I caught him with my question before he could continue to rant.

"Well, no."

"Then until you can, he will stay at my home."

Hugo started to interject but RC cut him off.

"You can't have Mr. Wainwright living at your house. Have you read the papers? Have you seen the scandal it has already caused?"

"Oh RC, you couldn't buy publicity like this. It has already guaranteed that *Samson and Delilah* will be a monumental success. In the copy I read, they called Hugo 'dashing.' That means the press already likes him and he hasn't uttered a single word in your talkie yet. My guess is, now that you've been given the opportunity, you will be playing up the angle of, what was it they said, 'love songs and movie reels?'"

I knew I had won because I knew how men like RC thought. I bet he'd already been on the telephone to my father planning out everything. Hugo and I sat down in the two chairs in front of RC's desk. He knew I was right, but he wasn't ready to concede quite yet, so I needed to let him bluster on.

I was looking out the window at the fountain shooting a stream of water at least twenty feet in the air. I was thinking how wonderful it would be to sit behind RC's desk and be mesmerized by its grace and beauty when a truck pulled in front of my view. Two men were in the cab and two younger men sat on the open tailgate. A large banner attached to the

wooden slatted sides read, "Eales Bros. Electrical Services."
"Are you expecting electricians, RC?"

He looked out the window. "Good, it's about time they got
here. Seems you were correct, my dear. There is a short in
the electrical wiring on the tennis court. I know you saw the
lights going on and off the night poor Reggie died. But then
the next day it shorted out altogether. I had the gardeners
look at it and they told me the fuse box that controls the
tennis court lights was charred. I tried to call an electrical
service contractor the very next day, but it seems that every
one of them has been finishing up the work on the new
Beverly Wilshire Hotel. They have just now been able to get
to me."

I shot to my feet. "A short in the wiring on the tennis
court!" I flew from the room. I was out the front door and
sprinting my way around the house when suddenly Hugo
was at my side, matching me stride for stride. Only this
wasn't Hugo Wainwright; it was Detective John Lister.
Puffing well behind us was RC.

When we reached the tennis court, an older gentleman was
down on his knees. He had the door to the fuse box open and
was peering inside. The other mature man was stooped over
him with one hand on his knee and the other holding a
battery powered light. The two younger men who had been
riding in the back of the truck were hunched low to the
ground as they walked from one lamp pole to the next.

"Here is the problem," the young man on the far side of the
court called out.

I ran to see what he was looking at. It was then they
noticed us.

"Here, here," the older man in front of the fuse box yelled,
"What's the meaning of this?"

As I reached the point where the young man was standing,
I answered, "This is Detective John Lister with the Beverly

Hills police department," I said, pointing to Hugo. "That is Mr. Rodrick Crawford, owner of this property and currently your employer," pointing towards RC. "And I am Theodora Desmond."

"I'll be," said the young man as he looked hard. "It really is Theodora Desmond in them men's clothes."

Instantly, I felt four sets of eyes sizing me up. I continued on, "There was a man killed right here the other night. He was electrocuted. And, as of yet, the police haven't been able to figure out how. Would you please show me what you've found?"

"Yes ma'am," the young man said. "But the only way this could have electrocuted anyone is if he was holding on to it."

He pointed down to where a black wire protruded from the ground. Its insulation was frayed, and I could see that a good portion of the copper wire inside had been exposed and was charred. It was only about an eighth of an inch away from the chain-link fence, but it was clearly not touching it. While I was investigating the wire, Lister moved over and began inspecting it closely too. Our faces were inches apart.

"Montgrieve was on the other side, so he couldn't have reached back and grabbed it by accident," Lister said.

"You're right about that," I continued to stare at the exposed wire. Then it hit me, and I stood bolt upright. I shoved my hand in my pocket and pulled out a wad of bills. I looked at the young man next to me whose eyes were now fixed on the money. "I'll give you five dollars if you can go fetch the head gardener who is working in the front lawn by the fountain and have him back here in less than five minutes." His eyes lit up and he took off in a dead run.

"What's going on?"

Before I could answer him, RC spoke up, "What the devil are you doing with all that cash in a jacket pocket?"

I was still holding the money. "Well, Coco Chanel may

have designed a line of men's clothes for women, but she didn't design a wallet to go with them," I shrugged.

Running back at break neck speed came the two men. When he reached me, I peeled off a five-dollar bill and handed it to the young electrician's assistant, who was now panting hard. He took it gratefully. I looked at the gardener.

"Is there a watering system that waters the landscaping around the tennis court?"

"Yes, sir," he answered and then noticed I wasn't a sir. "Yes, ma'am, I mean."

"Where are the valves that turn it on?"

"In a little house, next to the back wall, hidden by those bushes down there," and he pointed.

"There is a five-dollar bill for you if you can get the water turned on around the tennis court in less than five minutes. Then leave it on until I wave at you."

The man smiled and tore out for the little house behind the shrubs.

"What on earth is going on?" demanded RC.

"I'm not sure yet, but I have a hunch. Everyone should stand back. We don't want to get soaked. And be sure that fuse box is turned off." I said to the older gentleman now getting up from the ground.

"Already done."

There was a hissing and sputtering as the watering system came to life. The water spouts had been cleverly hidden behind the shrubbery. A fan of water sprayed out of each. The fans were pointed away from the tennis court, thereby watering the entire flower bed. All except one. The water coming from it came out in a stream that shot through the fence and onto the court itself. Detective Lister and I moved in closer to it. The pressurized stream of water was pushing the exposed wire against the fence.

"There's your killer, Detective."

"I'll be damned, you're right. Montgrieve was passed out from booze and drugs when the gardeners turned on the water. This broken valve acted as a conduit between the live wire and the fence. The fence was electrified until the fuse tripped."

I waved back at the gardener and the water shut off.

"That brings me to my next suspicion."

"What's that?"

"RC," I called across the court. "Where is your closest stash of bar glasses?"

He thought for a minute and called back, "Under the bar at the pool. Why?"

I peeled off another five-dollar bill.

"Give this to the gardener when he gets back up here." I gave the bill to the young electrician standing next to me.

"I'll show you," I called back to RC. "Let's go." I took off back across the lawn in the direction of the pool.

When we reached the pool bar the first cabinet I tried was locked.

"That one has liquor in it," came RC's voice, panting from the exertion of trotting across the grounds. "Try the one next to it."

When the cabinet door opened, displayed on four deep shelves, were every kind of glass imaginable.

"Now point to the glass you found by Reggie's body," I told Lister.

He pointed to a square rocks glass and I sat one of those on top of the cabinet.

"That can't be right," said RC. "Reggie only drank Beefeater Gibson's up."

"So?" Queried Listor.

"A Gibson served up is always served in a martini glass, not a rocks glass," I said, setting a martini glass on top of the bar and pointing to it. "You know what IS served in a rocks glass?" I tapped the rim of the stubby square glass.

"What?"

"Scotch."

I let him ponder my answer for a moment. Then his eyes lit up and I smiled.

"And I found a bottle of Scotch yesterday in Reginald Montgrieve's medicine cabinet. Are you thinking what I'm thinking?"

"If you are thinking that our dead man is not Reginald Montgrieve but his twin brother Martin Musgrave, then yes, you are thinking what I'm thinking."

"That would mean…" Lister trailed off.

"That would mean that Reginald Montgrieve is still alive. And if he's alive, he would need a place to hide."

"His house!"

"My thoughts exactly," I said, nodding my head once in affirmation.

"We need to get to that house as quickly as possible."

"You've got the key."

"Let's go!"

Lister began to run towards the front of the house.

"Thanks, RC," I said, as I grabbed the man, planted a kiss on his forehead and ran after the detective.

Detective Lister was nearly to the Mercedes. I called across the distance, "You drive!" Lister turned and a huge smile came over his face as he vaulted into the driver's seat and fired up the engine. I reached the car and vaulted into the seat beside him.

"My dear Miss Desmond, I don't know what has gotten into you," he said, with a smile

"I would say the thrill of the chase."

And with that, gravel flew into the air as the detective punched the throttle and we shot off.

24

In less than ten minutes time, we were pulling up to the gates of Reggie's villa. I got out and pulled the latch up and pushed the gates open. I got back in the car and we took the crazy curvy driveway around to the house. Even though the day was bright and cheery, for some reason, today the house felt ominous. Detective Lister put his hand in his jacket pocket and pulled out a revolver.

"I didn't know you carried a gun."

He looked at me as if I had lost my mind. "I'm a policeman. Of course, I carry a gun."

We both got out of the car. This time we both opened our doors and climbed out warily, Lister brandishing his revolver. When we arrived at the front door, Lister put two fingers in his vest pocket and produced the key. He handed it to me while he scanned the area.

"Chivalry may not be dead, but it sure seems to be in a bad way." I said giving Lister a grimace.

"I'm a gentleman. Lady's first." And he winked.

I unlocked the door, turned the knob, and gave the heavy wooden door a shove. It creaked as it opened. I shuddered.

The Reluctant Doppelganger

I know it must have creaked yesterday when we were here, but yesterday we were searching a dead man's house for clues. Today, we were searching a murderer's house for the murderer. There was a decidedly different feel about it. We stepped inside. The dead quiet of the place was almost overwhelming.

"We need to go back to Reggie's bed chamber. I'm sure he must be hiding in the bootleggers keep, and I'm betting the entrance is behind the painting in his closet." I pointed down the hallway.

"What makes you think that?"

"Because the painting is big enough to hide a doorway and because a closet is a very strange place to display a very valuable portrait. Especially since that portrait is of Reggie and Reggie has an enormous ego."

When we reached the door to the bedroom, Detective Lister placed his ear against the door and listened for a long moment. He lifted the latch and pushed. Again, the door creaked, and shivers ran up my spine. We entered the room cautiously, with Detective Lister going first, his revolver in front of him. We both scanned the room. Detective Lister searched the bathroom, then came out carrying the bottle of Scotch.

"It's a sixty-four-year-old single malt scotch whiskey," he said, peering at the label as he came back into the room. "My guess is it's very expensive and I'm betting it's also laced with Veronal."

"Why would it be laced with Veronal?"

"I'm not sure, but since he had it in a bathroom cabinet, it's not a liquor he drinks, and it's not with all the other liquor in the bar in his study, so I'm speculating that something is different about this particular bottle. My bet is that it is laced with Veronal. I am taking it with us to get it tested."

He set the bottle on one of the night tables and we moved

towards the closet door with Detective Lister and his gun in the lead. He opened the door and, of course, it creaked.

Didn't this man own an oil can?

The Detective switched on the light. The closet appeared to be just as it was yesterday. I breathed a small sigh of relief. We moved towards the back of the room. There, standing before us, in the Dukes family tartan, was Reginald Montgrieve. He still stood beside a throne and the throne still held the golden crown with its legendary ruby. My eyes fixed on the crown. Something niggled in the back of my mind, but it wouldn't come into focus. I tugged at one side of the massive gilt frame, while Detective Lister kept his gun trained at the picture as if Reggie might jump off the canvas. The frame wouldn't budge. I tried the other side with the same result. The frame must have been six inches wide with a very ornate pattern carved into the wood. As I looked closer at the pattern, it appeared to be tree branches that encircled the entire perimeter, and, sitting on the branches were song birds. My eyes followed the tableau around the frame. Towards the top, I spotted it. The gilt on one of the bird's eyes seemed to be worn. I reached up, pressed the bird's eye and a latch released. The frame swung open about an inch. I pulled on that side of the frame. It would only open about two-feet from the wall before the edge came into contact with the massive cabinet that stood in the middle of the room.

Detective Lister was on the wrong side of the painting. He couldn't see that there was an open doorway behind the picture. I pushed the portrait back to the wall and the latch clicked into place. I motioned for the Detective to join me on my side of the room. He slid past to stand close behind me. I could feel the warmth of his body as he pressed against me. Suddenly the space seemed to be very tight. Once more, I reached up and pushed the bird's eye. The door popped loose. I pulled the frame as wide as it would go. We both moved right up to the edge of the darkened doorway. The smell of stale cigarette smoke wafted through the doorway causing my nose to rankle. I felt around just inside the door's opening. I found the light switch. I looked at Lister and he nodded. The switch had two buttons. The bottom button was down so I pressed the top button in. It gave a loud click and three bare bulbs on a dangling braided black cord illuminated a roughhewn wooden staircase.

I turned my head and leaned back to Detective Lister. He moved his ear close to my mouth.

"Just a thought. But perhaps since you have the gun you might want to go first."

The man actually snorted in my ear. We shuffled around until he was in the lead. Then he stepped through the doorway and onto the small landing.

"Be careful." I whispered.

He held up his gun and started down the steps. When we reached the bottom of the stairs, we were surrounded by brick walls on all four sides. It was a big room but not the size I had expected for a bootlegger's keep.

The bare bricked room was being used as a bedroom. There was a large four-poster bed on one wall with night-tables on either side. The tops of these nightstands were cluttered with books, eye glasses, a half-filled water glass, and even a couple of empty martini glasses with old toothpicks protruding from them. I'm sure they had formerly held skewered cocktail onions.

There were movie posters from all of Reggie's films hanging on two walls. A third wall was filled with pictures of Montgrieve with what looked like most of the women in Hollywood. There was even one of him with Theodora. In the middle of the back wall was a heavy metal door, it's white paint worn and chipped from use. I counted six locks running down its frame.

I looked around. "This obviously is not just a place where Reggie's hidden for the last few days. This is where Reggie has been sleeping for quite some time, it would appear. Why in the world would such a publicly known figure sleep in a basement?"

"In my experience, people live in confined and hidden spaces in order to instill a sense of security. To feel secure from something or most commonly, someone they fear."

"What would Reggie have been afraid of?"

"Something or someone that might attack him while he slept."

I noticed, peeking out from under one of the nightstands, was a thick book. I pulled it out, sat on the bed, and started leafing through it. It was a family photo album. The older pictures were all taken at either a photography studio or at carnivals and fairs where patrons posed for pictures with giant painted scenes behind them. Towards the middle of the album, pictures began to look like snapshots made with a Kodak Brownie. There were several pictures of the two brothers with an older man I assumed was their father. There were many pictures of jewelry. There was one picture where the older man was holding what looked to be a jewel encrusted crown, one worn by a princess or perhaps a queen. Someone had written at the bottom, "Out With The Old." In the picture next to it was the older man holding a different jeweled crown. This one was captioned, "In With The New."

"What do you think this means?"

Lister looked at the two pictures for a long while. "I think that this was a family of jewelers. Jewelers to Kings and Queens. In this case, one queen was out and a new one has taken over. The old crown is redesigned for a new Queen. Monarchies cannot afford all new jewels every time one changes or is overthrown. So, they use master craftsmen to

The Reluctant Doppelganger

recreate them. Much cheaper in the long run."

"I'm sure you're right. I had never really given it much thought."

I continued looking through the book. By now, Detective Lister had become interested and sat down beside me on the bed. We both fingered through the life of a man I now knew to be Tommy "Reggie" Musgrave, his twin brother Martin, and their father, whose name I did not know. On the next to the last page of the album, there were two pictures, again side by side. The man in each picture appeared to be the same man but I knew by having looked at all the previous photos that one was Reggie and the other Martin. I had, without knowing it, begun to be able to tell the difference between the two. This time they were not dressed alike. But each of them was sitting in the same location, a stone room with what looked to be three chairs with holes cut out of the bottoms. Charlie's castle's medieval privy. One brother must have posed for the picture while the other brother took the snapshot. In each photo the man looked overjoyed sitting on the middle seat and pulling a face for the camera. And the man in each picture wore a crown. A crown that looked just like the one in the portrait that covered the door to the bootlegger's keep, a golden medieval crown with a mammoth burnished ruby at its crest. Tommy and Martin Musgrave had found the long-lost crown with the giant jewel known as the "Rose of Kintyre." On the last page of the album were only two pictures. One showed two cigarette lighters, two cigarette cases inlaid with mother of pearl, two sets of cufflinks, two tie bars and two signet rings, each bearing a monogram of either an M or a T. I knew that all the items in the photo were made of solid gold having seen Reggie's cigarette case and lighter. The second picture featured only a single object: the "Rose of Kintyre".

"Oh, my God!" I exclaimed. "The cigarette case and the

lighter you have in custody were made from that amazing piece of history. I can't believe they would do such a thing."

"Damn! Rather than answering all of our questions, this just creates more." Lister looked dejected.

"I'm not so sure of that. This may answer most of the questions, if we can fill in just a few missing pieces of the puzzle. When the crown was discovered, the two brothers were as thick as thieves, so to speak. Using the crown, they made two of everything. But there was only one ruby. Somehow, my guess is, Reggie ended up holding onto the ruby. Then he came to America with the Duke, stole money from his Grace, and stayed. He must have brought the ruby with him. When he didn't return, maybe his brother thought he died. His brother went on to become very successful designing elaborate costume jewelry."

Lister picked up the story, "Until the day he learns his brother is alive, living in America, and a famous film star. That's when he realizes he has been double-crossed. He writes his brother, threatening him. That scares Reggie, who moves into the bootlegger's keep. Sounds a little farfetched to me. Doesn't it to you?"

"They say truth is stranger than fiction." I looked back over to the door with all the locks. "Do you think that leads to a tunnel that opens up on the far side of the back wall?"

"Only one way to find out." Lister walked to the door and pulled it open.

I couldn't see inside. The door was blocking my view.

"Holy Cow!" Lister let out a long whistle.

I hopped off the bed and walked around the door. "Now this was what I was expecting when I thought of a bootlegger's keep." It was an enormous underground warehouse. And on the far side were double doors.

"I would imagine that's your outside entrance," Lister said.

"So, I'm guessing this bedroom was maybe the accounting

office?"

"That sounds about right. We might as well go over there and see if that is really a door to the outside, and if so, exactly where outside it is."

We started across the warehouse when I thought of something. "I didn't see you unbolt any of the locks. Did you turn the lights on when you opened the door?"

"Nope, they were already on."

"Then I bet Reggie was here when we got here. When he heard us trying to figure out how to open up the painting, he made a hasty exit."

"Quick, then! Let's see if he's still around." We broke into a run. When we reached the door, we found it too, to be unlocked. We pulled it open. The exterior of the door had been made to look like the wall that surrounded it. The seams to the door were carefully camouflaged with the placement of two palm trees. One would have to be standing looking right at the doors themselves in order to see them. There were only a few footprints that led from the door to one of the palm trees.

"Look! He climbed the tree and hopped over to the wall. I'm betting he headed for the front gate."

"He still might be on the grounds. Remember RC saying that the estate is twenty acres and most of the land was behind the house."

For a big man, Detective Lister moved like a flash of lightning. He shot out of the open door; monkey walked up the smooth bark of the palm tree and hopped up on top of the wall. He stood with his hand shielding his eyes as he scanned the estate.

"Nope. He's long gone. I need to get some men posted out here in case he tries to come back." With that, he leaned out and placed the palm of his hand on the tree trunk, then, lowering his other hand to the top of the wall, he lifted his body into mid-air, balancing there for a long moment, finally lowering himself slowly and gracefully to the ground. It was an amazing display of strength.

Once back inside, the Detective closed the doors and bolted them. We retraced our path back to the hidden bed chamber. Lister locked all of the locks on the door that led into the warehouse. As we started back up the wooden steps, I ran back and collected the photo album. I wasn't sure why, but my gut told me it was important. I switched off the lights and pushed the painting back into place until it clicked.

Detective Lister found the telephone and made arrangements for uniformed policemen to be posted at the front gates, around the perimeter of the house and at the hidden entrance along the back wall.

I telephoned home and Seedy answered. I told her that Detective Lister and I were on our way back and would like Mrs. Reid to prepare lunch for at least a dozen. I also wanted to know if there were reporters still in front of the house. Seedy informed me that the reporters had gone after it had registered on them that they had been duped and Theodora Desmond and Hugo Wainwright had both been in the shiny red Mercedes that shot out of the driveway and had gone in the opposite direction.

"Seedy, would you call RC and see if he can contact the Duke and Viscount and ask them if they might be able to attend lunch? And please make sure Mr. Truman knows we are coming. The last thing I want to do is tarry at the gates in case there might be any stragglers from the press." With a quick, "See you in a bit," I hung up.

25

I drove us back to the house. Once there, Claudette insisted that I change. Leaving Hugo in the long gallery, I made my way to my room. There, my mannish clothing was stripped away, the blonde Marcel wave was gone, and I was back to a bob. Claudette brought out the Chanel black dress with the huge white collar. I nixed it, remembering what a nuisance that collar had been the night we were at the police station. Instead, I opted for a simple silk sheath. It was the barest hint of jade green. It had a matching wide brimmed silk hat, but I passed on it. The look was completed with a three-strand pearl choker.

The red-cradled telephone rang, and Claudette picked it up. Wallace was announcing that our guests had arrived, and he had put them in the long gallery with Mr. Wainwright. He also told Claudette that Mrs. Reid was ready with lunch.

"Have Wallace show everyone in the long gallery down to the dining room. And have everyone in the household meet us there as well."

"You want the servants there too? To dine? Are you sure, mademoiselle?"

"Yes, Claudette, the detective and I have some news and I want everyone there. I don't want to have to say everything twice."

When Claudette and I reached the steps, I could see everyone was standing in the foyer. Seedy was in the doorway of the dining room giving directions to whom I assumed were Georgie and Randel on the other side. My father and Gertie were among the guests who arrived while I was dressing. That put our number right at twelve.

"There! It's done," Seedy pronounced.

As I stepped off the bottom step clutching the photo album under my arm, it was Hugo's hand that came up to assist me. "Would you allow me to carry that for you?"

I handed him the album. "Thank you, kind sir." I nodded at Hugo as he took the book from me. We took up our places at the rear of the procession that Seedy was now herding into the dining room.

My father was holding Gertie's hand. First, they were together at the party, now at lunch? Something was up. They were right in front of me in the line. My mind was working on the possibilities when Gertie leaned back.

"That girl is a wonder at her job. She's a natural at taking charge and getting things done."

I smiled. Seedy really had come to life in the position of the personal secretary.

If anyone objected to me putting everybody in the same room for a meal, they kept their thoughts to themselves. Once everyone was almost finished eating, I pulled the photo album over in front of me.

"Detective Lister and I, with the help of RC, have made a few discoveries today. Since everyone in this room has been involved with at least a part of this tragic chain of events, I thought it would be appropriate to let everyone in on those discoveries. The death of the man we all believed to be

The Reluctant Doppelganger

Reginald Montgrieve was an accident. He was electrocuted by an exposed lamppost wire and a misaligned watering system outlet. The pressurized water forced a live electrical wire into the metal chain-linked fence, thereby electrifying the entire tennis court enclosure. The man police believed was Reggie had been drugged and had passed out while leaning against the fence for support."

"What the devil do you mean, 'The man we thought was Reggie'?" Father demanded to know.

It was Lister who spoke now, "The man we've all thought was Reginald Montgrieve was, in fact, his identical twin brother, Martin Musgrave. Reggie's name used to be Thomas Musgrave before he took Reginald Montgrieve as his stage name." Everyone began to speak at once. Detective Lister raised his hand to quiet them. "Let us explain and I think you will have most of the answers to your questions." The room fell quiet. "We think the motive for it all is one of the oldest in the book. Greed."

I opened the album to the pictures of Tommy and Martin each wearing the crown. "We are not sure when, but we are guessing it was shortly before the Duke brought Tommy Musgrave, as he was known then, to New York as his valet. Tommy and his brother Martin found the long-lost crown that held the Rose of Kintyre in one of the castle's medieval privies."

The Duke and Viscount both began to speak at once. Lister again raised his hand to silence them. I went to remove the pictures from the album to show them, when a letter wedged behind one of the photos fell to the floor. Lister bent to retrieve the letter as I passed both pictures over to the Duke and the Viscount. Everyone near crowded around to see.

"Due to their upbringing as jewelers, I'm sad to say, they didn't view the crown as an artifact. They only viewed it with a monetary eye and with a vision of how it could be redesigned." Detective Lister went on with a hint of regret in his voice. "Together they removed the ruby from the crown. They melted down the gold crown and made themselves several personal items from it."

I pushed the pictures of the cufflinks, cigarette cases, signet rings and lighters across the table so everyone could see them. There was a good deal of muttering and head shaking.

"We think Martin came to the states to have it out with his brother over the ruby," I was saying. But before I could continue, Lister put his hand on top of mine. I looked up, and he was reading the unfolded letter.

He began to read aloud. "Brother, I hope this finds you well. After so many years apart it seems strange for me to finally speak to you once more. I know we had our differences after Father died. You told me he said nothing to you of his sack of treasures the day he left this world. But my path crossed that of our father's former housekeeper two weeks past. She told me that on his death bed he gave you a leather pouch. I knew immediately that you had lied to me. That pouch contained the jewels that Father spent his entire life collecting, one by one, from the arrogant and pompous aristocracy all across Europe. You have chosen to cheat me out of my share of our family's legacy. You laid claim to the ruby because you found the crown, and I thought that fair; but to cheat me out of my inheritance is the act of a scoundrel, brother or not. I demand my fair share and I am coming to America to get it."

"It sounds to me like their father was stealing jewels from his clients," The Duke ranted.

Everyone was nodding in agreement.

"But each brother was wealthy in his own right. I am somewhat puzzled why they would bicker over a few jewels."

"It's like Mr. Wainwright said, 'greed' can make men do

horrible things." The Duke's rage had toned itself down to mere fuming.

"We now have another answer to one of our unanswered questions." Detective Lister was smiling at me now. "Why he had waited so many years before coming after the Rose of Kintyre. He wasn't after the ruby at all."

"How did he get the Veronal bottle with my finger prints out of my studio?" When I looked up at Georgie, I saw that Randel had his arm around his shoulder holding him close, as if he were protecting him. Somehow that just seemed right to me.

"That one is easy," I said. "He had been planning this encounter with his brother for some while. He knew he was coming. He planned to drug his brother and leave him to be found in a public place. He would switch out his brother's identification papers for his own. His brother would be arrested for drugs or public drunk, it didn't matter which. Everyone would think it was Reggie being arrested. That would give the real Reggie time to flee using Martin's identification papers. He must have seen the Veronal bottle on one of his trips to your studio. The last time he was there he dumped the beads into the drawer and took the bottle. I'm sure if he'd known the beads were twenty-four karat gold, he'd have taken those as well."

"Why would he want to change identities with his brother? He's famous." RC queried.

It was my father who answered. "Reggie is getting old. He's been playing the handsome leading man for nearly two decades. The movie roles were coming further apart, and he didn't have the voice for the theater or talkies. All that would be left for him would be character roles. He saw those as beneath him. Pride goeth before a fall. He saw the handwriting on the wall. I'd bet he'd already converted all his American assets to precious metals and gems. He's comfortable with those and knows how to trade in them as easily as cash. Once he was in Europe, he could just disappear."

Detective Lister nodded his agreement.

"The question Detective Lister and I haven't been able to answer is, why didn't he follow through with his plan? Granted, his brother died by accident; but why didn't he just leave? He has had nearly a week. He could have been on a boat to anywhere in the world by now, but instead he's stayed around. We know he was at his house this morning. Thanks to Randel, we found the bootlegger's keep." Randel smiled and gave me the thumbs up sign. "That's where he's been hiding."

The red-cradled telephone rang, and everyone gave a little jump. Since everyone else was in this room, it had to be the front gate and Mr. Truman. Seedy was closest and picked up the handset. She listened briefly and said, "Thank you, Mr. Truman." Then hung up. "Mr. Truman says that one of the reporters has climbed over the wall and is now on the grounds."

"I doubt he suspects so many people are in the house. Let's go get him," my father said as he rose. Everyone else followed suit.

"I'm not so sure this is a good idea," Detective Lister admonished.

"Poppycock!" grizzled RC. "He's the one that entered private property. He deserves what he gets."

Everyone moved out of the dining room in two different directions. Some headed for the front door and the rest made their way through to the kitchen door.

The gang at the front door caught sight of the reporter first, striding across the grounds near the garages. They yelled at him as they began to give chase. When the man saw them coming at him, he broke into a run. He ran past the garages

The Reluctant Doppelganger

aiming for the back of the estate. He was running right for us as we came out of the kitchen. He tried to turn and bolt in a different direction but tripped on his own feet and went down hard.

Detective Lister was the first to reach the man who was lying face down in the grass, panting. He grabbed the man roughly around the shoulders and rolled him over. The rest of us gasped in surprise to see Reginald Montgrieve. Detective Lister pulled Reggie to his feet, then escorted him back into the house.

"Where's my ruby?" bellowed the Duke. I guess greed wasn't just limited to the Musgrave brothers.

While Wallace called the police station, Detective Lister quieted everyone, then turned his attention to Reggie.

"So, Mr. Montgrieve, do you want to tell us what's going on?"

"I've got nothing to say," Reggie said, biting out each word.

After that, Reggie just sat there fuming. When the two policemen arrived, they took Reginald Montgrieve by the arms and led him to the front door. Everyone followed behind. When we reached the front landing, we could see a police wagon waiting with its doors open on the driveway below.

"Wait just a minute officers," I said, just before they started down the stairs with Reggie. "I just have to ask you Reggie, why in the world have you waited around here? You could have been long gone?"

Straight away his eyes went feral. He looked hard at me and then over my shoulder through the open door. I turned to see what he was looking at but there was only the open entry and it was empty. Another question came to mind. *Why did Reginald Montgrieve come to my house? This used to be his house.* Came my answer.

"Officer," I called out. "Would you check his pockets to see if he has a key?"

Reggie began to jerk. One officer held him fast, while the other patted him down. The officer slipped his fingers into one of Reggie's trouser pockets and produced a key.

"Could I see that please?" I took the key from the officer and walked over to the massive oak door, inserted the key into the lock and turned it. A giant bolt popped into view. I looked hard at Reggie. And then I knew. He must have seen the dawning of recognition on my face. Enraged he yelled, "NO!" He broke free of the two officers and ran towards me. His eyes burned with fury, anger and rage.

For me, everything slowed down. He doubled his fist and cocked back his arm, ready to strike. Out of the corner of my eye, I could see Detective Lister spring into action, but he was going to be too late. He wasn't going to be able to stop Reggie from getting to me.

As Reggie reached for me, I turned to the side and thrust my elbow up into his gut while bringing my hand up, smashing into his nose. I wasn't sure if I heard it or felt it crack. Either way, I knew I had broken it. I grabbed his still balled up fist, turned into him deeper, and flung him over my shoulder and right into the two policemen trying to come to my aid. His body bowled them over and I heard a ripping sound as I realized that the jade green raw silk dress had ripped up the seam. I didn't pause. I rushed into the house and flew up the stairs. Detective Lister was right behind me. At the top of the stairs I turned, never slowing. I passed the door to the long gallery as I made for my bed chamber. I flung the double doors wide, shot to the center of the room and turned.

Lister did the same. "What is it?" he gasped, out of breath.

"Look!" I exclaimed, breathless from running, I pointed at the portrait of Theodora.

The Reluctant Doppelganger

"It's a beautiful picture. So what?" Lister was panting, doubled over with his hands on his knees.

"It's not the picture. Reggie gave me that frame. He told me they were paste."

At the top of the frame was the massive oval ruby as big as a chicken's egg. The rest of the frame was covered with gems and pearls of every conceivable shape, size, and color.

"That's why Reggie didn't leave town."

"Oh, my God!"

Soon everyone but the two policemen and Reggie had filed into the room. The room echoed with a cacophony of stunned voices.

After everyone had been cleared out of the room save Lister and me, I said, "It really was shear genius. Hidden in plain sight where no one would think to search."

"Yes, but it was still a big risk."

"His entire family were master jewel thieves. They were used to taking big risks. You know, I've always hated that frame because I thought it was garish. Now that I know they are real I am beginning to see its appeal." I smiled.

"I see just how you rich people really are. If it's valuable, it's pretty." He grinned at me.

I slugged him in the arm.

"Ouch!" he just laughed, rubbing his bicep.

26

We had only learned two things from Reggie. He talked Martin into coming to the party dressed alike so they could create mischief like they did in their youth. And that the four one-hundred-dollar bills had been placed in Martin's pocket after he'd passed out from the Veronal-laced Scotch. He'd told Detective Lister that it was to cover his brother's half of the jewels.

Four days after his apprehension, Reginald Montgrieve died in jail. He had been taken off Veronal and went into serious withdrawal. On the fourth morning, he was found dead in his cell having choked to death on his own emesis.

After his death, it was discovered that all of Reggie's bank accounts had indeed been emptied and closed. Going on my father's hunch that Reggie had converted all his wealth to precious metals and jewels, RC literally tore Reggie's villa apart looking for them. The upside is that the villa has been completely remodeled. The horn chandeliers with their stained-glass globes along with all of the old rustic wood has been replaced with sleek, modern, art deco chrome and glass. It is soon to be the residence of one Hugo Wainwright.

The Reluctant Doppelganger

Georgie's gold bead was returned to him and all the charges against him were dismissed. That meant I got my two-thousand dollars bail money back, too.

Detective Lister left the police force the day after Reggie died. He took a lot of ribbing from his former colleagues and friends over the next few weeks as he publicly and legally became Hugo Wainwright.

The Rose of Kintyre was returned to the Duke and his family. There was no way to determine the rightful owners of all the other gems; since they had been freely given to me by their last known owner, the courts awarded the jewels to me. I had them appraised so they could be insured. Remember, the four hundred bucks? Turns out that was only a tiny fraction of what the jewels were actually worth.

Samson and Delilah took just over four months to shoot, twice as long as any silent movie. Then it took another three months to edit, add musical tracks, and re-record some scenes where the sound didn't work correctly. They were calling these re-takes. It appeared that "talkies" took a lot longer to make and they were going to cost a great deal more to produce. But, like Pandora's box, once the lid had been opened, there was no closing it again. Talkie's are here to stay.

I was initially worried about Delilah's costumes, but Georgie advised me to throw a temper tantrum and refuse to wear anything that might "impugn the character of Theodora Desmond." Much to my amazement it worked. A large ruffle was added to every harem-style costume which included most of Delilah's wardrobe. It made the job of hiding my rather sizable credentials much easier.

Edward William Morgan was born on April 1, 1928. I hoped sincerely that being born on April Fool's day wasn't a bad omen. Molly had told me in a letter that if the baby was a boy, she was going to name him after me. I wondered on that day if little Edward would ever know his mom was really Theodora Desmond, the famous movie star, or would he be forever scarred knowing that his crazy namesake uncle was the infamous Theodora Desmond. My father and Gertie had gone to Texas for a visit when the baby was born. Yes, Father and Gertie were officially seeing each other. At first, I wasn't sure how I felt about that, but later I decided that she had been the closest thing to a mother I'd ever had. They were good for each other. Besides, she kept him occupied and out of my hair.

The jewels in the frame that surrounded Theodora's portrait had been replaced with paste replicas for real this time. I had given the portrait its rightful place of honor, ugly frame and all, above the mantel in the long gallery. In its place in Theodora's bed chamber now hung the painting of Reginald Montgrieve. RC was going to burn it, but I came to its rescue. RC was still mad at Reggie for hiding his money where he couldn't find it. The thought of Reggie thumbing his nose at the aristocracy until the end of time amused me. I often caught Claudette looking at it. She said he had nice legs, and I had to agree.

27

Tonight, at eight o'clock is the premier of *Samson and Delilah* at Grauman's Chinese Theater. Everyone has been on pins and needles all day. I arranged for the entire household to attend the opening and even borrowed two of the studio limousines to carry them to the theater. Georgie made sure they all had the proper attire for the evening, and I got VIP tickets on the main floor for each of them.

It had taken Seedy several inquiries, but she finally was able to run down the taxi driver who had brought us to the house that first morning. His name was Gerald Thorn and I hired him to drive the Daimler that evening so Randel could attend the movie along with everyone else.

Georgie had been telling me for months that he was working on something special for me to wear tonight. He commanded that I be in my room no later than five-thirty, having eaten enough beforehand that my stomach wouldn't make unladylike noises during the movie, but not so much that I might appear bloated. He said I could eat all I wanted at RC's opening night party after the movie; so it appeared that it was all right with Georgie if I made a pig of myself in front of hundreds of people at a party, but it was unheard of that my stomach should gurgle during the movie. I just did as I was told.

Claudette started my make-up at five-thirty sharp. Delilah had been a brunette, and tonight I was to be a brunette too. A brunette with a Marcel wave. At six-fifteen, Georgie arrived with a hanger covered by a long cloth dress bag and a large black velvet box.

"I want to see," I said excitedly.

"First things first." He held up my new custom-made foundation garment.

Getting into said foundation garments had not gotten any simpler in the last six months. There were so many different versions and it was always a struggle, but at least it didn't require me to poke holes in my credentials. Once I was secured into this one, he unveiled the dress. It was mother of pearl. The entire dress was beaded from top to bottom with shimmering mother of pearl beads. It seems that Georgie, Claudette, Mrs. Reid, and two other seamstresses had spent the better part of two months beading the gown by hand. The simple sheath dress was backless, sleeveless and had a décolletage that dropped nearly to my navel.

I stepped into the dress. Georgie and Claudette worked it up past the foundation garment until I put one arm in, then the other. When the dress finally came to rest on my shoulders, I was startled by how heavy it was. Now it was time to accessorize. First came the pearls — the long strand of small pearls that fell all the way down to just above the dramatically low neckline and lay cool against my bare skin. No one ever seemed to notice I had no cleavage. Next, Georgie produced the large black velvet box.

"The Duke had this made for his wife. It is with the Duchess' permission and blessing that you wear it tonight."

He held the box in front of him in one palm, and with the

other hand he opened it. There, set into a choker of marquise cut diamonds the size of your fingernail, all banded together in a spider's web of tiny seed pearls, was the Rose of Kintyre. It was an eye-popping mixture of the old and the new. The ancient unfaceted ruby polished to a burnished luster hung as a pendant at the base of the choker where its more contemporary faceted companions twinkled in the light. While Georgie held the case, Claudette removed the necklace and fastened it around my neck. And lastly, a jeweled head band with a large ostrich plume went around my forehead.

Georgie and Claudette stood back, taking in their handiwork.

"C'est magnifique!"

"Yup! Pretty damn impressive, even if I do say so myself," Georgie nodded his head in approval.

I turned to the mirror to see for myself. Looking back at me once more was Theodora Desmond. This time she portrayed the role of an angelic vision in white. This angel wore her heart for all to see. The ruby glowed like a red-hot ember. Not for the first time, I wondered to myself how beautiful women ever got past that sense of awe when they saw themselves in a mirror.

"One last thing," Georgie drawled, snapping his fingers as he stepped back out of the bedroom door. When he returned, he was carrying a huge shiny turquoise box. He set it on the bed. "It's an opening night gift from RC."

He opened the lid and folded back the paper, exposing a white fur cape. Georgie lifted it from the box.

"It's white chinchilla with bands of the same beads as your dress. It's to wear while getting out of the limousine and until you step onto the red carpet."

"I'm not sure I understand you," I said, with a puzzled look on my face. "It's to wear just to get out of the auto?"

"Yup, and then only over one shoulder. The right

shoulder. You stand looking like a bored goddess while photographers snap your picture. Just before Hugo steps up beside you, let the fur cape drop off your shoulder and slide towards the ground. Here's the tricky part. You have to catch it without showing any effort on your face and without looking down. That's why the right shoulder. Since you are right handed, it should be easier for you to snare it as it drops. As you and Hugo walk the red carpet, you drag it behind you."

Georgie placed the cape over my right shoulder.

"Give it a try."

My first two attempts failed, but on the third time, I caught it. I repeated the move several more times, catching the cape every time.

"I think she's got it," Georgie said to Claudette.

Georgie took the cape and draped it over his arm. "Like I said, its only to wear from the auto to the theater. You'll want to check it the minute you get inside." With me dressed and my instructions given, he moved to the open bedroom door. "It's time to go. Break a leg tonight. I guess that's what you say for a movie opening. It's in a theater after all." With a twinkle in his eyes and a smirk, he motioned me towards the open door with a cock of his head. "I am pretty sure Prince Charming is in the long gallery," he said, as I passed.

Prince Charming had become Georgie's pet name for Hugo. I was sure if Hugo was there, he wouldn't be alone.

When I reached the long gallery with both Georgie and Claudette in tow, Georgie stopped me just outside the doors. Claudette took hold of one doorknob and Georgie the other. Seems I was about to make an entrance. Suddenly both doors swung open and all eyes were on me. I could have sworn I heard Hugo gasp, but I'm sure it was just wishful thinking.

"Hail, Hail, the gang's all here," bellowed RC with a smile. And he was right. There was Hugo, of course, my father and

The Reluctant Doppelganger

Gertie, RC and the Duke, and Charlie with his date for the evening, Regina Banks. Regina's eyes were shooting daggers in my direction. I took that as a sign Georgie and Claudette had outdone themselves. Charlie and Regina were becoming quite the talk of the town. Would Regina Banks soon become The Viscountess Regina of Kintyre and Lorne? Only time would tell. If so, Charlie's new title would be Viscount Husband the Sixth, or would that be Husband the Sixth, The Viscount. With European aristocracy, who knew?

"What do you think of the cape?" RC asked, drawing me back from my reverie.

"Forgive my manners, RC. It is absolutely spectacular," I gushed.

"Well, I was thinking of some nice earrings, but Georgie said the cape was just what you needed."

"And as usual, Georgie was right." I smiled, first at RC and then at Georgie.

"And while we're on the matter of Georgie's must haves, I brought you these," Hugo said as he held out a long floral box.

Inside was the biggest corsage I'd ever seen. It had three white cattleya orchids surrounded by baby white roses and lily of the valley.

"I think it might be too big to wear on my dress."

"Dear God, NAW!" came Georgie's horrified drawl. "It's an arm band."

In minutes, Georgie had the floral band fastened to my left bicep. It wouldn't do for it to get in the way of the cape dropping ceremony.

"Since I'm betting you called the florist and ordered this for poor Hugo, you must have told the florist I was a float for the Rose Parade." Everyone laughed politely. "It really is beautiful," I amended.

The front drive was filled with a procession of cars, each

complete with its own chauffeur. The household had already assembled on the drive by the time we came down from the long gallery.

Mrs. Reid rushed over to me. "Oh, Miss, I've never worn such a beautiful dress." She gestured to the peacock blue silk drop-waist dress that sported a matching lace ruffle. "I just wanted to say, thank you."

There was an elderly lady I didn't recognize, but since her arm was twined through Mr. Truman's, I assumed she must be Mrs. Truman. The staff was loaded into the two studio automobiles and sent on their way.

"Those servants of yours are going to start expecting more than they are due," RC whispered to me as the cars pulled onto the road and were lost from sight.

It took three cars to convey the rest of us. RC, the Duke, my Father and Gertie rode in RC's Rolls Royce. The Viscount and Regina were in her Rolls Royce, and Hugo and I were in my Daimler. When our automobiles arrived at the theater, we were directed into our proper position in the queue. Seems the exiting of the automobiles was a show in and of itself, and there was a pecking order. Hugo and I were to be the last car to disembark. Having never done this before, I hadn't realized that this would take the better part of a half hour.

When the car in front of us, which carried RC, pulled away from the curb, it was our turn to proceed slowly, the nearly two full blocks to the red carpet. That gave the people already on the red carpet enough time to collect the proper amount of adoration and then get out of the way.

Then we were there.

"I know you are an old hand at this, but I'm kind of nervous." Hugo said.

"To tell you the truth, this feels like my first time too. So, get that smile in place, don't blink or close your eyes to the flash bulbs, and wave. Always wave." Hugo helped me put

The Reluctant Doppelganger

the fur over my right shoulder as I had been instructed.

The door opened and a hand came inside the door to help me out. The valet was standing to the side so that, as I stepped from the automobile, I would be the first thing everyone saw. As I stood up and stepped onto the red carpet, the crowd went wild. There were reporters and photographers lined up behind red velvet ropes held by brass poles all the way up both sides of the red carpet. The red carpet stretched from the curb to the front doors of the theater. Temporary bleachers had been setup to hold hundreds of people who had won tickets to the movie premiere through locally sponsored contests and give-aways. They would be sitting in the balcony and were not allowed in the theater until of the VIPs and their guests were seated. People yelled my name so I would turn to face them for a picture. There were whistles from men in the bleachers. I did as Georgie had commanded. I arranged my face as if to look consumed with ennui, as flashbulbs popped all around me. Hugo was preparing to exit the car. It was time for part two of "Theo Goes to the Movies." I turned my body the slightest bit, the cape dropped from my shoulder, and I caught it, just as planned, never reacting to the fact it had fallen. There was a thunderous uproar from the crowd and the photographers redoubled their picture taking efforts. I moved up to where Luella Parsons was broadcasting her radio show live from the red carpet.

"Oh, Theodora." She gushed.

She stood in front of a large star-shaped microphone.

"What was it like working with your new dashing co-star, Hugo Wainwright, on Colossal Studio's first talking motion picture?" She asked me, beaming.

Wow! How in the world did that woman get so much information into one statement? And that statement being a question to boot.

"Oh Luella, he is simply divine. He is just the bees-knees!" I gushed back.

Her next question was drowned out by the screams of the women. I knew, without turning, Hugo had stepped from the car. When I did turn, I saw him blowing kisses to the girls in the bleachers which caused them to scream even louder. He bounded up the carpet and offered me his arm.

Louella was not going to let him get away without asking him at least one question. "Hugo, what do you think of your first red carpet walk?"

"Just smashing, Louella. I cannot think of any other place I'd rather be." He gave a hearty wave to the crowd, then he turned his beaming smile back on Louella and gave her a wink.

I thought she might faint. He gave my arm a slight tug and my cape glided along behind me as we made our way inside.

Once inside, Hugo checked my cape and we moved to where RC and my father were waiting for us. RC took Hugo around, introducing him to the movers and shakers of Hollywood. Presumably, I already knew these people, so for me, it was just a matter of shaking everyone's hand while my father whispered their names in my ear. RC was an old hand at this game. He introduced Hugo as he worked us towards the stairs. We ascended to the third floor where the private suites were located. They were all reserved for RC tonight. They would be filled with producers, directors, and of course, movie stars. When the door opened, the huge room was truly filled to overflowing. I had forgotten about the most important people invited to the suites — investors: those who had invested in *Samson and Delilah* and those who would be investing in upcoming talkies.

Most of the people in the room had been here for quite some time. Champagne flowed like water and waiters

The Reluctant Doppelganger

serving hors d'oeuvres moved through the undulating crowd like ducks bobbing up and down on a pond. When we entered, we were given a round of applause just before the well-wishers closed in around us. Ten minutes later we were still shaking hands and kissing cheeks when the lights blinked several times, indicating that the motion picture would begin in ten minutes. The clutch of people surrounding us broke apart as they made their way to their seats. Theater ushers were now opening the massive movable wall between the private suite and the theater. We were shown to our seats as the lights began to dim. I was seated between Hugo and RC, center stage just in front of the now open wall. Best seats in the house.

The news reel was, of course, a talking news reel, a full ten minutes long. We had all come to expect those. When it finished, the theater darkened completely, music boomed as the screen lit up and the title appeared. I wasn't looking forward to this at all. I hated the way I sounded, as I told RC weeks ago, but he had just laughed and kissed me on the forehead.

RC leaned across me and motioned for Hugo to lean in. "If you want to know how successful your movie is going to be, don't watch the picture. Watch the people in the balcony. They are the true movie goers and what they think of your movie will determine its fate." Hugo gave him a firm nod and sat back up. As RC sat up, he gave me a wink.

I did as RC had told Hugo to do. I watched the balcony. That way I didn't have to watch myself as Delilah. What the balcony was seeing was a story from beginning to end. What I saw, on those rare occasions that I looked up, were scenes we had shot over and over again because I couldn't get the lines right or I had gotten distracted and lost my train of thought. Not to mention the constant starting and stopping because there were issues with the sound equipment.

Nick Hilliard

There was only one scene in this entire film I wanted to see. It had been a planned mistake on my part. *We had shot so many scenes over and over, what would one more be?* I'd thought. But it hadn't worked out that way. When I broke from the script and created my own dialogue and my own actions, the director kept the cameras rolling.

Two Philistines guards were holding Samson as he struggled. The part about his eyes having been gouged-out had been rewritten so as not to leave a flawed impression of Hollywood's newest leading heart-throb in the minds of his adoring public. The locks that Delilah had shorn while Samson slept were clutched tightly in one of her fists. A third guard crossed to Delilah where she stood across the tent. He handed her a sack of gold.

"Why, Delilah?" came Samson's anguished cry in his deep rich baritone.

"I did it for my sister's honor, but most of all I did it for the money. And even now, after all of this," she said, holding up his shorn locks, "you still love me." But even as she said it, Delilah looked visibly shaken.

"I do love you." Samson cried out, as tears filled his eyes.

This is where I had broken from the script. I was supposed to say, "I loved you too, Samson, but I loved the money more." jingling the bag of coins at him and then saying to the guards "Take him away. I'm done with him."

But instead, I threw the locks of hair and the bag of coins to the ground. I ran to Samson and threw my arms around his neck and hugged him tightly, pressing my face against his bare chest, his muscles flexing taut under my cheek as he struggled to pull himself free from the guards holding him fast. I leaned back, cupping his cheeks in my hands. I lifted my face to his and, sliding my hands behind his head, I pulled our lips together, kissing him long and deep and hard.

As I recalled the moment, I could have sworn he was

The Reluctant Doppelganger

kissing me back.

I released the kiss. Our faces were only inches apart. Looking into his face, I saw a man lost and broken. His eyes were clouded with tears that had begun to stream down his face.

"I'm sorry my love," I said, as tears filled my eyes too. "But know this Samson: I will love you until the stars grow cold."

The guard that had been standing across the room, where he had originally handed Delilah the sack of coins, now crossed back to her, pulled her away from Samson and threw her to the ground. All three guards pulled the struggling Samson from the tent. The camera panned back, showcasing Delilah alone and crumpled on the dirt floor, surrounded by Samson's tresses and a broken bag of coins littering the ground around her. The screen went dark and the words "The End" appeared.

On the day that we shot that footage, what came next was the director yelling, "Cut!"

I had begun to profusely apologize to everyone for going off script and that I knew we would need to reshoot the scene.

RC strode across the room. "Reshoot? That was brilliant! That's a print and a wrap!" He broadcasted loudly to the crew.

"But RC," I interjected. "That's not historically accurate."

RC turned to me with a look of surprise on his face, shaking his head. "Theo, honey, we are not selling history. We are selling movie tickets." Then his face split into that huge Cheshire Cat grin. "And that scene will sell movie tickets by the tens of thousands."

"But RC!" I pleaded. "I'm sure I plagiarized that line from Shakespeare or Dante or some other long dead poet."

RC waved his hand dismissively in the air as he headed off

the set.

"My dear girl, that's why we have an entire legal department."

And so it was, thinking only of myself, I had changed history – both for Samson and Delilah, as well as for the movie and perhaps even for me. Now it all depended on what the American public thought.

As the screen went dark, I found myself thinking of that stolen kiss and how no matter what happens in the future, I would always cherish it. I was shaken from my reverie as the theater erupted in applause. The sound was tumultuous.

RC leaned over, his lips just inches from my ear. "It would seem my dear, that we do indeed have a winner."

I smiled.

The orchestra in the pit had struck up once again, allowing us time to make our way to the stage for the opening night speeches.

28

My entire household, a group I'd come to think of as my merry men, were waiting backstage, smiling and ready with hugs.

RC was to speak to the movie goers first. He strode onto the stage waving both hands in the air. He walked to a microphone that had magically risen to center stage from the orchestra pit. Hugo and I stood just behind the curtain's line of sight. We would be next.

Hugo put his lips close to my ear and whispered, "I hope you don't mind, but we need to make a few changes before you head out there."

He reached over and pulled the long ostrich feather out of my head band.

"Give me your arm."

I did as he commanded, and he removed the huge floral piece that was adorning my bicep. He walked over to a big work trashcan and dropped them in. He returned to my side dusting his hands together.

I looked puzzled.

"Georgie is a master, no doubt about it. But when his

subject is already the most beautiful creature in the room, there is just no need for embellishments."

I was completely taken aback for a moment.

"I do think, my dear Mr. Wainwright, that that might be the most incredible thing anyone has ever said to me." And I'm pretty sure I blushed.

I was still staring at Hugo when RC began his introductions. I was first out waving to the crowd and gliding along just behind me in tandem was Hugo. When the audience saw us, the room erupted again, and everyone was on their feet. We bowed and waved.

RC finally motioned for everyone to sit down. As the crowd quieted, a man in the balcony yelled out, "Say it Theo! Say it!"

I had to admit I was at a loss. What was this man wanting me to say? I was going to ignore him and then it started to come from all over the theater. "Say it! Say it!"

Hugo leaned over and whispered. "I think they want you to say the line about the stars. I'd say it if I were you, before they bring the house down."

As I looked to RC, I could tell his eyes were telling me the same thing. "Say it!"

I turned to Hugo. I lifted both hands to his cheeks. The room fell silent. Loudly, and trying hard to mimic my movie delivery, I spoke the words once again. "I will love you until the stars grow cold."

I lifted myself onto my toes and pressed my lips against his. His arms slipped around my waist and he pulled me into him. This time I was one hundred percent sure he was kissing me back. I had no idea how long an appropriate stage kiss should last. But right then I didn't care. When I released the kiss and stepped back, the audience flew back to their feet and the room shook with the applause. Hugo and I parted, my hand sliding down his arm. He was quick to catch my

The Reluctant Doppelganger

fingertips in his before I could break away. He clasped them tightly in his hand as we took another bow.

Standing in front of this admiring throng of people, my mind whirred. I was filled with a jumble of thoughts and feelings all hitting me hard at once. I was excited, happy, scared; but most of all I was feeling guilty. With one careless kiss (well, I guess it's two now) Eddie Standish had turned America's silent screen sweetheart Theodora Desmond into America's most tantalizing talking temptress. And neither she nor her world would ever be the same again.

I was relieved when RC thanked the crowd and we exited the stage.

RC kissed me on the forehead once we were backstage and then shook Hugo's hand vigorously.

"This movie is going to make us all even richer." RC was rubbing his hands together with glee. "I will see both my shining stars at the party." And with that he headed back up the stairs to the private suite. His job had just started. With a successful opening, investors would be easy to snare, but one must strike while the iron is hot.

I looked up to see Seedy headed our way.

"Wow! Miss Schofield, you do look spectacular tonight," Hugo praised as she stepped up to us.

"Thank you." She blushed slightly and twirled around. "I told that man of mine that he'd better whip me up something special tonight if he ever expected me to cook for him again." She was, of course, talking about Georgie. The need for their engagement had passed after the charges for murder had been dropped, but Seedy still gave him a hard time about it. With her pronouncement, she was back on task.

"Here is the way I have lined things out. All four cars should already be in the alley."

"Four cars? I thought the household brought two and Hugo and I brought one. That's only three." I questioned.

"We did," she said. "But we need four to make a clean get-away. The Viscount and Regina will leave through the front like everyone else. They will take her auto to the party. Your father, Gertie and RC will be traveling in RC's Rolls Royce later because they're still working on collecting investors for your next motion picture."

"I still don't see why we need four automobiles."

"I made the request, Theo." Hugo said. "Seedy, why don't we just show her."

"Sure thing." Seedy smiled, turned back to our little family and started herding them towards the backstage door.

When I entered the alley, I could see why we had four autos. It had nothing to do with need. The fourth vehicle was my bright red **Mercedes-Benz Armbruster Cabriolet**. It sat with its engine idling facing the back alley that ran behind all the buildings. The other three automobiles faced the street that ran along in front of the theater. According to someone's grand plan, I was going to sneak out.

We were all in the alley between the two buildings, far away from the crush of fans mobbing the theater's entrance. Seedy started running down her list. Tonight, she wasn't carrying a clip board or a notebook, but I could tell she was still checking off a mental list. She had Randel help the Truman's into the lead car and it was off. Next, Mrs. Reid and Wallace climbed into the second studio limousine, but not before hugging me, thanking me for a wonderful experience and wishing me a good-evening.

Last, but not least, came my very own chorus line. Claudette hugged and kissed me on both cheeks, thanking me for a great evening followed by Georgie carrying my fur cape.

"Make the same dramatic entrance at the party," he said. "There will be a whole new crew of reporters and photographers there." Georgie smiled as he moved over to the car to wait for Randel.

Randel and Seedy were last. Seems they were all riding together with our former taxi driver, Gerald, as their chauffeur. Seedy climbed in next to Claudette, leaving the jump seats for Randel and Georgie. I guess that meant Hugo was riding with me. I walked over to the driver's side of the Mercedes.

Hugo had just reached the passenger door when he called out to me, "wait there a minute". He started back towards my side of the car. As I turned, glancing into the side mirror on the Mercedes' door, I glimpsed Randel slip his arms around Georgie's waist. His lips moved to Georgie's ear, and he was speaking softly. I could not hear the words, but it looked like he said, "I will love you until the stars grow cold."

Their lips met. I quickly averted my eyes; it was a very intimate moment and none of my business. I wasn't sure how I felt about people using my underhanded plagiarized deception as a term of endearment, but I figured God would make me atone for that sin at some later date.

Jolted from my contemplations, I was swept off my feet. Hugo had me cradled in his arms as he smiled down at me.

"I wouldn't want to be accused of forgetting my manners again. I know how much you like to vault into this car. But I felt you might need to present yourself as more of a lady tonight. So, I thought I'd help you out a little. And I must say, you are right; this dress is exceedingly heavy." He winked and gave me a huge grin.

"You'd better be talking about the dress, you cad. A man should never ever comment on a lady's weight." I gave him a light slap on the cheek.

He smiled as he lowered me into the seat. His lips moved close. I could feel his hot breath on my ear. He spoke softly.

"Thank you, Theo. À cause de toi, est la vie en rose ce soir pour moi."

"What does that mean? You know I don't speak French." I said, smirking up at him.

"'Because of you, for me, tonight is life in pink.' Sounds better in French," he said, with a shrug. He kissed me lightly on the cheek, then ran back around the Mercedes and vaulted into the seat next to me. He smiled at me, a smile that went all the way up to those arrestingly beautiful blue eyes.

I wasn't sure what tomorrow might bring, but for tonight I *was* Theodora Desmond, the movie star. I was with my Prince Charming, Hugo Wainwright, and together we were living life in pink. I released the parking brake and opened the throttle. The magnificent red machine purred as it charged into the night. And with a cool California breeze caressing our skin, the inky darkness swallowed us up.

The End

The Book Review:

Book reviews are the life blood of any author. This is the first book of a series. If you enjoyed this debut book please let others know. Reviews are available wherever you purchased your copy. Reviewing is also available on Goodreads. Your reviews are greatly appreciated.

Join Nick's Mailing list:

www.nickhilliard.com

All That Glitters

Life in Pink Book 2
Sneak Preview

Chapter One

The gatekeeper at RC's estate must have seen us coming, and even in the dark remembered the sleek red Mercedes Roadster that had raced the electric gates' abilities the last time it was there. Before we even got close, the massive gates began to swing open. The tires screeched to a stop in front of the gatehouse. Because the Mercedes was an English drive, I was across the car from the gatekeeper himself.

"Good evening, Curtis."

The man looked taken aback and then beamed. I was fairly confident it was the first time ever anyone had used his name.

"Good evening, Miss Desmond, Mr. Wainwright." He grinned and tipped his hat.

"Okay if we head on up to the party?"

"Yes, Ma'am! From what I hear you two are the guests of honor." And he waved us on with a flourish.

The Reluctant Doppelganger

I drove through the entry and up the drive a short way, then pulled to a stop again.

"Hugo, be a dear and help me get this cape back over my shoulder."

Hugo did as I asked. If anyone saw us, they would think we looked like two monkeys at play, our arms and hands flailing in the air and batting at each other. My right shoulder was farthest from him, and the gear shift and handbrake were between the seats. When the deed was finally done, we sat for several minutes just laughing.

"What women won't do to get noticed."

"Oh, my dear, the correct line is: What a movie star won't do to get noticed. Just wait. You're only getting started." I put the car in gear. I hit the throttle hard enough that we both jolted back in our seats. Gravel flew up behind us as we shot down the driveway.

We rocketed to the front of the house. I pulled the little red car up to the red carpet so quickly that some of the photographers actually jumped back a bit. All eyes turned to us. Most, if not all, of the other guests had arrived in their chauffeured limousines. I was certain no automobile had been driven by a woman. Flashbulbs popped the second the photographers recognized us. The young valet in his tuxedo with tails, the same one assigned this task every time I had been here before, opened my door. The roadster's door swung open at the front, placing me in full view of the photographers.

The valet proffered his hand. I took it. Stepping from the roadster, I said, "Thank you, Bobby."

The young man looked at me with an astonished look. "You are so welcome, Miss Desmond. I can't wait to see your new picture." The smile he gave me was dazzling.

I palmed Bobby the five-dollar bill I had pulled from my purse while we were stopped back down the driveway fussing with my cape. "Would you mind seeing that my car gets parked since I don't have a driver tonight?"

"You bet Ma'am," he said excitedly with a quick bob of his head.

"And Bobby, I am so grateful for you taking care of this matter for me that I'll make sure you get two free tickets to *Samson and Delilah.*"

"Ma'am, that's not necessary."

"It is necessary to me. If I don't get them to you tomorrow, call my house and talk to my secretary, Cecilia. Tell her that crazy actress boss of hers promised you two tickets and you're guessing she forgot."

Bobby chuckled. "Yes, thank you, Ma'am."

I stepped away from him and stood posed as I'd been instructed, except I just couldn't seem to look bored. I could not keep from smiling as the flashbulbs popped. I tilted my shoulder, the cape dropped. Out of the corner of my eye, I saw Bobby reach to grab it, but it fell into the palm of my hand and my fingers closed around it. There were audible gasps and a new volley of bulbs popped. I dragged it behind me about halfway up the walkway and turned back as if to say to Hugo, *I'm waiting.*

I noticed that Bobby had closed the driver's door to the Mercedes. Using the top of the windscreen and the back of the driver's seat, Hugo lifted himself into the air, pulling both feet up. He extended his legs across the auto until he was standing in the driver's seat, raising his hands in the air waving to the photographers. Flashbulbs popped and some of the reporters were even clapping. With his arms outstretched, he bent his knees. Suddenly his entire body was in mid-air. He landed flat footed on the red carpet amid a torrent of flashes and applause. Straightening his legs, he pretended to dust himself off and stood while photographers went wild. He nodded to the photographers before bounding down the walkway to my side.

"Why, Mr. Wainwright, I do believe you are enjoying your new job." I gave him a wicked grin.

"Why, my dear Miss Desmond, I would say that is an understatement. I am loving my new job."

He slipped his arms around my waist, leaned forward and kissed me. Photographers went into a frenzy. The space around us was instantly as brilliant as day. I thought that surely the photographers would run out of flashbulbs.

As we turned and moved toward the open doorway to the house, he leaned close to my ear. "Besides, I didn't want some movie star goodie-two-shoes upstaging me." And his face split into a wide smile.

"We are going to be in so much hot water tomorrow when that picture hits the papers across the country." Then I winked mischievously up at him.

"I'm sure you're right. Without a doubt, we will most certainly be called to the headmaster's office."

"Don't you mean the throne room?" And I winked again.

When we were within earshot of the front doors, I could see they were flanked by the same two doormen as before.

"Good evening, Oscar, Tom." I nodded to each of them.

They both smiled broadly. "Good evening Miss Desmond. Good evening Mr. Wainwright," they said in turn.

As we stepped through the doorway the scene was familiar. It was almost indistinguishable from the first party I had attended in this house. The coat check stand had reappeared, music floated down from upstairs, and there were people everywhere. And many of those people were the same people who had been at RC's party for the Duke. This was getting easier.

Hugo guided us towards the coat check. He lifted my fur from where it trailed behind me and handed it to a coat check girl in a geisha costume. She handed me the ticket. It was then I remembered I still had the little handbag.

"Thank you, Tilley," I said, as I took the ticket. "I would like to check my bag as well."

As she took the tiny purse, she looked bewildered. "You know my name?"

Before the words had finished leaving her lips, RC's butler was at her side.

"Yes, Tilley, Miss Desmond knows everyone's name it would seem." He gave me a curious smile.

"Thank you, Tilley," I said, holding up my ticket stub. "And thank you too, Samuel." I smiled and gave the butler a quick wink as I tucked the ticket into Hugo's jacket pocket. I slid my arm through Hugo's and leaned against him. He began to maneuver us into the crowd.

When we reached the staircase, I pulled my arm from his to better navigate the stairs. As I pulled free, Hugo's hand slipped around my waist. I lifted the hem of the heavy dress to avoid tripping as I climbed. Stepping slightly in front of Hugo, I took the first step. This put Hugo directly behind me, and as I mounted the second step and he the first, his hand moved almost naturally down to my bottom.

Oh, God! I thought. I started doing long division with double digits in my head, willing my body NOT to react to his touch. The thought had never crossed my mind as to how intimate that particular touch could be. *Divide four thousand three hundred and twenty-four by twelve. Twelve goes into forty-three 3 times, leaving seven. Bringing down the two makes seventy-two.* It was during my calculations that I took in the identical twin staircase on the far wall. I had never paid any attention before, but that staircase seemed to be the "down" staircase and we were on the "up" one, just like the escalators in some of the large department stores. Funny what your mind chooses to notice when it's trying desperately not to notice the elephant in the room. I snickered slightly to myself, thinking what that might imply as I mentally thought of my own very well hidden and tightly secured elephant's trunk.

"What's so funny?" Hugo asked, smiling and giving my bottom a squeeze.

And now I was back to long division.

At the top of the stairs, we stepped into the massive ballroom. My father, Bertram Standish, stood next to his now-constant companion, Gertrude Myers. Gertie had been my father's secretary since he opened his office some twenty-five years earlier. She had known me all my life. I would have never imagined my father, who had intimate knowledge of almost every actress in Hollywood, ever having more than a business relationship with Gertie. Yet here they were, together and pretty much inseparable. And right now, the inseparable duo was staring sternly at both Hugo and me and headed our direction at a marching pace.

It was my father who spoke first when they reached us. "Have you lost your minds? What in the devil were you thinking, kissing each other? It's gotten all over this room in less than five minutes. It'll be all over the world by morning."

As if to acknowledge my prophecy, Hugo gave my bottom another squeeze as he took my father's rebuke.

"And get your hand off his bottom." He barked out in a hiss.

He had said his. Oh, God!

"I don't have my hand on his bottom?" I said indignantly, covering my father's faux pas.

"I meant to say, Hugo take 'your' hand OFF Theodora's bottom," he amended with a stutter.

For the first time ever, I wasn't sure whether it was my father or my agent talking. I cocked an eyebrow. As if in answer to my question, my father cocked his as well. I smiled. It was the protective father I was seeing. And like a young man caught getting too familiar with his sweetheart, Hugo removed the offending appendage instantly.

"Come on, the both of you. RC has asked me twice where you were and why it was taking you so long to arrive." He spoke in a stage whisper, like we could be overheard amidst the cacophony of conversations and music.

As if on cue, Gertie moved around and took Hugo by the arm, with my father following suit with me. And just like that the misbehaved children had been separated. I looked up at Hugo and a smirk shot across his face.

This time, as we made our way across the room to where our host was holding court, I found it a great deal easier mingling with the rich and famous people clustered in their cliquish clutches.

"There you are at last!" RC exclaimed, in delight.

He gave me a hug and what had become his trademark kiss on the forehead. He moved to Hugo and shook his hand vigorously.

"Well, well, well, Mr. Wainwright. Perhaps instead of playing leading man to Hollywood's newest temptress, I should cast you as a swashbuckling pirate. It would appear from tonight's entrance you think you might rival Fairbanks." RC's tone was both bubbling over and chiding all at once.

Still clasping RC's hand from the shake, Hugo turned the back of RC's hand skyward and bowed his forehead to it. "Your wish is my command, My Liege." His face radiated sincerity, accepting the reprimand for jumping out of the Mercedes in front of the press, but not apologizing for it.

In response, RC clasped his other hand around Hugo's and pumped even harder. RC's cheeks turned rosy and the smile that lit his face made him look more like jolly ole Saint Nick than the head of one of Hollywood's largest motion picture studios.

The Reluctant Doppelganger

"You are going to make it big, my boy," he said, almost laughing out loud. "Now both of you get over here, I have some gentlemen I want you to meet.

We didn't really have to move so much as re-orient ourselves. My father and Gertie had placed themselves next to the Duke, who stood just behind RC's left shoulder, while to RC's right were three men lined up in a row. All three were in tuxedos, but one stood out. Tall, slender, and ruggedly handsome, he was wearing a black cowboy hat with his tux; and instead of the usual loafers or wing-tips, his feet were clad in shiny black cowboy boots with a high heel that made him even taller.

If I ever get to be a man again, I might need to buy a pair of those.

"I'd like to make some introductions." RC started with the gentleman closest to him. "This is Ezra Blum. Ezra is a diamond merchant from New York City."

Mr. Blum nodded to us.

"Next to Ezra is Grady Chesterfield. Grady owns about half the state of Montana. He deals in cattle and thoroughbred horses. More than one of the horses he's bred and trained has won the Kentucky Derby."

"I can only take credit for breeding and training them. I have to give all the credit for the races to their current owners and jockeys."

His humbling words didn't exactly ring sincere.

"And last, but far from least, is Raymond Housley Overholser. Mr. Overholser is an oilman from the great state of Texas." RC sounded like a politician introducing a candidate from Texas at the Democratic convention. "Gentlemen, I'd like to introduce Colossal Pictures' most adored actress and soon to be America's most sensual temptress, Miss Theodora Desmond. This is her co-star, our newest leading man, Hugo Wainwright."

Hugo was the first to shake everyone's hand and then it was my turn. Like most perfunctory handshakes, it was an extension of the arm, a clasp of hands and a single firm pump. At least with both Mr. Blum and Mr. Chesterfield it happened that way. However, when I extended my hand to Mr. Overholser, he held it.

"You can call me Tex," he drawled out, with a Southwestern twang. His voice was almost as oily as his profession, and he was still holding my hand.

"I have acquaintances who own a rather large ranch in Texas. Their names are William and Margaret Morgan. Do you know them by chance?" I was trying to make polite conversation.

He gave a slight laugh. "Oh, honey, Texas is a mighty big place. No, I'm afraid I don't." He was still holding steadfast to my hand.

"Well, Tex," I drawled back, mimicking his accent, "they have a mighty big ranch."

I didn't like him calling me *honey*.

"Well, little filly, in case you haven't heard it before, *everything's* big in Texas."

The corner of his mouth turned up into something that was between a grin and a sneer. He gave me a wink. Then he rubbed his thumb slowly up and down the back of my hand. I nearly cringed in revulsion.

Instead, I dramatically feigned embarrassment, with a slight turn of my head. I caught my father's eye. He had that look. Then, I noticed so did the Duke as well as did Mr. Chesterfield. And to my pleasant surprise, so did Hugo. And I would bet that my own face mirrored that same expression. I'm not talking about a look of rightful indignation because the man had brazenly propositioned a woman in public. I'm talking about the look of challenge.

Most men would tell you that the fairer sex consists of

The Reluctant Doppelganger

complicated creatures. But I find men equally baffling. A band of men will gladly concede which man is the wealthiest, which is the most handsome and which is the strongest. They will even concede, as to which has the greatest prowess when it comes to the fairer sex. But let one man in that band boast about the size of his credentials and suddenly there is an overwhelming need for proof. And at this very moment, there were five men within earshot ready to throw down the proverbial gauntlet of challenge to this braggart, and I was one of them. If this had not been a public forum and had we not been in mixed company, I'm sure there would have been a wager followed by a laying down of the cards, so to speak. And quite confidently, my money would be on the Standish boys.

Feeling an almost uncontrollable desire to fight, I snapped my head back abruptly and locked my eyes with the arrogant cowboy. "Well, then Tex, I guess all it will take is one of those Texas-sized checks invested in my next movie to throw that big ole Texas-sized hat of yours into the ring." And I gave him an exaggerated wink.

"Now why would I do that, Li'l Filly?" A tight, almost wicked smile creased his face. "Just so old RC over there can overpay his cute little pet actress?"

"My dear Tex, I have now made seven films. My very first movie was wildly successful, and each one thereafter has earned more than the one before it. In *Samson and Delilah*, Theodora Desmond the commodity has gone from being America's sweetheart to America's most wanton femme fatale. Do you know what that means, Tex?" I hissed his name and landed hard on the X.

I took a step in, holding on to his hand tightly. "It means, with the release of this new talking picture, every red-blooded American male will LUST after Theodora Desmond, the sensual siren, and every red-blooded American girl will long to emulate Theodora Desmond, the sexual goddess. And that translates into dollars and cents."

My voice was nearing a low growl now. I stepped even closer and glared up at him. I squeezed his hand as hard as I could. Due to my judo training, I have a very firm grip. His eyes popped open wide. He tightened his own grip in return.

"And it only takes the slightest bit of business acumen to know, the smaller the group of investors in a sound and successful venture, the larger the profit for said investors. So Tex, know that I, Theodora Desmond, have three more years left on my contract with Colossal Studios. If you are not seeing dollar signs by now, you are never going to see them. And you need to understand this, Tex. No matter how much money I get paid, I'm worth *every* penny!"

I immediately regained my composure and extricated my hand from his. I looked over to Hugo.

"Dear Hugo," I said as sweetly as I could. "I am truly parched after all this business talk. Would you escort this li'l filly to the bar on the veranda? I would just love some fresh air and a glass of champagne."

Hugo nodded his good-nights to each man in turn, moved over to me, and proffered his arm. I slipped mine through his, slunk against him as I had all evening, and we moved away from RC and his money coalition.

"I think I'm with Theodora," Gertie said. She was right behind us as my father shook every hand before scurrying to catch up with her.

Available now on Amazon